Wakefi

The Ho

Simon Butters is a screenwriter in film and television. His credits include *Wicked Science*, *H20 Just Add Water* and *Mako: Island of Secrets* among others. Simon lives in the Adelaide Hills with his two hilarious kids, a very busy wife, and a scruffy little dog that definitely doesn't talk but does do a weird grunt when you pat her behind the ear. *The Hounded*, Simon's first novel, was shortlisted for the 2014 Adelaide Festival Unpublished Manuscript Award.

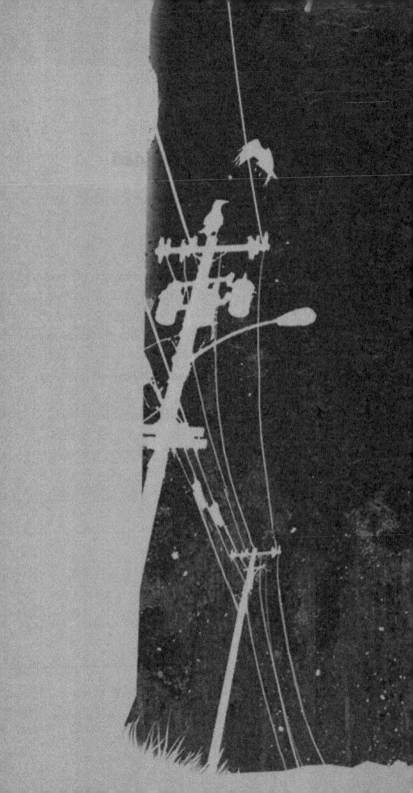

THE
HOUNDED

SIMON
BUTTERS

Wakefield
Press

Wakefield Press
16 Rose Street
Mile End
South Australia 5031
www.wakefieldpress.com.au

First published 2016

Edited by Margot Lloyd, Wakefield Press
Cover designed by Liz Nicholson, designBITE
Text designed by Clinton Ellicott, Wakefield Press
Printed in Australia by Griffin Digital, Adelaide

National Library of Australia Cataloguing-in-Publication entry

Creator: Butters, Simon, author.
Title: The hounded / Simon Butters.
ISBN: 978 1 74305 395 9 (paperback).
Subjects: Young adult fiction.
                Depression in adolescence – Fiction.
                Mental illness – Fiction.
Dewey Number: A823.4

CORIOLE
McLAREN VALE

Wakefield Press thanks
Coriole Vineyards for
their continued support

For Penny, Zoe and Charlie. My light.

Chapter One

Alias: @The Full Monty
Date: Thursday February 14, 6.15AM
There's something in my room. Time left to freak out:
four, three, two, one ...

I was freaking out. I don't know how long it had been there but when I opened my eyes it was staring right at me. It was silent as night, the black dog.

I sat up in bed and squinted, trying to wipe away night's lingering shadows. It had a long snout, a shiny black coat and deep, sorrowful eyes. Those eyes were empty pits; black holes in space and time. It held my gaze and I fell away, getting a sick feeling in my guts like I'd gone over the top on some killer rollercoaster. Stupid dog.

I thumbed out my bewildered status in SpeedStream and, as usual, nobody responded. This was the all-new, worldwide, social networking freeware that practically every teenager on the planet live streamed on their smart phones. I'd been on it for two months now, and had the grand total of three connections: one guy in New Zealand, one in Greenland and one guy from Germany who was I guess the closest thing I had to a friend, which was odd because he didn't speak a word of English. We conversed by converting text into one of those online translation sites. Our conversations were like decoding a series of warped Chinese whispers. We were perpetually lost in translation.

Alias: @The Full Monty
Date: Thursday February 14, 1.25AM
I can't sleep. I think it's the full moon.

@Gutentag
I wouldn't eat that if I was you being.

@The Full Monty
I don't plan to. Besides, it'd need a lot of salt ☺

@Gutentag
Must retire now. Pondering cheese limits my understanding.

What did I tell you? Totally random, huh? Still, I didn't mind. I was connecting with someone; a real person, no matter how far away, had attempted to share their innermost thoughts with me. That was worth something, even if it was just nonsense.

The dog?

I thought maybe it was a birthday present. It was my fifteenth birthday, so it was possible, I guess. Mum and Dad could have slipped it into my room during the night. Deep down, though, I knew better. Besides, the dog looked too old. Normal people gave each other puppies; something cute and innocent to care for and give wise instruction to. This creature looked as old as time. The thing just sat there and looked at me. No expression. No playful wagging tail. Nothing. It had to be a stray.

It wasn't unusual to have a stray animal suddenly appear in our house. This sort of thing had happened before. Once, a feral cat took up residence in my mother's underpants drawer. How it got in nobody knows but it had kittens in there. My mother was furious. All her undies were in there, soiled by the gross bits that come out when an animal has babies. It was a nasty cat, that feral cat. It hissed and growled and threw its paws about when you walked down the hallway. It was crazy. Its eyes were wild and the noise that came out of it was the sound of pure insanity. I loved that sound. I'd walk past the open door, goading it to scream and yowl at me one more time. My mother hollered at me to leave it alone. We had to wait until my dad finished work and came home to scare it out. He took one look at it, and raced at it carrying a cricket bat. It took off out the window, leaving its kittens mewing away, helpless. Why it chose to have its kittens in my mother's undies remained a mystery. Maybe it knew it wasn't cut out for motherhood and left them there in hope we'd care for them. The next day they were all gone. There was a fresh hole filled up in the garden. I would have liked a kitten.

I ignored the dog and shuffled past it to the loo, passing my reflection in the mirror. Things today were bad. I'd grown a zit the size of a walnut. Okay, maybe not quite the size of a walnut, but it was big. It shone a brilliant, painful red.

In the rest of nature creatures painted in such a fierce colour are considered dangerous, filled with some kind of toxic venom, like red-back spiders, or those yellow frogs from the Amazon that lost tribes used to make poisoned darts. Me? I wasn't considered dangerous. I'd just get punched out. There'd be no way to keep a low profile with that throbbing red light on the end of my nose.

The rest of me didn't fare much better. My hair was

mussed up from another sleepless night and my teeth were in dire need of braces, a luxury my family could never afford. Teeth grew out of my mouth at awkward angles. The older I got, the more twisted and shameful my smile. I grinned in the mirror and repulsed myself.

I had taken a vow never to smile in school photos. Everyone always blamed me for ruining them because of my sullen expression. They had no idea I was doing them all a favour, sparing them the sight of my rancid set of chompers.

It wasn't always this way. I used to be quite good-looking as a kid. I was even in a glossy brochure once, selling bicycle shorts for a local sports store. That was the first money I'd ever earned. I never saw it of course; it was gone before we even got home, replaced by cartons of cigarettes. My mother smoked them in quick succession: two, then three at a time. The cigarettes poked out of her face like giant fangs. I hated cigarettes. I could always smell her charred insides from across the room. The scent of burning lung was ever-present in our house. Whenever you walked in the lounge, you'd disappear into a dense fog hung with the sickly, sweet smell of decay.

The mirror bent and swayed, mocking me. My chin had a little bit of teenage growth on it. My first real whiskers had erupted out of me, daring to enter our world. They were malformed at birth, so thin and delicate they'd practically blow off in a good wind. Other kids thought their first whiskers signalled their ascendancy into adulthood and took to shaving, more in an effort to promote further growth than to look tidy, I guess. Me? I didn't bother with shaving. Mine were so downy and pathetic I could just rub them off with the back of my hand.

I was a skinny kid. My cheekbones sunk. Ribs protruded

out my sides. I don't remember when controlling the urge to eat started, but I had limited my food intake for years, I guess. Don't get me wrong. This was no sort of pathological disorder, I was sure of that. I could eat if I wanted to. I just didn't *want* to. It took an enormous, concentrated effort of will. My mind and body were at constant war over the subject. My brain had to force my body into submission. It was a daily chore to ignore nourishment, to forget chocolate existed, to wipe the memory of vanilla ice cream from my mind. Something in me enjoyed the sacrifice, I guess. It made me feel stronger, the weaker I became. I thought I was in control. I was an idiot, of course, but I didn't care.

The dog watched me as I dressed for school, putting on a pair of faded jeans and a dirty t-shirt from the day before. I was slightly annoyed now that it hadn't gone away.

'What do you want? Go on. Get!' I snapped.

It sat there impassively, watching me squeeze my face in the mirror. The zit refused to pop. It stubbornly held on to its bonanza, preferring to ambush me at some later opportunity. The dog maintained a silent vigil. From its curious expression, I half expected it to laugh. But it just sat there, staring into me.

I went to the kitchen and allowed myself breakfast. Today's ration consisted of a quarter slice of toast with one smear of jam in the corner. I concentrated my efforts and imagined a banquet before me. If I had enough determination, I could get through the day without anything further.

The dog didn't beg or anything. It didn't slobber on my leg looking for a bit of toast. It hadn't even wagged its tail yet. It just sat and watched. I tossed it a chunk of toast. The dog glanced down and I was sure it rolled its eyes in disdain.

The crust dropped to the floor to find itself among friends.

Years worth of breadcrumbs were taking up residence down there, unswept, threatening to create an ecosystem of their own. Those crumbs might clump together, I thought, to one day form little planets made entirely of crumbs. And on those little crumb planets, maybe a whole new civilisation of tiny creatures would evolve. One day, they'd become so advanced they'd send up little spaceships to explore their universe and come to the startling conclusion that they were all just crumbs. They were nothing but some other person's refuse, left lying on their kitchen floor. This shockwave of self-doubt would send their world into anarchy. Riots would break out. Governments would fall. A once proud and intelligent race would succumb to the crushing realisation they were nothing more than a bunch of worthless crumbs. The dog ignored the toast.

'What kind of dog are you?' I asked.

'Black,' said the dog.

I choked. Unless I'd just suffered a brain injury, I heard the dog speak. Now at this point I had a choice to make. Various possibilities exploded in my mind like a mouth full of popping candy and Coke. Talking dog? Hmm. Okay. Scientific miracle, secret government experiments, genetic mutation, alien body snatcher, my ear canals could simply be full of wax, could be a dream, god is dog spelt backwards, maybe I've been hit by a car and I'm in a coma, maybe I'm just …

'No, you're not crazy. Not yet anyway,' said the dog.

'Don't you like toast?' I asked.

'If you're planning to make this hard on yourself, keep that up. I don't mind. I'm very patient,' it warned.

My mother burst into the kitchen in her usual frenzy of cigarette smoke and worn out slippers.

'Someone's been in here! And moved the toilet paper!' she bemoaned.

A complaint like this wasn't unusual in our house. My mother was dead-set certain someone had sneaked in the previous night and moved the toilet paper. There was none left in the loo and none under the sink in the laundry. That was strange because she swore she just bought a new pack the day before. The only possible explanation was we'd been burgled. Some diabolical man had invaded our house, crept past our sleeping bodies in the dead of night with the sole intention of moving our toilet paper.

The fact that he'd left all our valuables where they were – Dad's wallet, Mum's antique jewellery – didn't mean a thing to my mother. She was certain someone was playing tricks. She looked under the kitchen sink to discover the offending pack of toilet paper, hiding there all along.

'Ah-ha! See? Someone's been in here!' she cried.

I grew up with this sort of thing on a regular basis and used to wholeheartedly believe that if you lost anything, it meant that some stranger had come into the house to move it about, just to annoy you. I pictured this evil wretch, delighting in his latest trickery. He'd have a black cape, a long moustache and sit outside the house wringing his hands in pantomime glee, listening as his latest Machiavellian plot came true.

It was only about two months ago that I finally realised my mother was just making all this up. In her mind, she couldn't cope with not remembering where she'd put the toilet paper, so she invented this strange burglar guy to explain the mystery. Smart really. The idea that you could create someone so real that other people around you believed in him too astounded me. You just had to believe in them so much, there couldn't be any reason to *not* believe in them. Sure, I was annoyed at myself for not waking up to this sooner but, to tell you the truth, I was in awe of her inventiveness. I continued the ruse. I didn't do this to placate her. We just had an unspoken rule, I guess. Judgment was never allowed.

'Yep, he's getting trickier Mum,' I offered.

She lit up another cigarette, breathed in her breakfast, and made her way back to the loo. She walked out without any mention of my birthday.

That was actually quite normal in my house. My parents hadn't mentioned birthdays since I was six. They never told me why, but I figured they thought birthday celebrations were for little kids. By age six they must have deemed I was old enough to celebrate birthdays on my own. Either that or they'd just plain forgotten how to parent. Maybe both.

More disturbing than not mentioning my birthday, was the fact that my mother hadn't mentioned the dog. Its impassive stare gave me the creeps but, at the same time, its presence felt somehow warm and reassuring. I knew this creature intimately. It knew me too. We were like old friends reuniting after a lifetime apart: a century lived of war, love, torment and joy, only to come together again at the final hour. This strange creature understood me. But as I looked closer, the dog began to shift and change. The longer I looked at it, the less it seemed like a dog at all.

I squinted, trying to exorcise it with my mind. My eyelids shut out the world. Everything fell away and I travelled to some other space, some other time. I floated there, in that shadow world. I lost my arms and legs. My body merged with the nothingness. I was free.

If you haven't noticed by now I suffer from some kind of affliction. My mind tends to wander. I don't mean this in the figurative way, like I'm constantly daydreaming, although most of my teachers believe this is the case. I mean it in a very literal way. My mind *actually* wanders. It leaves me. Sometimes for hours.

It can happen anytime, anyplace. There's no trigger, no rhyme or reason, it just happens. I have no control. It's like an out-of-body experience. I'm on autopilot. I could be just about to cross a busy road, or discover one of humanity's enduring secrets when my mind will simply disappear. My eyes roll back into my skull. The world around me fades. A numb feeling spreads all over my body. I have no sense of touch, no sense of taste. Nothing. I can still see and hear, but that's about it. It's as if my head has suddenly been separated from my body. I am decapitated, and my mind dropped into a jar of thick jelly.

Meanwhile my body is left to its own devices, left standing like a headless shell. To its credit, my body will often try its best to run the show while I'm gone. It will often walk me around like some kind of zombie, pretending to still be a part of the living.

Once, when I had to stand up in front of the class to give a talk, I got sidetracked by one of life's multiple tangents and my mind abandoned me for over thirty-five minutes. There I was in front of everybody, drool hanging from my mouth, eyes rolled up at the ceiling. People giggled. Someone threw a blunt object at my head. Nothing brought me out of my stupor.

Eventually my body got so annoyed, it decided to give this thinking thing a go. It couldn't be that hard, after all. My actual brain hadn't done that much to impress it, I guess. My body tried to force me to speak. But without a brain to formulate any thoughts, the best it could do was mimic actual words. My jaw hung open and my tongue flapped about, but all that came out were some weird barnyard sounds. I moaned and groaned and everybody stared. More blunt objects.

Somewhere, off in the distance, my mind watched on. I could hear the sounds, but they sounded far off and alien. No matter how much I concentrated, I couldn't understand what I was saying. From the expressions on everyone's faces in the classroom, they couldn't understand what I was saying either. Was I even speaking English? Or was I just standing there mumbling incoherently? I had no idea. Eventually, I fluttered back into my brain and took the wheel over my rambling tongue. Suddenly the words became English again. Somehow, I always made it back to my body before anyone called the police, or an ambulance, or worse, my mother.

So there I was with the dog in the kitchen, my brain in a jar of jelly.

'Are you still with me, Montgomery?'

Okay, stop right there. Yes, my name really is Montgomery. But everyone calls me Monty for short, which is just as bad really. My mother, seconds after she'd given birth, decided to call me Montgomery in a fit of idiocy. It was only six months ago that I understood why during sex education. When mothers give birth it's really painful so the doctors often give them so many painkillers they don't know which way is up. Yep, my mother was drugged out of her mind when she decided to call me Monty. My father was apparently confused at the time.

'Didn't we decide to call him Bob?' my dad had muttered.

'No!' wailed my mother, writhing about like Medusa with her snakes cut off. 'He's Montgomery, can't you see? Montgomery! I'll never forgive you if we don't call him Montgomery. The world will end if we don't call him Montgomery!'

And on and on she had ranted until my father shrugged at the nurse and quietly looked for the exit.

My eyes came back into focus. The dog was still there.

'Yes. I'm still here,' I said. 'What do you want?'

The black dog narrowed its eyes and snarled, looking menacing for the first time. I realised if this were a feral dog, it could bite my face off before I even raised an eyebrow. That feral cat could move fast. Maybe this thing had decided toast wasn't going to be enough and it was going to have *me* for breakfast instead. I backed away a little. The dog's face softened.

'I'm not going to hurt you,' it chided. 'Not unless you want me to.'

The dog trotted to the kitchen door that opened to the rear yard. It batted the screen door open with one paw and turned around.

'Take some eggs with you,' it grumbled.

Wow. I was just visited by a talking dog and that was it? Take some eggs with you! That's all the wisdom I was going to get? It was clear that if I was going to gain any under-standing of life, it wasn't going to come from a talking dog. I watched it head out. The screen door slammed shut behind it like an abrupt full stop.

Talking dog? Pathetic. Who needs it?

I opened the fridge and stuffed my pockets with every egg I could find.

Chapter Two

Alias: @The Full Monty
Date: Thursday February 14, 7.55AM
When you're dreaming, you think you're awake, right?
So when we're awake, does that mean we are really
dreaming?

@Gutentag
You tempt the absurd dream. Fate makes the riddle
known to you.

@The Full Monty
Right ... I can always rely on you to make things clear!

Our house was called the ghost house. There's usually one
in every neighbourhood, I guess. Little kids whispered
stories about it as they went past. One of them would
always get spooked and break into a run. It was odd to
watch. To my knowledge nothing bad ever happened in our
house. There had been no gruesome murders, no children
snatched away in the middle of the night, no ghosts had
ever rattled their chains, but the stories persisted. I could
see why it attracted attention. It stuck out like a beacon of
misfortune in an otherwise pretty street.

The house was a weatherboard shack built over a hundred
years ago, which kind of impressed me really. Who would
think a house made essentially of sticks would last that
long? It had an overgrown garden that probably looked
amazing once. There were about a hundred different types

of roses all matted together, like jungle vines. Most of the year the garden looked positively evil. The thorns threatened to pluck your eye out if you gave them so much as a sideways glance. But in spring, the entire place bloomed. I tried counting all the different colours one day, but by my sixty-fourth flower I got distracted, followed one of life's tangents and found myself six blocks away trimming my nails with a razor blade.

Razor blades interested me. I collected them out of old box cutters, the rustier the better. I used them for all sorts of things, from cutting paper, shaving pencils, to seeing how fine I could cut a single human hair. It was always my personal goal to slice a human hair right down the middle. So far, I hadn't succeeded. Old people generally think razor blades are dangerous. They're probably right. I sliced my fingertips clean off on more than one occasion, completely by accident of course. The blood that came out was thick and bright red. Redder than you'd expect. It's not something I wanted to do again. Doing homework with peeling scabs on the end of your fingers was damn annoying.

The rest of our street demolished their weatherboard shacks years ago and replaced them with modern two storey jobs that oozed warmth and wealth. You could hear the widescreen TVs and smell the gourmet cooking from the street. The sounds and smells would travel out, taunting me, hinting at a life unlived.

I'd lift my nose and sniff out lamb roast, exotic curries and bubbling casseroles wafting from those lofty mansions. It'd make me so hungry I swear I was turning savage. Despite my best efforts to ignore nourishment, I secretly longed for this type of cooking. Any sort of cooking would do, really. The most I could hope for was some baked beans on toast. My parents let me fend for myself. If I were a wolf pup this would probably be a good survival strategy. For me, all it did was make me feel alone. Food is about sharing, comfort and human interaction. We had none of that in our house. We certainly didn't have a widescreen TV, or any sort of TV. We had one once, but that was before my mother heard the Prime Minister swearing at her.

The names were shocking, foul-mouthed curses; the sort of names truck drivers and wharfies mutter to themselves when they think nobody is listening. The sort of names that if spoken to a mother like mine would send her into utter hysterics. Which, of course, it did. Dad and I listened but all we could hear was the Prime Minister droning on about the economy. Still, my mother was adamant it was all directed at her. She ranted on about the Prime Minister being out to get her until my dad simply nodded and put his foot right through the middle of the screen. That was the last TV we ever had.

The other reason kids called our place the ghost house was that it did look remarkably like an angry face snarling at you. The rotting weatherboards curled around like a deep, furrowed brow. A pair of glowering eyes consisted of two large windows. The front door was, of course, the nose. The varnish had peeled off giving it a cancerous appearance. A small porch out front made up the mouth. The exposed beams looked like bared fangs ready to devour passing children. If you got too close, legend told, the ghost house would swallow you whole and add your bones to those we supposedly had stored underneath.

To me, the house was just in a terrible state of disrepair. I imagined it was once clean and ordered, the weatherboards straight and painted a fresh coat of white, the windows warm and inviting, and the garden tended and flourishing. Children would play in the street, friends would come together for weekend barbeques, parents would chat over low fences, songs would be sung around the piano, hot roasts would be carved and families would tell each other they loved them.

I crept out of the house and the eggs in my pockets clunked together, threatening to crack and leak their gooey remains all over the insides of my pants. I began to walk carefully, taking each step in slow motion like I was walking on the moon. Either that, or people would think I had just pooed my pants. I must have looked ridiculous. And ridiculous people gain attention.

'What do you think you're doing?'

It was Eliza.

Eliza Robertson lived at the far end of my street in one of those designer homes that consumed houses like mine. She was about half a foot taller than me and a whole head wiser. We were the same age, but Eliza Robertson was wholly a woman. She had made the change and grown up long ago. This happened in the blink of an eye over the summer holidays last year. One day she was a little kid, riding her bike with pink tassels on the handlebars, the next she was a towering beauty, summoning the dark forces of sensuality. Eliza Robertson held the quiet confidence reserved only for those educated in life's ultimate mystery.

I froze in her commanding presence. Authority came naturally to her. Her kind never spoke to mine, so this was unusual. There was nobody else around, so I guess she felt she could entertain herself with me for a while. Eliza stood atop the hierarchy at our school. Boys became stupidly extroverted in her presence, driven mad by her sullen beauty. Girls followed her every move, desperately hoping that some of her allure would rub off on them. She never said much. She didn't need to. Her eyes were dark green jewels and when they locked on to you, you had nowhere to hide. She could peer into the very depths of your soul, could Eliza Robertson.

Eliza's school clothes were always clean and fresh, ironed so crisp I swear you could hear them crackle with electricity when she moved. She always wore white cotton shirts that were just transparent enough to allow a tantalising glimpse of lace underneath. Her silky brown hair draped down over her shoulders and finished in fine twirls just above her breasts. And those breasts? They were like coconuts. I always wondered why guys said that about girls. Breasts like coconuts? Not a bowl of jelly? Or a ripe mango? No. Always coconuts.

'Stop staring,' she said. 'You're giving me the creeps.'

'Sorry. I was just thinking about coconuts.'

She seemed to get the meaning straight away, and smiled curiously as if she understood the secret boyhood code for coconuts. Either that, or she could read my mind. I tried to test her. Guess what's in my pockets, I thought.

'What's in your pockets?' she asked.

I gasped. She seemed to sense my fear. I told myself it was a simple coincidence and showed her the eggs. She nodded as if she understood, which of course she didn't. Maybe.

I had often imagined myself to be Eliza Robertson, transforming overnight on a full moon. I'd tear at myself and scratch out my eyes in agonising pain. I'd howl at the moon and shake off my old body, like a wet hound after a rainstorm. The old bits of me would fly away and splat against the walls of the old house. I'd be renewed. I'd be clean and fresh and smelling of a sweet salty breeze. I'd stand before my mirror and admire my long silky brown hair and perfect white teeth. And those coconuts ...

'Are you alright?'

'Huh?'

'Your eyes are doing that weird thing again. You know, when they roll back in your head.'

'Oh. Sorry.'

She looked past me now, like she was hoping to find someone else to talk to. Bored I guess. I would be too, if I was talking to someone like me. She checked her phone and thumbed out about sixteen instant messages in quick succession. That was the usual sign that you were too excruciating to endure anymore and should quietly slink away.

Eliza Robertson was on everyone's friends list. SpeedStream constantly listed her as someone I'd like to connect with. I wanted to send her an invitation, but couldn't. I was stuck with Gutentag. I didn't mind. He was an oddball, but an interesting oddball. I liked that.

'You going to egg the teacher's car or something?'

She looked up at me, interested now. Despite her pleasing visual appearance, Eliza Robertson held a dark and menacing heart that fed on other people's misfortunes. Most people couldn't see the evil streak in her, dulled into submissiveness by her beauty and all. But I could. I could see past her outer shell. I could see the coldness inside; her hunger to watch as someone else suffered. I knew that it somehow made her feel better about herself.

That didn't scare me though. I actually liked the fact that I knew something about her that nobody else on this earth could possibly understand.

'I was thinking of Mr Rooney,' I lied.

She smiled appreciatively. Mr Rooney was our science teacher and was about 400 years old, I swear. He looked like a leathery old toad in safety boots. He sniffed and shuffled and stank of mints and alcohol. We all knew he drank before class, in a little room containing all the chemicals at the back of the classroom. He was a hard man and gave no quarter to slackers and misfits. He enjoyed making everyone's life a misery by constantly forcing us to sit old tests from the sixties and recount the entire periodic table from memory. He was also a huge perv and spent most of his time staring at coconuts. Eliza despised him. Most girls quit science after just one year, sick of having his eyes constantly down their tops.

Eliza narrowed her eyes at me, summing me up like a cat does prey. I felt her sense the lie. I had no idea why I had the eggs. What was I supposed to tell her? A talking dog had visited me on my birthday and told me to take some eggs to school? She'd think I'd gone mad. Maybe I had but, in my bubble, I just hadn't noticed it yet. She looked past me again, as if communicating with some silent force.

'Do it, Monty. I'd like that,' she said.

I smiled and the king zit popped on my nose. That zit had waited until the worst possible moment to discharge its horrors. It exploded into a little ball of pus right in front of Eliza Robertson. It was involuntary, I swear; I had no control over it, but it was as if my body had secretly done this on purpose.

Eliza grimaced and stepped away. I could see the disgust

catch in her throat. She was saved as the school bus arrived, spraying us with dust and diesel fumes.

I didn't like taking the bus. It went on such a circuitous route, winding through suburban streets and cul-de-sacs, that my mind almost always drifted away. I would end up riding that bus all day if I wasn't careful. A couple of times I missed getting off at school, only to realise I was still on it at lunchtime. By then, I was miles away and had no choice but to ride it all the way home. But that presented the exact same danger. On the way back, my mind would eventually slip away once more, and I'd miss my stop all over again. I'd come back to consciousness just in time to watch the sun go down.

The door slid open and Eliza hurried onboard, welcomed by the shrill greetings of all her school friends. She looked back to me as if to check if I was getting on too. But the driver knew all about me, and my tendency to ruin his bus schedule, and quickly shut the door in my face. Eliza took her rightful place among her adoring friends, holding court like the queen that she was. The bus drove away and a thick film of dust settled over me. I knew what I had to do.

Rooney's car was a blue, sporty two-door thing. It was old though. I'd heard someone say it was a classic. I liked the look of it. It was decorated with shiny chrome bumpers and had side mirrors that poked out like those clipped ears on expensive show dogs. The car sat at attention, listening for its owner's whistle. I hunkered down low beside the car and waited for the bell to sound. I was often late to school so that wouldn't be out of the ordinary. I waited until everyone went to class so I could act unseen. Finally, the bell sounded. I had my chance. I lifted my first missile.

Mocking laughter echoed out behind me. The sound made my skin crawl.

Tony Papadopoulos had a head the size of a pumpkin and a nose with a peculiar shaped mole perched right on the end of it. I swear it looked as if that mole had made its way from some other part of his body, in sheer disgust at being part of him, and was going to end it all by throwing itself off. Sometimes, during science class, I'd secretly goaded the mole to do it.

'Go on. Jump!' I'd whisper to that mournful looking mole. 'Nobody would blame you. End it now while you still can!'

This would usually end in Tony looking at me kind of strange and punching me in the kidneys. Tony was Greek. He grew up playing football, going to the gym and eating copious amounts of salty cheese and dried meats. He was enormous. He held the school record for most things sporting and could bench-press a hundred kilos. He shaved for real and his armpits stank of yeasty bread. He oozed testosterone. Meaty pheromones hung about him in a grey fug. He was a frightening predator, ready to devour innocents like me.

His two friends were grey, tepid reflections of him. They wanted to be like Tony so much, they almost appeared like caricatures of him. They ate the same food, wore the same clothes, and hit the same people. These two morons didn't have what it takes to pull it off though. On their own, they'd be nothing. Jordan and Rhys were their names. They were inconsequential and they knew it.

My guts bellowed as the first punch hit home. The wind inside me gushed out and I couldn't suck it back in. A tight cramp wound itself around my chest as my lungs went down for the count, paralyzed. I was winded. It was a feeling I had become accustomed to; a beating from Tony Papadopoulos was a common experience for me.

This part of a beating I didn't actually mind. Being winded was an experience I almost actually enjoyed. I think it has something to do with lack of oxygen to the brain. If you forgot about the crushing pain in your chest and focused your mind, you began to float. The air in front of your eyes would solidify and fall like snowflakes. Pretty soon your mind dripped downhill and you found yourself watching the rest of the beating from afar, feeling no pain whatsoever. I imagined this other self put his feet up and grab a bowl of popcorn to watch the game.

'Go on. Kick him in the guts one more time,' I'd shout. 'I can't feel a thing!'

It must have been a reflex action, I'm not sure, but somehow all my eggs found themselves mashed up in Tony's face. He stood there, stunned, with creamy yellow goo dripping down the front of his designer soccer shirt. I had come back to my body just in time for him to murder me. But the weirdest thing happened. He looked down at his shirt and squeaked.

'Dad's going to kill me,' he gasped.

Tears threatened. He suddenly looked pudgy and young. The fat around his cheeks congealed, making him look like a chubby little eight-year-old. For a second I imagined he was going to call for his mummy. I took in some fresh air and resisted the urge to daydream about this delightful prospect. Tony wasn't the forgiving type. I took my chance and ran.

Eliza would have to wait another day for her revenge on Mr Rooney. It was my first real encounter with her since we were kids, and I had failed. That was going to be it, I was sure. The next time we would pass each other by and she'd politely snub me with the silence I deserved.

Alias: @The Full Monty
Date: Thursday February 14, 9.00AM
I just made a big mistake. Got any advice on how to avoid a beating?

@Gutentag
If you fear losing control, you have already lost yourself to blame.

@The Full Monty
Actually, that's the first thing you've said that makes sense!

Chapter Three

My father, if you haven't guessed by now, was the strong and silent type. He worked for a local mechanic shop and spent long hours under the bonnet of every sort of car you could imagine. To this day, I don't really know if he actually liked cars or loathed them. If you were driving around with him, going to the shops or something, he'd point them out. Not directly to you, or even to himself really. He'd just point them out.

'Toyota Camry, corroded master cylinder,' he'd mumble. 'Ford Mondeo, new fuel injector.'

And on and on like that. For years, I took these statements to have some hidden, dramatic meaning. There, in the tiniest parcels of his vocabulary, was the answer to all life's problems if only I could fathom the deeper meaning. The way he intoned these mysticisms was so deadpan that, for all my keen sense of hearing, I could not detect the slightest amount of emotion. Undaunted, I took to noting them down. When I got home I'd cut and paste the names together looking for a pattern, a secret code that would reveal some universal truth. I'd been fooled. It was simply a list.

Disappointment is harder to deal with when it's directed at someone else. Self-disappointment for me was a comfortable set of pants. I didn't understand it at the time; I had never harboured expectations of my father. He was just there, like an old pile of bricks in the corner of the garden: a solid and continuous presence, cold and maybe covered in a little bit of moss. I was disappointed. My father didn't think about the world how I did. I guess I'd always hoped that, as I grew older, I'd somehow learn his mysterious ways, or he'd learn mine. I looked upon him with more than my customary fleeting glance. My father suddenly appeared robotic, going about his daily life in such a monotonous fashion I swear all it amounted to was moving around a bit until he died. Perhaps that's all everyone ever did? No matter what you achieved, you could be president of the free world, discover the cure for everything, walk on Mars, whatever, in the end all it amounted to was moving around a bit until you died. Maybe he did have it right after all? Maybe he had seen a deeper truth and had emptied his head of all the unnecessary stuff of life? Maybe he wasn't distracted by everything he came across? Maybe he just let things be? Life to him was a list of objects. The thought horrified me. I didn't want to be an object.

I observed my father, deeper than my usual fleeting glance. His arms were solid and thick. Auto grease had ground its way into his fingers. His face was square, his chin thick with stubble. His hair was parted the same way it had been since he first sprouted a crop on that impervious head. I longed to get into that head. Yet the thought I'd find nothing more than a list of auto parts was more than I could bear.

Alias: @The Full Monty
Date: Friday February 15, 2.43AM
Have you ever seen a coconut?

@Gutentag
You mean a breast?

@The Full Monty
What? This thing works now? Can you understand me?

@Gutentag
I am of thought that you lead disaster with sleeping.
Better the cohesion of tomorrow.

@The Full Monty
Yeah. That's what I thought.

The next morning the black dog sat under a bramble of
roses in the backyard. We stared at each other for a while,
me from the vantage point of my bedroom window, it from
underneath the safety of a thousand daggers. I walked out
to meet it.

'You knew about Tony?' I asked.

'The eggs. Yes. Did they work?' asked the dog.

'I'm still alive, aren't I?'

The dog lowered its eyes. It almost looked disappointed.

'Did you see the girl?'

'Have you been watching me?'

'Did you see the girl?' the dog asked, looking almost as
deadpan as my father and his lists.

'What about her?'

'Did she say anything? About your birthday?'

'No,' I said. 'Why would she do that?'

The dog looked away, reflective, and I could see the
passage of a thousand thoughts behind those dark eyes.
The dog reminded me of somebody. Me.

I'd once seen a video recording of myself, sitting at my
desk in school. A couple of arty types from the drama
room were making what they called a warts-and-all docu-
mentary about the school. I guess I was a wart. They
showed the film after school one day. It was pretty dreary

stuff. The narrator rambled on about sexual stereotypes, school cliques and underground movements in political awareness. It was wholeheartedly a bore until I suddenly appeared on screen. I had no idea I'd been filmed yet there I was, on the big screen for all to see. The camera wobbled into my classroom, shakily passed a few students, and zoomed in so my ugly mug filled the screen.

I could actually recall what I was thinking about, during those fifteen minutes of fame. The teacher had been banging on about genetic modification and I was pondering the significance of my own gene pool. I was busy wondering which parts of my mother I had inherited and which parts of my father. Like most teenagers I was sure I was adopted and bore absolutely no resemblance to either of them. Yet the more I thought about it, the more I could see how both their beings were tightly interwoven in me. We were all locked into our own genetic prison. Was that it? Was life just a prison? Are we just a random mix of genes, a list of parts, giving us the mistaken impression that we're free? Or maybe we just follow a pattern that's already been laid out for us? We move about a bit, until the puzzle is completed, then expire.

'And here we have the coolest guy in school,' the narrator giggled. 'Line up girls! He's got charm, wit, and such fabulous good looks.'

On cue, a little bit of drool dripped out of my mouth. About half the school was watching this on a hastily set up screen in the cafeteria. Laughter echoed off the walls. Heads turned towards me. A couple of oranges bounced off my head.

Now, most people in that situation would feel embarrassed and sorry for themselves. Okay, I did, but that was secondary. What concerned me most was that the film-makers had got it wrong. Right there, on bright celluloid, my eyes told the true story. They were flitting back and forth, every so slightly, as if I was reading a giant scroll, a stone tablet of such cosmic importance that wiping a bit of drool from my mouth didn't matter.

That's how that dog looked.

'Next time you see her, give her one of these,' said the dog.

It turned away and disappeared into the brambles. Its black coat quickly dispersed into the darkness of those untamed vines. I peered in after it and saw a rose. It was so perfect I wondered if it was plastic, like the decorations you see outside hospital wards. I picked the rose and lifted it to my lips. The perfume was light, the petals were soft, but the main thing that struck me was its evenness. Its symmetry was astounding. Each petal was perfectly reflected on the opposite side, like two identical twins fused together.

Okay, maybe I was making a bit much of the rose but it was a nice flower. It was certainly good enough to give to a girl. But *that* girl? I was taking a huge chance.

My mother snapped her thumb over her cigarette lighter. The flame gushed up bright yellow and blue. She shot a quick glance at me as she lit up. Her eyes betrayed an emotion I'd never seen in her before. Annoyance.

This was highly unusual in our house. Most of the time my mother and I passed each other by like two acquaintances in the street. We would stop and chat, talk about things that concerned us both, but neither judged the other. My mother never told me what to do. She never scolded me. She'd certainly never given me any parental advice. Her sudden attention was unnerving.

'What are you doing with that?' she asked.

'I thought I'd give it to someone.'

'A girl?'

I nodded. Why did I feel like this was a betrayal? My mother sucked on her cigarette and looked upset.

'I'll put it back if you want, but I think the damage is done.'

'I don't care about the rose, Monty. Do I look like I ever cared about the roses?'

Quite clearly she didn't. They were as wild and unruly as her hair. She had a hairbrush somewhere in the house, but I hadn't seen it in years. I pictured it hiding under the floorboards, turning feral from living so many years in the wild. That mangy old hairbrush would swing from vine to vine and strike terror into the hearts of every cockroach under the house. The sad truth was, though, it had just lost its way. It was no monster, and would secretly yearn for the day to brush my mother's hair once again. Without its true purpose, it had descended into chaos.

'Whoever she is, she's going to disappoint you,' said my mother.

She stubbed her cigarette out in the perpetually full ashtray, lit up another, and turned her back on me. I waited for a few moments before I realised that was it and headed out the back door. The dog was gone. This was up to me.

'What the heck is this? Some kind of joke?'

Eliza glared at me. I'd found her back at the bus stop. I had anticipated sarcasm, humiliation, maybe general ambivalence, but not outright hostility. She came at me. Instinctually, I recoiled and hid my face. I thought she was going to punch my lights out.

'Someone told me to give it to you, I'm sorry!' I blurted.

It was weak of me. Confronted by an angry teenage girl, I panicked and blamed someone else. Pathetic, I know. She narrowed her eyes suspiciously.

'Who?' she demanded.

An eloquent soliloquy flew overhead but my tongue was a dull rock. I couldn't tell her about the creature in the roses. I realised how stupid I was. There was no dog. I had made all this up. It was all my own illusion, just like my mother and her strange intruders. I wanted to run and hide in those thorny bushes. Shame is a damaging emotion. Its cousin, self-loathing, is more overt and destructive, but shame chips away at you, breaking tiny bits off you until your insides become visible.

'I don't want it,' she sighed.

She tossed the rose away and stood on it. A second before her shoe ground that rose to dust I admired its symmetry one last time. It delighted me, like wondering how a salt crystal knows how to build such a delicate shape, or how a bee knows how to make perfect hexagons when the rest of nature hasn't heard of a straight line. The rose disappeared, broken forever, and my eyes travelled up to Eliza's. It struck me right then. She too had perfect symmetry. Her eyes were equidistant, her mouth perfectly reflected, her high cheekbones a complete match. I was an idiot. I was standing there smiling at her.

'Geez, Monty. What the hell is wrong with you? You think this is funny?'

'No, I'm sorry. I shouldn't have done it.'

I lowered my eyes back down to her shoes, where they deserved to be. She paced back and forth for a few seconds, like a caged animal deciding whether to go on the attack or turn and flee. She sighed and her anger dissipated. Maybe I was a complete lobotomy case or just plain deluded. Either way, I was no threat. I obviously didn't mean any harm.

Up the road, the school bus turned the corner. A flurry of messages shot into her inbox, making a series of gleeful little buzzing sounds. I wondered how such a cute little sound could hold so much importance. It was the buzz of recognition, the buzz of being noticed. Eliza's entourage was moments away on that bus. Soon I'd be left alone on the roadside again, covered in dust. She looked to her phone and turned it off.

It was a momentous act. Not left on silent, vibrate, or just plainly ignored; she had actually turned off her phone. This was an act of pure abandonment. It was sheer recklessness. Anarchy. I don't think I'd ever seen a girl turn off a phone before. Not on purpose anyway.

'They can live without me for one day,' she said and moved off.

I wondered if this was just a statement of fact, or an invitation.

'You coming or what?'

An invitation then.

Eliza wasn't at the bus stop that morning. The bus drove right on past and all Eliza's friends peered out to see where she'd gone. It was a mystery. A scandal. Texts were sent. Posts were uploaded. A flurry of activity spiked. Eliza's disappearance was the hottest trending topic online. People knew something was up, but what?

Nobody knew she was with me, Montgomery Ferguson, the lowest of the low. We headed off, leaving that crushed rose to rot in the dust. So it was that I first got to hang out with Eliza Robertson, the hottest girl in school with a heart of sheer contempt. I couldn't have been happier.

Chapter Four

Middleford was perched right on the edge of suburbia. The perpetual urban sprawl had swallowed this once semi-rural town and turned it into another Lego-land paradise. The place used to be the domain of wild bushrangers and hardened farmers. Now it was filled with cul-de-sacs and rows of identikit houses. There wasn't much to it, other than the highway. It finished abruptly at the end of civilisation, as if the town engineers thought there was nothing beyond Middleford worth heading for and suddenly downed tools. The furthest reaches of humanity were marked by nothing more than a big mound of dirt, the off-ramp to Middleford. Our house, the ghost house, was the last of its kind in Middleford. I used to wonder if there were any others still like it, hiding in the untamed lands past the suburban boundary. I was about to take my first look.

Eliza led me beyond the edge of suburbia. The other side of civilisation was a corrugated iron version of the Great Wall. The good folk of Middleford were protected by a battlement of identical rear fences, keeping out marauders and feral goats. Over those fences people had hot running water, air conditioning and electric toothbrushes. On the wild side, there was nothing but needle grass and rolling hills. We ventured into the wilderness. Out there, in the shadow lands, we didn't exist.

A hot northerly blew dust and flies. The dry desert wind cut through my clothes, searing my skin. Middleford was a thousand kilometres from the desert but on days like this, the inland heat moved permanently south. My sweat evaporated instantly. I longed to stop but I pressed on against the onslaught. Eliza seemed to know where she was going. She didn't look back, but I guessed she knew I was still there as I took time to curse the needle grass that invaded my socks.

Those little knights, I thought, had declared war. They were riding hard into battle, thrusting their tiny lances deep into my flesh. I picked them out, like some terrible giant, and tossed them away. Ha! They were helpless against such power. I was king of this forsaken land. I had control over their meagre destiny. I would be a harsh and vengeful god. I'd play games to amuse myself with their fates. They'd send armies into battle. They'd lose entire cities to my whims. I'd stomp them to dust and think nothing of it.

A sharp sound made me jump back into my body. Eliza had picked up a stick and rattled it against the steel fences as we walked. The stick bounced against the metal corrugations, mocking the world we'd left behind. Dogs began to bark. Soon the entire neighbourhood was filled with their bluster. The sound spread like a contagion. Eliza smiled at the havoc she had wrought.

She took me to the old park. It wasn't much of a park really, more like the last remains of some ancient scrub. Giant gum trees stood watch. They were full of possum hollows and magpie nests. In that small remnant of bush, native creatures still clung to life while all their city cousins had been eaten by cats or run over by ice-cream vans. They were rebels against extinction. This was their last outpost. I felt right at home.

Eliza led me up a small rise to find a train tunnel. A lone track wound its way through the hills. It was the interstate line and was hardly used these days. Only the occasional freight train would rumble slowly through, on its way east.

The tunnel was deep and cold. As we entered, we left the summer heat behind. The place gave me the shivers, though that probably wasn't all due to the cold. My eyes reeled at the dark. I stumbled, only able to follow blindly ahead. The tunnel was framed by the opening at the other end. It seemed so far away; a small circle of life amid the gloom. Eliza led us deep into the heart of the mountain. We skipped over the tracks. The occasional scurry in the dark signified we were not alone. There must have been an entire ecosystem of rats down there, living out their lives in the dark, curious about our sudden invasion.

Deep in that cavern, we found the middle. The light at both ends appeared exactly the same size. We stood half way, in the middle of all things, in the space between space. The light looked close enough to touch, yet far enough away that if you broke into a run you'd never reach it in time.

It struck me then. If a train came we were gone.

Fear gripped me. The rush was intoxicating. Adrenalin surged into the balls of my feet and I let out a little gasp. I was also certain a little bit of wee came out too, but I wasn't about to tell that to Eliza.

'Why are we here?' I asked.

'Relax,' she said. 'You're shivering. What's the matter, you cold?'

'I'm okay,' I lied.

I heard her rummage about in the dark. The sound of paper. The crunch of twigs. The rasping hiss of a cigarette lighter. The sound was so loud I could have sworn it was amplified, or something. Yellow flames gathered pace to push back the darkness. Flickers of light bounced around the tunnel. I could see where we were now. Red brick walls reflected sharp, glorious patterns. The flimsy heat offered only a momentary comfort. Eliza looked at me, shivering beside her. She poked my ribs and ran her finger down a few bony notches. Her finger bounced along, just like that stick against the corrugated iron fence.

'Geez Monty, don't they feed you?'

I didn't want to let her know about my theories on food. Self-control meant nothing if you had to blab about it. My guilt had unfortunate timing though. It meant I couldn't concentrate on the fact that this was the first time a girl had actually touched me. On purpose even. Not the kind of accidental touch you get while pushing for the door at the end of class. This was intentional. Normally, something like this would have sent me into far off realms of imagination. My eyes would have rolled back and I would have lived a whole lifetime of births, deaths, marriages, famine and war. A hundred years would pass in a few microseconds. But not now; I was in the moment. Eliza moved away from the fire and fished about in the tunnel. There, in the darkest recesses, was a cache of secrets. She pulled out a pack of cigarettes.

'Want one?'

I thought of my mother – the acrid stench, the winter cough that rattled the house – and shook my head.

'Suit yourself,' she said.

She lit up and warmed herself over the fire. I watched her peer into the flames. She regarded it vacantly. There was no sense of relaxation for her. This was a lonely place.

'There's something else you might like,' she said. 'Some guys must have left it here.'

She fumbled through the secret cache and revealed a crumpled old magazine. On the cover was a woman, all coconuts and pouting lips. I recoiled. The image wasn't that confronting, I'd seen stuff like that before, but it was the look in Eliza's eyes that made me nervous. She was a cold person, I understood that, but this was something else. It was an accusation.

'What's the matter?' she asked. 'This is why you're here, isn't it?'

Sure, I desired her, who wouldn't? But those kind of thoughts, for me at least, were always thin and far away. The real temptation was to think about the middle times, like the simple act of walking past her house, or hanging out with her behind someone's back fence, or sitting with her in a train tunnel. That was the real joy. I threw it on the fire.

I caught her smile in the gloom. Whatever was going on with her, I knew I'd just passed some kind of test. Clearly I was not, under any circumstances, to picture her on the front cover of such a magazine. I'd leave that to our science teacher.

'What do we do if a train comes?' I asked.

'Why? You scared?' she teased.

'No.'

'Liar.'

'I just want to know, that's all.'

Eliza gave an exasperated sigh and I caught her roll her eyes in the firelight. She suddenly pulled me close to her. A sudden heat surged through me. Eliza pressed me flat against the brickwork of the tunnel, and inside a small cavity. It was an old safety refuge, made by the original tunnel makers. They must have had delinquent kids of their own back then. Either that or they could foresee far into the future when a stupid boy would follow a beautiful girl to his demise. The refuge was small and only made to accommodate one person. We squeezed in together, wedged so tight that I could feel her breath against mine. My heartbeat soared. I could feel hers racing too. We were suddenly warm and protected in our little brick bubble.

'See? We're perfectly safe,' she said.

'Yeah. Safe.'

Then she pushed me away.

Our street was empty, expect for the two of us returning together. It was getting late. Still, the sun shone well into the night at this time of year. We had spent most of the day underground and our eyes were still getting accustomed to the daylight. We were like two sleepy bats emerging from their cave to scowl at the world. Middleford was like a desert mirage, it pained us to look at it. I wanted to run back to that cave and hide in its darkest reaches with her forever.

'Don't tell anyone about this. Okay?' she asked.

'Eliza, if you haven't noticed, you're the only person who talks to me,' I told her.

'That's not true. And you know it.'

The screen door to the kitchen announced my arrival with its usual dull thud. My mother was in the front room of the house, clouded in a blue screen of cigarette haze. I found her behind the couch, gripping a tennis racquet in defence. She looked scared.

'Someone's been in here!'

'Did he steal anything?' I asked.

'What? No!'

'Nothing? Not the scissors? Or the knob to the washing machine? Don't tell me, not yesterday's newspaper?'

Belligerence was unlike me. Honestly, I don't know what came over me. Until that moment, I'd been happy to play along with her inventions but there I was, openly mocking her. It was cruel yet something in me wanted to see her feel pain. I wanted to dispel her somehow. She looked confused. I could see she was genuinely fearful. While I watched, my mother became a child, full of doubt, fearing the unknown.

'It's not that. It's something else,' she hissed.

She tentatively pointed with her cigarette up the hallway, towards my bedroom. I nodded and crept along the rickety floorboards. Slowly, I pushed open the door to my room.

'Hello,' said the dog.

'You scared my mother,' I said.

'Did she like the rose?'

'Eliza? No. No, she didn't.'

The dog nodded in agreement. It knew all along, I thought. We looked at each other for a long time, waiting for the other to speak first, both unwilling to give the other the satisfaction. The dog finally tired of this game.

'You like her, don't you?'

'Everyone likes Eliza,' I said in defence.

'It's fine to admit it. It will make everything easier.'

I'm not sure what had changed between us but I suddenly felt wary of that dog. When I'd first met it, I found it strange, but comforting. The creature talked to me. It understood me. I think I liked that dog. Yes, I liked it. But the rose? I sensed the dog knew more about me than it was letting on. It had some purpose of its own, I swear, but what? The dog sat, watching me watch it. It was on to me. It could see through me. It could hear me.

'Yes, I can,' it replied.

I baulked. I wondered if I had said this out loud or just in my mind. My concept of what was real and what wasn't spun. Everything merged. Outside was inside. Inside was out. I was a confused mess. The dog simply looked amused.

'Just be yourself, Monty. She wants you to be yourself,' it said.

'It was just an open window,' I told my mother. 'A bird must have flown in. It's gone now. I chased it out.'

'A bird? No, this was bigger.'

'Like I said, Mum, it was just a bird.'

Doubt flooded through her. Her understanding of the world had been undermined. She fumbled for another cigarette. She couldn't light it and kept dropping it to the floor. I picked it up for her, calmly lit it, and passed it to her lips. She suckled on it greedily.

'Thank you,' she whispered.

A mournful self-pity washed through her eyes. Anger suddenly filled me. She wanted my help? I was stung. I couldn't recall the last time she'd moved a finger to help me in any way. Someone must have changed my nappies as a baby, fed me, kept me alive until the time came that I could fend for myself. All this was far away in the past. I'd been on my own for so long, forging my own way through life. Yet there she was. Dependent. I didn't want her to make it a habit.

'You should quit. Those things will kill you,' I said.

Her face contracted into a tight ball of agony and she began to shake all over. Her head nodded in agreement as the sentence I passed down struck home. She was guilty. She knew it. I knew it. She sucked that cigarette down in one breath.

I was back in the cave. Eliza smiled at me over the fire-light. We huddled over the tracks, eager for its warmth. Flames reflected in her eyes, redolent with promise. We moved closer. Suddenly, a deep rumbling sound walloped my internal organs. The sound was so low it penetrated my bones. My skull split and began to sing in time. A high-pitched squeal rang out in warped harmony. Metal wheels screeched the kind of sound feral cats fear. It made the hairs on the back of my neck stand up, like listening to a thousand fingernails run down a blackboard. Eliza quickly kicked out the fire. Darkness reclaimed the tunnel. The fire was reduced to a small pile of glowing embers, sending up little flares of distress. Eliza instantly disappeared and merged into the darkness. I didn't know where to go. I didn't know where she went. I was lost.

'Hurry up!'

Her voice seemed far off, calling from the shadows. I realised where she'd gone. The refuge! I followed the sound of her voice and found her pressed into that tiny gap in the wall. I hurried in to meet her. We flattened ourselves against each other until our breath fell in time. I wanted to grab hold of her, but my hands were paralysed. She grabbed mine instead.

'It's coming,' she said. 'Go on, look! Put your head out!'

I dutifully followed and looked out to see daylight dis-appear, replaced by the front of the train. The headlight burned white hot, tossing the darkness aside. The driver must have spotted the remains of the fire and sounded the horn. The noise blared through the tunnel, so loud it threatened to make my ears bleed.

Instinct kicked in. Survival is a stubborn force. My body involuntarily took over and tried to go back into the refuge.

I fought the urge and stayed with her. Her hand gripped mine and we calmly stared our mortality down. We were impassive. We were unafraid. We had control.

We dived back into the refuge as the train passed us by. It was a tight fit for two and there was only just enough room. We flattened ourselves against each other and held our breath. The rail cars flashed by. The sound was mortifying. I thought I was going to lose my mind. The banshee squeal of those steel wheels admonished our presence. I lost my grip on the world and was swept away. The train sucked me under its wheels. My body was destroyed. Blood and gore. Poor dismembered Monty. Gone. The last image I saw was her face, smiling.

Alias: @The Full Monty
Date: Saturday March 22, 12.12AM
Wow. This is freaky! I just had a dream that I died.

@Gutentag
Can you be assured this is a dream?

@The Full Monty
Good point. Maybe I should pinch myself to see if I'm awake?

@Gutentag
I am of agreement. Pain means you are having this life.

@The Full Monty
Yeah. Got it. That kinda sucks though, huh?

Chapter Five

Alias: @The Full Monty
Date: Friday April 11, 5.23AM
Hey, what do you think's on the other side?

@Gutentag
Nothing and something give to cancel.

@The Full Monty
You mean it's just like here, but the opposite?

@Gutentag
No. Not like here but the same ☺

I'd often wondered why my parents never had another child. Of course I assumed it was my fault. Somehow I'd been such a bothersome baby that my parents were sworn off bringing another one into this world. I imagined myself, needy and crying in the middle of the night. In my version I'd be pathetically small, weirdly no larger than an eggcup. My father would grunt in his sleep leaving my mother to tend me, swearing hot curses under her breath. Her nerves were so shot after giving birth to such a horrific creature, that she reached for her first cigarette. I was the cause of her anxiety, I was sure.

I'd once seen some old pictures of my mother, young and fresh looking. What struck me wasn't her youthful face, without the wrinkles and dark rings that stained her eyes now. It was the fact that she always appeared without a cigarette. In one picture she was laughing at a fair ground, in another she was holding a pet rabbit she once had, in another she was sitting on a beach in her bikini. In none of these images did she hold a cigarette. This compulsion came later, after I was born. It was all the proof I needed.

'You ever been to Germany?' I asked the dog.

'If you haven't noticed, I'm a dog,' it said.

'Yeah, but you're not a *normal* dog, are you? Who knows where you've been?'

It sat there watching me pull on yesterday's shirt. There was a long stain down the front. It had been there for a few days now, some glue from school or something I guess. I tried to wipe it off by licking a handkerchief and dabbing at it, like a mother does a child's dirty face. That only made things worse, so I gave up.

'Well?' I asked. 'Have you ever been to Germany?'

The dog suddenly bared its teeth, and its hackles went up. All the hairs on its back stood on end like sharp bristles.

'You think he's your friend?' snarled the dog. 'You don't even understand what he says. And he doesn't understand you. Don't waste your time with him.'

I grimaced stubbornly down at the dog. Talking to Gutentag was like reading a cryptic fortune cookie. Nothing ever quite made sense but you always had the feeling he knew more than what he was letting on. Surely there was meaning there before the translation mucked it all up? Or was the dog right? Was Gutentag just spouting incomprehensible babble, even in German? Was he locked up in some mental hospital in Berlin, his arms pinned in a straight jacket, writing to me by punching a keyboard with his nose?

No. I refused to think of him like this. He was the only friend I'd ever had.

'Forget about him. She's what you want,' said the dog. 'I'm here to help you.'

Its demeanour softened. The hairs on its back relaxed and it tilted its head to one side. It almost looked cute enough to pat. Still, I didn't dare.

It was unusual for our family to do anything together. Most weekends were spent apart. Even if we were all home at the same time, we'd all find separate rooms in the house to do whatever. But on the odd occasion, duty won out and we'd visit Dolly.

Dolly was my grandmother, my mother's mother, and a gregarious extrovert. She liked to wear bright purple everything. From her hair to her frilly blouses to the fluffy slippers on her feet, everything was a lurid purple. She'd been a nurse in her working life and had seen her fair share of pain and suffering, so I guess that was her way of coping.

'Why are you so purple?' I had asked when I was little.

'Oh. I just like to brighten things up a bit,' Dolly would say. 'How about we go ride a unicorn?'

Dolly liked the unicorns at the Royal Show. She used to take me there when I was little and we'd go round and round on the carousel. She'd always pick the unicorn, so I could hold onto the horn while we ate fairy floss. Those days were long gone. A few years ago Dolly had a fall and broke her hip. Now this once proud and independent woman couldn't get herself to the toilet on time. She tried her best to cope, but after a while she couldn't manage her house. That's when the trouble started. She blamed my father.

'Is he out in the car?' asked Dolly.

'Yes,' said my mother.

'You shouldn't have let him come. He's not welcome.'

'He'll only come in if you say so.'

'Well, I won't say so!' she spat. 'Did you bring any biscuits?'

Dolly's own mother lived through World War Two and had instilled in her a pathological fear of throwing anything away. Back then people had to make do with what they had. When something broke, they mended it. There simply wasn't the option of buying a replacement. Dolly kept everything. Her house was a mad collection of refuse. There was probably a lot of valuable stuff in there, hidden under piles of yellow newspapers. Collectors paid top dollar for old gear like that. But when Dolly was put in the retirement village, Dad just backed a truck in and took the lot down the dump. Dolly was furious. She never forgave him. He had thrown her life away. She had no idea it was all my mother's idea. Dolly needed full-time care so, forced to choose between caring for Dolly and sending her to a home, my mother chose the home. Dad took all this on the chin. He never once tried to explain that it wasn't his decision. Whenever we visited Dolly, he'd just sit outside in the car and read the paper.

Dolly's retirement village was a small collection of units, all lined up next to one another. It had tended gardens and nurses on call. Each unit held someone's grandmother, or grandfather, and they'd all sit in their little houses and wait for someone to visit. They waved hello to each other in the morning and sometimes played cards in the evening. There was a dog there too.

It was a greyhound, an ex-racing dog, purchased to give the elderly residents some company, I guess. Normally dogs like this were put down once they were too old to race, given some sort of lethal injection. But this one was saved. This geriatric dog lived with all the geriatric people. But it hadn't spent much time with humans, so it had no idea how to behave like a pet. It didn't care for a pat or a game of fetch. All it did was sniff the old people. And when one of them was about to die, it sat next to them and watched. It was never wrong. If that dog sat with you you'd die, guaranteed. Maybe it could smell cancer cells, or pheromones given off when your body shuts down, or maybe it could just smell death? Needless to say, none of them liked it.

The greyhound crossed the yard in front of Dolly's unit and she nearly choked on her biscuit. A look of terror crossed her face. We all watched out the window as the greyhound paused a moment, sniffed the air, and then moved on to another unit. Dolly breathed a sigh of relief. Her hands trembled as she sipped her tea.

Dolly never let you pity her though. When you'd been there for about an hour, she'd abruptly tell you it was time to go. She was almost rude about it.

'Go on then. Off you go!' she'd say. 'I'm a busy person. I've got much better things to do than sit around and have tea and biscuits all day!'

She'd see us off at the door and scowl at my dad waiting in the car. That was just a ruse though. We all knew that as soon as we drove off, Dolly would just sit there and wait until our next visit, surrounded in purple. Waiting is always the hardest part.

Alias: @The Full Monty
Date: Monday April 14, 6.45AM
Hey, what's your favourite food?

@Gutentag

I prefer sustenance for good thought.

@The Full Monty

I get it. You like a good idea? Food for thought, you mean?

@Gutentag

Unless your thoughts are to punish.

@The Full Monty

Why would I do that?

@Gutentag

When don't you?

I was determined to try and cooked a boiled egg for breakfast. I wasn't sure I could eat it without puking.

About a year ago, I'd found a block of chocolate dropped outside a supermarket; the owner must have let it slip from their shopping bag, or something. It lay there on the bitumen, still in its shiny red wrapper, promising delight. It was a momentary weakness in my otherwise successful campaign of self-sacrifice. I hid behind a bush and ate the whole thing in one go. The taste was extraordinary. I hadn't eaten anything remotely that wonderful in years. But it was too much, too soon. I was horrendously ill and puked all over the gutter. Chocolate-flavoured goo flew all over the place. People came out to watch and point at me. I was sure they thought I was drunk or something. I stumbled around like a hobo, trying to hold myself up on a parked car. The sugar rush gave me an instant headache and my skull throbbed in agony. My brain decided it wasn't going to hang around to be punished like that and took off who knows where. I woke up an hour later two streets away inside a bin.

I had to take this easy.

I pondered the egg, steaming in its cup. A whole slice of toast waited for me too, buttered thick. I cut the toast into soldiers and dipped one in the creamy, soft yolk. I ate just one corner. It was good. I could feel nourishment coursing through me. It was energising. My body craved more. But I knew too much, too soon, was going to be the end of me. I had to take this slowly. I could feel the sick rising in my throat. I sat back and let my fingers bounce across my ribs. No. That wasn't going to be enough. I had to do better, and not just for me. I held the nausea back and ate some more.

'Hello Monty,' said the dog.

'Do I smell like I'm dying?' I asked.

The dog paused a while, as if considering how much information it could tell me.

'That's a matter of degree,' it finally said. 'Everything dies. Eventually.'

'What about me? Do I smell like I'm dying?'

'That's not for me to tell you, even if I could.'

What was that? Doubt? Maybe it didn't know anything after all.

'You look different,' said Eliza.

'Yeah? How?'

I was almost proud. I was bursting to tell her about my morning success. She shrugged, suddenly non-committal, and lit up a cigarette as she waited for the bus. She flicked her hair back as she breathed the calming smoke in. She looked beautiful, like one of those old time movie stars when they filmed them with the soft lens, surrounding them in that dreamy, far away look. Everything about her was perfect – except for the cigarette. She noticed my look.

'What? You don't like smokes?'

I shook my head timidly. It wasn't my place to judge. Eliza narrowed her eyes and took a long, pensive drag. She blew the smoke in my face.

'Fine,' she said defiantly and tossed the smoke down and butted it out with one shoe. 'See? I can do it too.'

I was full of panic. Was I that visible? Was I that transparent? I had eaten one boiled egg and she had understood me. She had seen right through me. Nope. I realised I still had some egg on my chin.

The bus came and went. Eliza disappeared with it. We wouldn't spend the day together. I had been a fool to hope.

I sat by myself at lunchtime. Once, years ago, I had a friend who used to sit with me. His name was Tim Smith.

Tim Smith was a good guy. He was honourable, friendly, trustworthy and all that. But those qualities weren't why we became friends. It was his name. Tim Smith. That name was so incredibly ordinary that nobody took the slightest notice of him. He blurred into the background, literally disappeared when anyone else entered the room. He was such a forgettable person that, if you asked around, nobody could remember ever laying eyes on him. He was nothing. Invisible. Not even the teachers could put a finger to him. Tim Smith knew how to get through school, that's for sure. Tim Smith. I longed for a name like that. What did I have? Montgomery Ulysses Ferguson? I swore, one day, I'd change my name but, no matter what, I couldn't think of anything better than Tim Smith. The world wouldn't care if there were two Tim Smiths in it, surely? If I were a Tim Smith too, I could be just as invisible. But the more I thought about it, changing my identity jarred with me. Deep down, I knew I couldn't rub out my existence that easily.

I never really knew what happened to Tim Smith. One day he was there, eating his salad roll, the next he was gone. I never saw him again. Perhaps he fell down a mine-shaft somewhere and nobody could hear his paper-thin cries, or maybe he's still at school, going about his studies so quietly that he's practically a ghost, a walking corpse among the living.

I was knee-deep in thoughts about Tim Smith when I did something stupid. I was on autopilot again. My body must have enjoyed breakfast and decided more food was in order. The fact that I didn't have money wasn't going to deter it. Before my brain knew what was going on, my body lumbered up to the canteen window and pushed in line.

Tony Papadopoulos never left the canteen during break times. He'd eat all the food from his mother's lunchbox then spend all the money from his father's wallet. And he didn't like being pushed. The pain was instant. I was pulled back into existence as something hard struck my back. I blinked and took a second to work out which way was up. I found myself pushed over a long, metal handrail. The cold steel had belted into my spine. It was like being king-hit with a baseball bat. The pain was intense. Tony stood over me, grinning.

'What's the matter? Don't like being pushed, huh?'

I scrambled to my feet and was about to leave, but Tony felt like adding salt to the wound. I guess he was still angry about his ruined soccer shirt so he punched me in the face.

I didn't expect it. Nobody did. There was a gasp of shock from all the kids watching as the punch landed home. Tony generally just hit you in the guts. Usually he was too smart to leave any clear evidence. He didn't want trouble from the teachers, so bruises were best avoided. This was a clear violation of that unspoken code.

I landed on the concrete floor. The hard surface stung the back of my skull. I've heard of people getting killed from this type of thing. It's not the punch that kills you. Death comes from the crushing blow as your head hits the ground. Your skull cracks open like a split watermelon, and your brain simply bleeds out while everyone stands around to watch, wondering what to do. Lucky for Tony, I wasn't quite dead.

He wanted more. That thing with the shirt must have really bugged him. He pumped his fists and ordered me to get up. I tried to obey, I really did, but my legs just wobbled underneath me. I looked like a broken puppet. Tony grabbed the front of my shirt.

'Leave him alone!'

Eliza pushed her way in between us. Tony instantly obeyed and wiped back his hair in an effort to make himself look palatable.

'He started it,' he explained.

He was right enough, I guess. I had started it. It all started with those eggs. The dog and the eggs. I could see a pattern forming. A pattern I had blindly followed.

Eliza led me to the safety of the teachers' office. Not to look for help from them of course, I could just hide out in the toilets nearby. I had a shiner on my eye like a pro boxer.

'How do I look?'

Eliza smiled. She liked it, I could see.

Chapter Six

Some ants were busy building an entire civilisation using nothing more than brains the size of a speck of dust. There were leaders and followers. The followers worked in perfect harmony, mindlessly going about their duties. The larger soldier ants quietly stood guard over the trail, protecting their weaker brethren. This was a revelation. Those tiny creatures had put their thugs to good use, for the betterment of the tribe. It was a simple survival strategy, but if the bigger soldier ants decided to push the other ants around for a bit of fun, soon the tribe would come under attack. The queen, hidden away in her mansion somewhere, would die a slow death. That would be the end of the tribe. Ants never questioned their purpose. They just performed it. Maybe that was our problem? We weren't meant to be self-aware.

'Monty! Hello! Are you there?'

Eliza stood beside me. How long she'd been there, watching me watch the ants, I didn't know. I was sitting on a bench outside the school, partially hidden by a row of bushes. All around us, kids were delivered home on a never-ending stream of school buses.

I knew Tony would be looking for me after school, but I also knew that his parents drove to pick him up. My plan was to lie low, camouflaged in plain sight, and keep an eye out for his parent's car. Once he was gone, I could walk home safely. My plan had one obvious flaw.

'Tony left half an hour ago,' said Eliza. 'I think you can go home now.'

'Thanks.'

'What's with the ants?' she asked curiously.

What had started all this was the school sign hung above the gates. A motto was emblazoned on it: *Vade Ad Formicam*. It was Latin and roughly translated to 'look at the ants'. Obviously some arrogant school founder came up with this quaint little quote to inspire students into an industrious work ethic. It hadn't worked. Our school had one of the lowest grade averages in the country. Most kids wouldn't even know what that sign meant, or care if they did. Who spoke Latin anyway? It was an extinct language. Still, it made me look at the ants. Eliza seemed to get bored waiting for an answer.

'I've got to go.'

Some girls turned a corner nearby. They were friends of Eliza's and flicked their hair with such perfect unison I could've sworn it was choreographed. They were headed straight for us. Eliza quickly avoided them and made sure she wasn't seen with me. I watched her scurry away. That wasn't right, I thought. Eliza Robertson didn't scurry.

'See what you've done to her?' hounded the dog.

It peered at me from under some bushes nearby. It kept its head low, as if it were stalking.

'What do you mean?' I asked.

'Those girls,' it said. 'They used to hang off her every word. Now she hides from them. She is desperate to remain unseen. Remind you of anyone?'

A sick feeling washed over me. I had turned Eliza into Tim Smith.

Normally, I'd walk home on autopilot. My body could usually handle this daily chore by itself. It knew how many steps to take, when to turn and when to avoid a pothole.

It'd only have to wait for me to guide it across a busy road. My body would often be spotted loitering aimlessly around pedestrian crossings, waiting for my brain to drift back to consciousness.

Not this day. I was firmly in place. I walked to the other end of my street and stood looking at Eliza's house. The two-storey mansion was clean and fresh. The front lawn was mown tight and happy topiary bushes were clipped into perfectly round shapes. Everything about it was new and perfect. Even the windows were clean. I never knew windows could be clean.

I rang the doorbell. The cheery ding-dong that sang my arrival made me smile. It was so simple, yet effective. It announced my presence with sheer delight. We never had the happy pleasure of a doorbell at our house. Visitors to our house sometimes looked around for a doorbell, but in its absence were forced to knock. For some reason they'd always bang extra loud, like they were trying to scare away the ghouls.

A middle-aged woman answered the door. Eliza's mum I guessed.

'Yes?'

She had a fresh hairdo, crisp features and wore pearls. I'd only ever seen a woman wear pearls in the movies. They caught my eye. I was transfixed, desperate to dive into thoughts about the lifecycle of a mollusc whose only purpose in life was to make a shiny ball for some two-legged land animal to wear around its neck.

'If you're selling something, I'm sorry, I can't help you,' she said politely and moved back to close the door.

'Is Eliza home?' I asked tentatively.

She looked me up and down for a few seconds, considering her options. I was obviously not Eliza's usual type of visitor. They would mostly be those girls from school: well dressed, perfectly preened and confident. Any boy to ring that doorbell would have been so handsome your eyeballs would shatter at the sheer sight of him. Not me. Lank hair drooped over my face. My pimples shone. My teeth jutted. My black eye bulged like a warning beacon. My entire body was slumped in under itself, trying not to be seen.

'She's upstairs,' she said. 'Come in.'

I entered the house. It smelt of lavender and air freshener and bleach. There was carpet underfoot. It was so springy it was like walking over freshly mown grass. The furniture was all brand new, and each piece matched perfectly. I had no idea furniture came like that. Our house was full of whatever mismatched pieces of junk we could get our hands on. Eliza's house had style.

I walked in carefully, trying not to disturb the order. Eliza's family smiled in their portraits, hung on the wall in perfect rows. Her father and mother stood behind her solemnly. They didn't look very happy in those photos. Being clean and having money didn't necessarily mean you had everything in life, I guess.

Past the household cleansers, I could smell something wonderful cooking. I suddenly realised I was hungry. I tried my best to ignore it, but my body was about to mount a military coup and take over for good. I broke out into a sweat. I was in a panic. I wrestled for control. If I lost, I knew my body would go feral and devour whatever it was in that kitchen like some mad animal. I wiped a little saliva from my mouth. Eliza's mother looked at me curiously.

'You have a nice place Mrs Robertson,' I said in my best attempt to appear normal.

She suddenly looked self-conscious and glanced down to her feet. In that split-second, I swear I could see her nervous system pump adrenaline through her body. The flush was momentary but vivid; the slight redness in her cheeks, the sudden quick energy in her step, the elusive tightness in her throat were giveaways to the trained eye.

'I'll just get her for you,' she croaked and backed away.

I wondered what I had done to offend her. Maybe I was drooling more than I thought. Eliza came down the stairs, her eyes wide in astonishment.

'Monty? What are you doing here?'

I realised my visit wasn't wanted. I had to leave but the front door suddenly looked far away. I stood there in no-man's land, waiting to be shot down.

'Why are you here, Monty?'

'I just wanted to say sorry, for turning you into Tim Smith.'

'Who the hell is Tim Smith?'

'Exactly,' I said.

She looked at me as if I was crazy. She was probably right, I thought. I couldn't think of one good reason why I should be there.

'Did anyone see you?'

She looked furtively out the window and peered up the street. There was nothing out there.

'How long were you standing out there?' she asked.

'Dunno. What time is it?'

'Nearly six.'

'I came straight from school. I'm not sure,' I said. 'It could have been a few hours.'

She hissed angrily and checked the street again. I had gone too far, coming over and all. I went to leave but she held me back.

'Wait. You're here now. You might as well stay. At least until it gets dark.'

Eliza's mother eavesdropped from the kitchen, pretending to fuss with the cooking. She was obviously keeping a close eye on developments and peered around the doorway to check on us. Mrs Robertson was a touch shorter than Eliza, her features more bird-like and pulled into an anxious, thin line. Little creases in the corners of her eyes betrayed a secret sense of humour, or perhaps she grew up in a really sunny place and was left with a permanent squint, or maybe her eyes were just half-closed to the world, fearful and suspicious. Eliza noticed her and pulled at my shirt. She led me upstairs towards her room. My heart raced. My breath quickened, as if I'd just run a marathon. In reality I'd only taken two steps but I was already out of air. I heard Eliza's mother drop a spoon.

Eliza's room was not what I expected. I didn't really know what to expect, I guess, but I had imagined a few possibilities. One vision was bright pink with hundreds of teddy bears on the bed and a large mirror so wide it could reflect her perfect face from any angle in the room. Stupid I know but, to me, it was more like a childish, romantic dream. Another vision, one that I expected to be closer to the truth, had her room painted black with the walls plastered in posters from some underground industrial rock band.

In reality there was nothing. The walls were painted dull beige, just like the rest of the house. There were no teddy bears, no posters; nothing to give the impression this was a teenager's room at all. The closest thing it resembled, I guess, was a hotel room. It was devoid of personality. That really threw me. Even my own room had certain objects that would give away something about me: science magazines, old toys, drawings I did when I was a kid. Eliza's room had nothing. It was barren and cold.

'Sit down,' she ordered.

I obeyed and sat on the end of her bed. This was the bed she slept in. The bed she disappeared in to dream. My hand felt the sheets, in some vague attempt to touch those thoughts.

'Does it hurt?'

'The eye? Yeah, a bit,' I admitted.

She smiled. That wasn't a smile containing pity, or empathy. She enjoyed the idea that I was in pain. She moved to a small ensuite off the bedroom and wet a face washer. She returned to sit beside me and wet my face with it, soothing that puffy dark bruise. My greasy hair fell down in front of my eyes a little and she had to push it aside to complete the task.

'Who cuts your hair, your mother?'

'Me actually,' I admitted, feeling like a total idiot.

I had cut my own hair for a long time. I'd sit in front of the bathroom mirror with a pair of scissors. It wasn't easy but I thought I was pretty skilled at it. When I was little, my mother used to take me to a barber at the local shops. Later, she tried to save money and cut my hair herself. I couldn't stand it: she'd always manage to burn me with her cigarettes, dropping hot ash onto my scalp. I remember hiding from her whenever she threatened me with a pair of scissors. Finally she gave up. After a few months of my hair growing wild, I took to tidying it up myself. It took a while to get used to moving your hands in reverse in the mirror. The back of your head is the hardest part to cut. I used a small hand mirror like a periscope to peer around the back. It was a disconcerting feeling, to look at the back of your own head. If you looked long enough, it began to look like the head of a completely different person.

'Who's in there?' I'd ask.

'You are,' said the head.

'Oh. How do you like your haircut?'

'Could be better,' said the head. 'Don't think I'm going to pay!'

Eliza touched my hair and flinched in disgust. She stared at me with contempt. I think she was simultaneously repelled, and compelled, to look at me. I was like some horrible car crash. You couldn't look away, no matter how horrible the scene.

'In here,' she ordered.

Again, I was to obey. She led me to the small bathroom and pushed my head down into the hand basin. She was forceful, like she was bathing a dog. Hot water gushed over my scalp. I recoiled. The pain was searing.

'Too hot?'

Something in her voice made me think she already knew that. She turned on the cold tap to bring the temperature down a little. She washed my hair in punishing movements and my head bounced off the side of the basin more than once. I tried my best not to cry out, even when she struck me right on my black eye. I took her blows without complaint. I realised for some reason she needed to hurt me. I shouldn't have come over. I deserved this. Eventually, her movements began to soften and I could feel her anger slip away. She tried to hold onto it, I could tell, but it drained out of her like the shampoo in the sink.

'Bet that's the first time in weeks you've washed,' she muttered.

The accusation held. She was right, but it had been more like months.

'Sit here. And stay still.'

Another order, but the intensity had gone out of it. Eliza placed a seat for me in front of her bathroom mirror and cut my hair. Her movements were fluid. She began to relax, unfettered by anger. She was somewhere else, I could tell. Her body was going through the motions, combing and cutting, but her mind had gone to that other place. I longed to go on that journey with her but I knew that was impossible. She suddenly looked up and our eyes connected in the mirror. She quickly finished up and grabbed a tube of face cream.

'Wash your face with this. Every day. It'll help with the pimples,' she said bluntly.

She tossed me the face cream and walked out to the bedroom. I had been cleansed. The haircut was good, stylish even. She knew what she was doing, that's for sure. She was much better at it than I was. I washed my face with the pimple cream and could feel the tiny particles grind away the grease and oil from my skin. It was like rubbing popping candy on your face. I'd never had a feeling like it before. My face tingled with excitement and I could feel the zits scurry back in fear. Their days were numbered.

'Thanks,' I offered.

'It's nothing.'

'I mean it. Nobody's ever done something like that for me before.'

'Don't get used to it. I'm not your mother.'

'Have you met my mother?' I joked.

She hadn't. Nobody from school ever came round to meet my mother. But she'd heard the stories. Everyone had. The woman from the ghost house was a local legend. She'd steal your babies and feed them to the house. And her son was a zombie. She'd taken his brain out as a child and kept it in a jar of jelly above the sink. That's why he's so mental. Of course, it was all just an urban myth. Still, I had to accept my own behaviour: if I were a normal, confident kid stories like that wouldn't have taken hold. But I wasn't any of those things. There was a soft, almost inaudible, knock on the door. Eliza instantly looked tense.

'What do you want?' Eliza snapped.

The door opened a little and Eliza's mother peered through the small gap, as if she was protecting herself from possible attack.

'Your father's home from work. He'd like your ... friend to stay for dinner?'

She phrased this almost as a question, hoping Eliza would accede to the request. The door softly closed and Eliza sat frozen, her eyes boring into the wall.

'I should go,' I told her, attempting to ease her mind.

'No. He knows you're here. He'll want to meet you.'

The table was laid like I'd never seen before. White linen. Silver cutlery. Matching china plates. Folded napkins. There was even a lit candle in the middle of it all. I never thought people actually ate like this. Busy sounds of electrical appliances whirled about in the kitchen. Rich aromas wafted through. The smells teased me, threatening my head to explode.

I was placed next to Eliza who dutifully sat with eyes on her plate, saying nothing. Her father held court at the head of the table and placed himself under a simple wooden crucifix on the wall. The austerity in that house suddenly made sense: they were religious people. Eliza's father wore a suit and tie and his light grey hair was neatly clipped. He had a broad smile papered to a crisply shaven face. He had the relaxed ease of a man in control of his domain. He appeared cheery enough, a bit like that doorbell. But his eyes never left me. I knew that meant trouble.

'Doreen tells me you live in my street?' he chimed amiably.

His street? I thought. What did he mean, *his street*? Our house was the oldest living relic around. It was a fossil, sure, but age garners respect, right? If anything, this was *my* street, I thought.

I simply nodded my head.

'That's great,' he said. 'So you two know each other from school?'

He sat forward, hands on his chin, smiling. He certainly seemed interested in how we met. He gave me the impression he wanted to be friends. Yep, this meant trouble.

I nodded again. He hadn't yet asked me about my black eye. Neither of them did. I thought that was odd, as if they knew I had something to hide.

'Strange. Elizabeth hasn't spoken about you, Montgomery. Montgomery? That's actually your name?'

Again, all I could muster was a nod.

'Am I meant to do all the talking here?' he joked. 'Come on, I like the name. I half thought of naming Elizabeth something extraordinary like that. Maybe Cleopatra? Or Clytemnestra? What do you think?'

He eyed Eliza with this. She just gave him a cursory nod, as if she'd heard this type of good-natured jibe way too often. I smiled, thinking that's what he expected of me.

'What? You think that's funny, Monty?'

He was still smiling but I could see this was no longer a joke. He was goading me. I didn't know what to do. Capitulation seemed like a safe option.

'No sir,' I said.

He suddenly laughed, sounding overt and strained. It was a honking bellow that was way too loud in such close quarters. He was trying hard to appear sociable yet I could see the cracks seeping into his veneer. He made my skin crawl.

'Sir? You don't have to call me, sir! We're not that formal here. Call me Derek,' he said magnanimously.

I simply nodded again, deferentially. Derek and Doreen? I thought. What wonderful symmetry. They were in tune, twins in alliteration. I wondered what our names would sound like together. Monty and Eliza? Eliza and Monty? Despite my hopes, we just didn't sound right. We had no simple-sounding connection. Our names were discordant, as if we were not meant to be.

The smells from the kitchen became more intense but I didn't care, I wanted to get the hell out of there. Eliza's mother entered carrying a platter with the biggest roast beef I'd ever seen. Roast potatoes and pumpkin surrounded it. She also laid out green vegetables and gravy that made my mouth water. I couldn't take my eyes off the food. It was a revelation. Derek grabbed a long knife and sharpened it over the beef. The sound of the knife scraping backwards and forwards seared the air. The whole time, he stood grinning at me.

He might be a middle-aged accountant but this man was one step away from slicing me up instead of that beef. He dissected the meat and the food was dispensed with precision timing. Eliza and her mother dutifully placed just the right amount of everything on each plate and passed them around the table. Maybe the good china and silverware didn't come out all that often, but these people certainly ate formally every day of the week, that much was clear.

'Monty was just agreeing with me Doreen,' her father said. 'I could have chosen a much better name for Elizabeth.'

She smiled politely, looking at little confused.

'Well, at least Eliza can thank you for being sensible Mrs Robertson,' I offered.

Silence.

All of them stared at me, shocked. I had that out-of-body feeling again, unsure if what I'd just said was English, or some language thousands of years old. There was a clink of cutlery and my strange outburst was seemingly forgotten.

They said grace. I'd never said grace before, so I just watched and listened as they thanked God for allowing them to eat one of His cows along with some of His vegetables.

I never thought much about a god. The idea struck me as absurd, really. After all, so many people from so many tribes had so many different gods. How could you tell if one was any better than the other? Most people grew up believing in the god their parents believed in, and that was enough for them. But what if you had a really stupid god?

I recalled my history teacher. He told us a story about some Polynesian islands and their cargo cults. These Pacific tribes watched the white settlers sit around and do almost nothing to survive. They didn't tend animals. They didn't hunt. They didn't even try to plant a crop. All they did was sit at a desk and pray to some strange box with a long wire hung out the door and, a few months later, a ship would come with all the cargo they needed to survive. Presents would be unloaded. Food. Timber. Furniture. Wine. Their prayers had been answered! Of course, those white folks were simply calling home on the telegraph line. But the tribal guys thought they must have talked to God. And God had sent them cargo. The weird thing is, this happened in loads of islands all around the same time. The islanders had no way to spread the idea of a cargo cult, it just happened simultaneously in every place where white people ordered stuff on the telegraph. So they worshiped cargo. I stared at the crucifix on the wall.

'You appreciate the Word?' Derek asked.

'Huh? No, I was just thinking how stupid it was.'

Eliza laughed, but caught herself and quickly passed the gravy. Derek stared at me coldly. I had made a fatal mistake. You don't insult someone's religion lightly, I knew. Wars had been fought for less.

I ate the food quietly. Bile instantly rose in my throat but, each time it did, Eliza looked to me reassuringly. She understood what I was going through and her simple presence was enough for me to go on.

The taste was all I hoped it would be. The beef was soft and salty, the potatoes were crisp on the outside and creamy in the middle, the gravy was thick and flavoursome. I'd never had a meal like this. Ever. It was the most I could ever remember eating yet, to look at my plate, you'd think I wasn't hungry. I'd just taken one bite of each thing.

'Don't be shy. Eat up!' Derek chimed.

He really did sound like that doorbell. Perhaps he'd go out in the middle of the night to press it? He'd hum its ding-dong greeting over and over and mimic the sound, perfecting it. I could've sworn he appropriated that happy tone so he could disguise his own dark core.

The bile rose again. A hunk of beef jagged in my throat. I knew I wouldn't last the distance. I gagged. My face went all puffy. My eyes watered and I suddenly ran from the table, holding my mouth. I think my plate fell behind me as I left; the sound of broken china was accompanied my Mrs Robertson's pained gasp. She loved her good china, I could tell.

I vomited in the bathroom up the hall. All that fantastic food was washed away. I sat on the edge of the bath and held my head. Shame returned to chip away at me. I wanted to flush myself down that toilet too.

I wanted to squeeze through the pipes, burrow deep underground, and take my rightful place with all the other excrement down there. Eventually, I'd be washed out to sea. Maybe I'd hit some swimmer in the eye, give him the fright of his life? Eliza knocked and came in.

'Maybe you're not ready. Maybe neither of us are,' she said.

She reached around the back of the vanity and pulled out a pack of cigarettes. She turned on the bathroom fan to extract the smoke as she lit up. Eliza sat beside me on the edge of the bath, blowing the smoke up into the fan. She always looked so cool.

'Your father's a nice guy,' I said, barely hiding my sarcasm.

'I told them you've been feeling sick,' she explained.

I had failed her. Again. I just wanted to run and hide.

'It's getting dark,' she said. 'You can go now.'

I was almost at the front door when Eliza's father appeared, coming at me from the shadows. He stood in front of me and blocked my escape. I turned to look for witnesses to the beating I was about to receive. There were none. Eliza had gone back to her room, and her mother was in the kitchen, attempting to glue her china back together.

'I don't like you,' he snorted.

His doorbell chime had evaporated and all that was left was raw animal instinct. I tried not to show fear. I tried not to run. Still, he could sense I was afraid.

'You're a rude boy,' he said. 'You come into my house. You eat at my table. I want you to show me some respect!'

He was trying to keep his voice down but his venom was clear.

'Doreen's very upset,' he muttered.

'I didn't mean to break the plate,' I whispered.

'This isn't about the damn plate!'

He looked exasperated with me now and sighed. He wiped back his clipped hair, attempting to calm himself. As his hand rustled through that low-clipped hedge, hot sparks of electricity leapt off his scalp, like angry little lightning bolts.

'Doreen isn't Mrs Robertson. Do you understand? Elizabeth's mother died two years ago.'

His eyes were thin points. There were so many emotions in there, all hidden, but grief didn't seem to be one of them.

'Cancer is a terrible thing, Monty. It makes your body waste away. The pain is excruciating to watch. It was a very hard time for us. But you have to live life. You have to move on. Doreen's been very good to me.'

I was a total idiot. My wise crack about Eliza's mother, calling her daughter Elizabeth, would have come across quite the insult. It all made sense. The framed pictures in the hall were all recent. There wasn't a single picture of Eliza as a child. Some small part of Eliza's pain was revealed to me then. She was incapable of telling me this herself. She'd left it up to her father.

'I'm sorry,' I said. 'What was her name?'

I don't know why I asked this, but it suddenly seemed very important. Derek looked at me as if I was truly an imbecile. He shook his head, perturbed by my insolence.

'Rose.'

Chapter Seven

'Dog!' I howled at the night.

'Dog!'

The backyard was empty of life. The bramble of roses hid many shadows. I peered in but could only see blackness. Nothing resembled the creature. I pushed my way through, hunting, clawing through the thorns.

I'd never felt this kind of rage before and the energy that rushed through me was intoxicating. It was more nourishing than any food. I quickly found myself in the middle of that thick undergrowth. Thorns stuck my skin. My arms bled. My scalp dripped with blood. I scrambled all the way to the deepest core of that bramble but found nothing. I looked out through that twisted vine, to the world beyond. I was the shadow creature now.

'Coward,' I muttered.

It had known all about Eliza's mother.

Alias: @The Full Monty
Date: Tuesday April 15, 4.13AM
Have you ever killed anything before?

@Gutentag
I was of wondering when you would have the courage.

@The Full Monty
Stop fooling with me. Just answer the question.

@Gutentag
I am for disagreement. You are the fool being.

@The Full Monty
Very funny. So, have you ever killed anything?

@Gutentag
Only one thing.

@The Full Monty
Yes?

@Gutentag
It was nothing. A dream.

@The Full Monty
Tell me!!!

@Gutentag
You.

I started the chainsaw. It filled the crisp morning air with rage. The sound was deafening, liberating too. I revved it hard. The mechanical roar gave perfect voice to my fury.

We had had this old chainsaw for years. My father used it to cut wood for the fireplace when I was a kid. These days, we'd all forgotten the comfort of an open fire and just slipped on an extra jumper to protect from the winter chill. The old chainsaw hadn't been started in a very long time. After countless, frustrated pulls on that ripcord, the frightening machine had suddenly roared back into life. Resurrected, I guess.

I took to the roses. I cut. I sliced. I chopped and hacked them down until there was nothing left but a line of dull grey stumps. I found no dog. The murder lust left me.

I looked deeper and realised the roses were originally planted in rows. There, like an archeological dig, was evidence that someone had once loved those roses. That dark bramble was once a neat promenade of colour. It was once a place of order and joy, a place where lovers strolled arm in arm. I killed the chainsaw and kicked at the stumps. They were surprisingly easy to dislodge. It was done.

I turned towards the house and saw my mother watching me, her mouth open in horror. Scared, I guess. What did she think? That I'd take to her next, and hack her to pieces with that chainsaw? It would be a fitting revenge, I thought. After all, I could plead my case to the courts. I was a poor only child, I'd tell the judge. I was malnourished and left to fend for myself fighting over bin scraps with the local sewer rats. The court would understand. The verdict would be simple. They'd place me in a nice foster home and I'd have all the food and kindness I could desire.

My mother turned away and disappeared inside. I put the chainsaw down and followed. I found her in the lounge and sat in front of her. She had no choice but to see me.

'I tried to kill something,' I told her.

She sucked in her smoke and disengaged. Her perpetual meditation removed the world from her sight. It washed away the pain of existence. All that was left was the inhalation, the exhalation. I wanted to feel that pain for her. I wanted to understand what it was that hurt so much. But her feelings were elusive as that smoke.

'Did you find it?' she asked.

She was there after all. Excitement rushed through me.

'No.'

'Too bad.'

'Yeah. Maybe it's gone for good?'

'Don't count on it,' she said.

She turned her back to me, and disappeared behind a wall of blue smoke. She looked like some ancient witch on the moors, sitting by her cauldron, fixating on future kings. Or maybe it was the past she looked into, observing in the smoke images of days gone by. She'd replay these events over and over, watching out for the split second when her life was ruined forever. She relived the moment of destruction. She rejoiced in it, I was sure.

Dad came home and found the chainsaw in the rain. I watched from my bedroom window as he calmly picked it up like an old friend and took it to the shed, turning on the light to look over the damage. He wiped it down and oiled it carefully. He unscrewed bits and laid them out in order, then put it back together with a comforted look on his face and started it. It purred beautifully, revving high and low. His job done, he turned it off and placed it back on a shelf. There. He'd performed his duty. The machine was taken care of. There was nothing else to do.

He came into the house and I was sure he'd yell at me for leaving it out in the rain. He didn't. I realised he'd forgotten all about that terrifying machine in the shed. Coming home to see it sitting in the rain was like meeting up with an old friend. It was odd. If anything, I thought he might thank me for reintroducing them.

'You killed my roses,' said the dog.

'It wasn't the roses I was after,' I told it.

The dog sat without expression, staring at me. I held its gaze.

'I don't think you should come to see me anymore,' I said.

'You don't get to decide,' it warned. 'You think I should have told you about her mother? You think I should have laid everything bare for you? How would you have acted with her, if you had known?'

I thought this through. I would have treated her with the same kind of humiliating comfort that most people would offer her. I would have been uncomfortable, knowing her suffering. I would have placated her.

If there's anything I could do . . . I would have said.

How stupid. Of course there was nothing I could do. There was nothing anyone could do. People only made offers like that to make themselves feel better. Those words would have been a selfish act. Eliza neither wanted my help or needed it, that much was clear.

'You see? She would hate you now if you knew.'

'You don't think she hates me?'

'Not like she hates the rest of the world.'

The rain continued all week. Summer gave way to autumn and Middleford began to take on a whole new charm. A lot of the new houses had cottage gardens, complete with trees that dropped their leaves in shades of deep red and yellow. It was all a pathetic attempt to make our suburb appear a little bit cultured, I guess. It didn't really work. Underneath the bright autumn leaves, the dull, grey monotony of Middleford persisted. Still, something was different. The winds had changed; the hot desert northerlies had died away, replaced by a looming squall from the Southern Ocean. The cold was coming.

I liked rain. It gave everything that fresh, green smell. Water pooled around my shoes as I walked to school. There were little cracks in the rubber of my soles and water had seeped in and soaked my socks. I'd squelch with every step for the rest of the day. This was a bad omen.

During the Vietnam War, the American soldiers swore blind their enemy knew how to walk through the jungle without making a sound. These little Asian warriors knew the art of camouflage so well that they could happily stand two feet in front of their assailants without being seen. They could pick people's blind spots and pass through a crowded room completely invisible. I practised this technique on a daily basis. It was a delicious insight. People were inherently selfish creatures. Not in the way that a two-year-old is selfish, although there are a lot of people like that. I mean in the way they literally see the world. People almost only think about themselves. Their concerns are about what affects them. And that is all. People's brains seem to be hardwired to ignore everything else. A juggling chimpanzee in a party hat could walk right past you, but as long as you are more concerned about how much money is in your pocket, or what your hair looks like, you'd never see it. That's how those sneaky Asian soldiers operated. They didn't hide. They just made themselves invisible. They knew how to be ignored.

It was a difficult skill to master. Even though people are selfish, they are still biologically hunters. Any sudden movement makes them snap to attention. The art of camouflage took patience and slowness. If you moved at the rate of a passing cloud, you could glide right past people without them ever noticing you were there. You'd be invisible. A ghost. This required utter silence. The hunter instinct was also attuned to the slightest sound. My squelching shoes were about to give me away.

'There you are, Monty. We've been looking for you.'

It was Becky McDormond. She was one of Eliza's friends. Eliza had lots of friends. People generally flocked around Eliza, to bask in her presence. They hoped her good looks and charisma might somehow rub off on them, I suppose. They would be beautiful by attachment. Becky McDormond was one of these people. Becky spent a lot of time preening and wore heavy perfume that smelt of artificial strawberries. Her thick make-up and sculpted hair always looked like something out of a fashion magazine. Yet underneath all the glamour, if you took the time to look, was a plain and simple fifteen-year-old, just like all the other plain and simple fifteen-year-olds who tried their best to be liked. I never tried to be liked. I didn't see the point.

'I know about you and Eliza,' she grinned.

I was startled. Not because she had found us out. It was the idea that there was actually something between Eliza and me that was startling. Until then, the concept had never crossed my mind. Not for real anyway.

'Amy saw you at her house. Didn't you Amy?'

Amy Fotheringham flanked Becky, looking eager to please. Amy was another hopeful, but more insipid and cowardly than the rest. A few years back, before she had discovered mascara, Amy was a champion chess player. Sadly, she was robbed at the state titles by a severe head cold. Amy Fotheringham never looked you in the eye when she spoke, always at some point far away over your shoulder. That confused me. On the few occasions when we needed to talk to each other, paired up by a teacher or something, she'd talk to this imaginary point across the room. I always found myself turning around, trying to figure out who she was speaking to. I wondered if she could see things I couldn't. In the end, I realised she was just incredibly shy. I was wary. Shy creatures, when backed into a corner, can be extremely dangerous.

'Yeah,' said Amy. 'You were there for hours. You stayed for dinner and everything.'

I turned around to see she was directing this at the fire extinguisher on the wall. I was an idiot. Amy Fotheringham lived not far from Eliza's, around the corner to our street. She had a perfect view of Eliza's front yard and would have noticed me standing there in the street. Eliza had been right to be worried. We had been seen.

'So what's going on?' asked Becky. 'It's alright. I won't tell anyone.'

Some people, I had come to understand, are very good at concealing what's going on in their mind. Take me for instance. Most people thought I had the IQ of a dead cockroach. Maybe it was because of my scruffy appearance, or the fact that my body was often seen wandering around by itself, bumping into the furniture: I was generally considered to be a bit thick. Not many people knew I actually had pretty good grades. Despite not listening to most of what my teachers had to say, I found textbooks and study quite simple. I read fast and did the work in double time. That meant I could spend more time thinking about the things that needed to be thought about. Eliza was obviously a master at this type of concealment. She was the ultimate in mystery. Not Becky McDormond.

'I won't tell anyone,' she said.

Her intent rang loud and clear. Of course she was going to tell everyone. I could see her eagerness, I swear. She was circling me, ready for the kill. Becky was second in line to the throne. In the girls' hierarchy at school she would rule if, by some unfortunate accident, Eliza was deposed or horribly maimed. Being associated with me would be enough for that to happen. I could destroy Eliza's entire social network. She didn't deserve that, just because of a haircut.

Years before there was a girl who suffered the ultimate humiliation at the hands of Becky McDormond. Her name was Fiona or Felicity, or something. I can't remember exactly. And that's the horrific thing. Even to me she became a shadow creature, a Tim Smith, once Becky decided her fate. Backs were turned, whispers flooded hallways, online rumours spread like viruses. Nobody really knew what this poor girl had supposedly done. It didn't matter. Teenage pregnancy, a debilitating drug addiction, a secret affair with someone's pet turtle, whatever; everyone knew the stories were false, but that didn't stop them. Once Becky set the wheels in motion, all she had to do was sit back and watch. A once popular girl was reduced to a nervous wreck in a matter of weeks. Finally she couldn't take it anymore and left. Nobody knew where she went, or cared even. She just evaporated. Gone. Forgotten.

Becky looked at me expectantly, waiting for my brain to come back to the world.

'Science project,' I said. 'We we're meant to team up. But she's going to do the rest on her own. She thinks I'm too stupid to help. Ugly too.'

I added this last bit to make it sound more like something Becky would say. She seemed to buy it. Her disappointment was obvious.

'Okay then. As long as you two weren't, you know, hanging out together or something?'

Or something. I used this term myself a fair bit because, to me, it could sum up an entire set of circumstantial events in two simple words. *Or something* could mean so much. *Or something* contained eons of time wrapped up in a neat little package. It could mean a whole separate existence, one that could be so much better. It was a universe of its own making. There, anything that could be, would be. I loved *or something*.

'Everyone's right. Talking to you is like talking to a zombie,' moaned Becky.

'Huh?'

'I asked you a *question*, remember?'

Her teenage sarcasm was pitch perfect; the heavy intonation, the roll of her eyes, the condescending tilt of her head asserted the natural order between us.

'No. We weren't hanging out,' I said.

My deflection seemed to work. She looked past me and saw some girls she'd rather make feel small. She headed off without saying goodbye, followed dutifully by Amy. In her wake, she left a scent of cheap perfume that made me gag. I hoped I'd done enough.

Jeers filled the school. Amy ran through the hallway, her face covered by schoolbooks. She pushed her way through gangs of boys who called out luridly, blowing her kisses. Teachers hurriedly whisked her out of sight, into their offices. A scandal had broken out.

I caught the screen of some boy's phone. On it were a pair of coconuts, close up, out of focus, but most certainly coconuts. They were beautiful, on free display. The girl's hands pushed them up into the screen. It was from Amy.

For some reason, she'd taken a picture of herself and sent it to everyone. And I mean everyone: kids, teachers, parents, everybody had this picture of Amy pinged into their inbox. Nobody knew why she did it. The boys loved it. The girls were horrified. Parents were outraged. Teachers flew into action. The police came around to ask questions. The Principal, Ms Finch, lectured us at assembly. She talked about online safety. Acts like this not only damaged the child in question, but the school. In future, electronic devices were banned. Kids groaned in horror. Becky McDormond went into a complete meltdown. It all happened so fast. Amy quit school that day. Eliza stood in the centre of this maelstrom and smiled.

I found Eliza by the old park. She sat on top of the train tunnel on the high, bricked ledge, her feet dangling over above the tracks. I climbed up to meet her. She blew some smoke my way.

'Thanks. Just what I needed,' I said.

'My pleasure.'

She puffed another one in my face for good measure. I coughed and looked out over the valley with her.

'Who did your hair?' she asked.

'Just some hack. Not a bad job, don't you think?'

'Maybe. It could do with a comb though.'

We sat in silence for a long while. Shadows crept up on us. A cold breeze drifted through.

'Amy saw me come over,' I said.

Eliza didn't look my way. She just crushed her cigarette on the ledge, letting the butt-end fall through the sky.

'She was going to tell everyone about us,' I continued.

Eliza glanced over at me. I could see she was appalled by the suggestion.

'I mean, not that anything *is* going on. Just that ... she was going to tell. Right?'

'Well, it doesn't matter anymore, does it? Amy's gone.'

Eliza uttered these words as a cold statement of fact. Her slight smile was chilling.

'I upset your father,' I said.

She gave me a tired look and went for another cigarette.

'I didn't know,' I told her. 'About your mother.'

'Right. You going to tell me you're sorry for me now?'

'Of course not. What good would that do?'

She looked to me. Her crisp vehemence dissolved. Her lips involuntarily came together, soft and sweet looking. She seemed curious, hopeful even. I wanted to reach out and touch those lips. She quickly turned away to stare over the valley.

'So when are you going to introduce me to this mother of yours?'

Chapter Eight

I had killed before. It wasn't on purpose but that wasn't the point; I had set a precedent, however small. I horrified myself and vowed it would never happen again. I was about eight I think, and I'd seen some kids in the neighbourhood with slingshots. I thought it was a fantastic idea, to be armed like that, and took to my dad's shed. The other kids' slingshots were pretty basic things, made out of twigs and rubber bands. I knew I could do better. First of all, I bolted two long pieces of metal together. Second, I replaced the pathetic rubber bands with a rubber tube from an old spearfishing gun in the back shed. I made a little pocket out of leather for the projectiles. Soon enough, I had a weapon that would strike fear into the hearts of all who crossed my path.

Armed with a glass marble, I looked around for my first target. I couldn't really find anything interesting until a little black sparrow sat on a tree about thirty metres away. It was a long shot. I didn't really think I'd hit it so I aimed and let loose.

The power in the spearfishing rubber was astonishing and the sparrow disappeared in a flash. All that was left was a puff of downy feathers floating around in the sky. I gasped and ran over. The body told the grisly tale. It had obviously died instantly: I'd shot its head clean off. I tried to find the missing skull, but it was probably on the other side of town by then. I thought of all its babies, lying in their nest waiting for food that would never come. I thought of all the other sparrows it knew, who'd sit on the wire wondering why there was a little bit more room now. What was worse was thinking that it wouldn't be missed at all, that all the other sparrows would get along just fine without it.

Eliza and I walked past Amy Fotheringham's place. The curtains were drawn and the lights were off as if nobody was home. I glanced towards the house, waiting for the slightest movement inside. There was none.

I searched Eliza's face but her gaze was impassive. The threat had passed and she no longer wasted her time thinking about it. She caught my look. I was staring at her again, like a young pup admiring its owner. She rolled her eyes and moved ahead so she didn't have to look at me.

I knew she didn't think of me the way I thought of her. But I hoped she thought *something* of me. I hoped she pondered what went on in my head, and why we were spending time together. Why, out of everyone at school, and how completely opposite we were in every respect, there was something, however small, going on between us. I hoped she thought about that. Us. I hoped she thought about us.

'There is no *us*. Okay Monty?'

'Sure. Of course not,' I lied.

'There is only you and me. Nothing else.'

'Then why are we here?'

We stood on the front porch of my house, ready to meet the disreputable mad woman who lurked within.

'Monty, don't do this,' she groaned. 'Not now.'

Her tone was exasperated. She didn't want to confront me. She didn't want to turn on me. If I pushed her too far she would cut me loose, I knew.

But what was this all about, this skulking around on the outskirts of town? She'd made a companion of me, I guess. That was it. I was someone to pass the time with. Whatever we did, for good or bad, we'd eventually come to the same end. One day, we'd simply slip away and forget we'd ever existed. She was right. Whatever we felt about each other would evaporate forever. Eventually.

'I get it,' I told her. 'No matter what we do, one day it won't matter.'

She looked taken aback, as if I'd spoken a refrain she'd heard some place before. Those words struck her somehow, I could tell. It wasn't as if I was trying to be philosophical or anything, but it somehow made her relax. She knew I understood. No matter what she felt for me, I wouldn't hold her to it.

Eliza walked past the stumps where the roses once lay, moving around them like headstones in a cemetery. She saw the pile of thorns I'd made at the back of the yard. I didn't really know what to do with their remains so I just put them to one side, to rot I guess. The vines had dried out into sharp sticks. If you went too close, they still had enough life left in them to tear the shreds off you.

'I guess I won't be getting flowers anymore,' she quipped.

The back door announced our arrival with a dull slap. My mother was sitting in the lounge room, as usual surrounded by a pall of smoke. Eliza and I moved up behind her.

'Mum, this is Eliza.'

My mother turned around and was shocked.

'Sweet Jesus, she's beautiful!'

I once heard that all mothers believe their children are beautiful, that it was all in the eye of the beholder, or something. Of course that isn't true. Parents of ugly children know their children are ugly. Facial features are genetic and usually their parents are no great lookers either. At school there were fat kids with glasses, whose parents were fat with glasses. There were skinny kids with sunken eyes, whose parents were skinny with sunken eyes. These ugly parents still loved their ugly children, no doubt telling them they were beautiful on the inside. But it was a con neither would admit to.

My mother? In one of life's spiteful quirks, she was actually rather good-looking, behind the wild hair and manic green eyes, that is. If you looked past her present state, she actually had a pleasing shaped nose and elegant, even features. While I resembled something of her, my genes must have had a flash of inspiration and decided to reorder things a bit. That was a terrible mistake. My mother knew I was an ill-formed version of her. She didn't hide it. She knew I was ugly and left it at that. She must have assumed Eliza would be equally ill formed. I'd never seen her more surprised.

She stood up and investigated Eliza's benign-looking face, inspecting it from all angles. She got closer and closer, looking for some mark of ugliness that would render her presence in our house comprehendible. For a while she didn't find any. Eliza's face was a work of art. My mother delved deep into Eliza's eyes. Finally she stood straight and smiled. She'd found what she was looking for. There was ugliness there, an endless pit of it.

'So you've come to see me for yourself, have you?'

'I've heard the stories, thought I'd see what all the fuss is about.'

'You're a brave girl,' my mother warned.

My mother offered her a cigarette. Eliza took one casually and they lit up together. They sized each other up as if waiting for the first to blink before going on the attack.

I stood frozen to the spot, wondering who would win

out in a fistfight. Eliza had youthful strength, so I had to give her the natural advantage. But my mother was a wily old thing with baleful eyes. You could never discount a look like that. Who knows what superhuman strength she could muster if the need should arise? I was in the middle of this thought, imagining the screaming and the hair pulling, when Eliza's words shook me.

'Monty, would you mind leaving us alone for a minute?'

They were both staring at me, and sucked on their cigarettes in perfect unison. Had they been rehearsing that while I was off in thought? No. It was instinctual, like the way people sit together with the same leg crossed, or copied each other's hand gestures, or patterns of speech. It was all a subconscious act. A signal they were united. They were connected. They were from the same tribe. I was in deep trouble.

'Yeah. Of course,' I said.

I headed to my room. I could hear their voices from up the hall, dim and far away. They were obviously talking in hushed tones so I couldn't hear the conversation. I thought of sneaking back to listen, but I knew my mother had ears like a wolf and would pick up the slightest creak of the floorboards. I had no choice but to wait it out. It was like a young child being asked to sit outside while their parents talked to the doctor.

'I'm sorry, madam. Your son has clearly lost his mind,' the doctor would say.

'Is there a cure?' the mother would ask.

'No. The humane thing to do would be to put him down.'

The sentence would be final. Whatever they were discussing, it would change everything between us. Eliza would discover something about me that I didn't know, or had blocked out of my mind, or just plain forgotten. This little bit of information would be vital, a one-line explanation for my whole life.

'Ah, that's why he's such a moron,' she'd realise. 'That explains everything. Thanks!'

Or worse. Eliza was right at that minute confessing to my mother all my insecurities, all my pathetic attempts at appearing as if I belonged in this world. These little anecdotes would combine, forming a pattern of behaviour that my mother could now rationalise, and finally make sense of her own son.

'Ah, that's why he's such a moron,' she'd realise. 'That explains everything. Thanks!'

'You don't have to sit there and take this,' said the dog.

The dog sat across from me. I blinked. I didn't see it come in.

'Where would I go?' I asked.

'Find a place of your own. If you can.'

It was a challenge. Was I really that insipid that I'd never even found a place of my own? The closest I'd got was Eliza's train tunnel, but that was all hers. I remembered the roses, how I used to sit under them as a kid.

'I cut down the roses. They're all gone,' I said.

'Yes. That was unfortunate,' said the dog.

'Do you miss them?'

'They had their uses,' said the dog. It stared at me, unblinking.

'You could leave now. Nobody would miss you.'

'Will you help me?'

'Of course I will,' affirmed the dog. 'I'm always here to help you.'

We moved down the hallway together. I walked down the line of nails in the floorboards, following the beam that supported the floor. The floor didn't creak so much this way. I made no sound at all and glided down that hallway, floating inches above the floor. I was invisible. A ghost. The dog floated beside me. Its eyes looked serene.

The rocks were slippery. Waves crashed up in a looping spray. Cold water slapped my face and I woke from my slumber. The dog stood next to me on the rocks, calmly looking out to sea. A fog was lifted.

I'd been to this beach before, on a school outing a few years back. Our class had taken the train there for Clean Up Australia day. We searched sand dunes and escarpments for plastic shopping bags and cigarette butts, avoiding dangers like blue-ringed octopuses and used syringes.

Even though these things were tiny and hid in small crevices, they both had the power to kill you. I desperately wanted to find them both, just to see what they were like. My goldmine would have been a blue-ringed octopus holding a rusty syringe. Now that would have been some prize. Despite my best efforts I found nothing but rubbish.

Most of the other kids just hid behind the dunes to goof around and smoke cigarettes. But I found the task interesting, like an archaeological dig on human nature. Every discarded scrap told a unique story about its previous owner. I picked up some chewing gum wrapper. It spoke to me about a six-year-old girl with pigtails who despised her older sister for leaving her at the mall when she was three. Ever since, she'd chew gum to conceal a nervous twitch she had developed. She kept chewing, well into adulthood, until one day her psychiatrist would question her relentless need for gum and she'd break down into sobs, recounting that her life's miseries were all her sister's fault and that's why she'd never been able to finish school or hold down a job or fall in love with anyone but her pet budgerigar Robert, who also chewed gum.

That was how I thought about rubbish.

'There's a shipwreck out there,' said the dog.

The dog looked out to sea. There was a small reef off the point we were standing on. A high sandstone cliff rose behind us. Chattering gulls nested along the cliff face. I suppose they thought a fifty-metre sheer drop was a pretty safe place to bring up a small, flightless chick. Still, those little chicks survived the wind and the rain and the ever-present danger of falling to their death. Most of them, anyway.

Beyond the point, a hundred-year-old shipwreck rested in peace under the waves. All you could see was a buoy, bobbing up and down with the rise and fall of the waves. But there were meant to be some remnants of the old wooden ship down there. Broken bottles and pieces of green copper could be found washed up after a decent storm.

Our class had done a worksheet on the wreck. It was a sorry tale of events. Despite their best efforts, everything on that fateful journey went wrong. Apparently the ship was held up in port an extra day while someone ran about trying to find the right kind of whiskey for the Governor. After finding the last case of it in town they set sail, right into a terrible storm. Usually, the Captain would turn back for port but he couldn't. The first mate suffered a terrible sneezing fit on his way past a barrel of pepper and accidentally blew all their maps overboard. The Captain, hopelessly lost, took to the Governor's whisky, not to drink it, but to make homemade flares out of it and light the way in the storm. But the fierce wind blew the flames back onto the ship's sails, setting the entire ship ablaze. The first mate, still in a pepper-induced sneezing fit, steered the ship for shore. They crashed on the rocks and a hundred little baby gulls dropped from the cliffs above, their downy feathers catching alight as they rained down upon them. Exactly one hundred men died that night, one for every burning chick. There was only one survivor, the cabin boy, who limped to shore to tell the story. If only one of those events had happened differently, if the ship wasn't held up in port, or the first mate hadn't sneezed, or the Captain hadn't decided to burn all the whiskey, then maybe those one hundred men would have survived. Maybe. Or maybe no matter what path they took, they were all destined to end up dead, with the bodies of those little gulls burning next to them on the rocks.

'There's treasure down there,' said the dog.

'The bottles?'

The dog nodded. Apparently it knew as much on the local history as I did. Those whisky bottles were extremely rare and an unopened one would fetch a small fortune. But they were all destroyed, surely. Plenty of divers had been out to that wreck over the years and found nothing. I told the dog as much.

'If one bottle was protected all this time, it could have survived,' said the dog.

I wasn't convinced. It was all too long ago, surely.

'Perhaps the bottle was in a wooden case,' continued the dog. 'And that wooden case was in a metal chest. And now, after all these years, the wooden case had rotted away and the metal chest had rusted through and that one surviving bottle, worth a small fortune, was right there for the taking, lying on the seabed under that buoy. Perhaps.'

'What kind of dog are you?' I muttered.

The dog looked back out to sea. Most dogs on a beach run around like complete lunatics. They roll about in seaweed and poo as much as they can. Not this dog. It just stood on the reef and talked to me about shipwrecks. It was disconcerting, but the idea of finding a priceless piece of history was tempting.

I was an okay swimmer but that stretch of coast was known for its rips and the occasional white pointer. The buoy wasn't far off shore. The waves rolled in and broke on the reef, but they were only small. I decided to brave it.

I took off my clothes and placed them on the rocks. I was naked, on a public beach, looking for sunken treasure with a talking dog. Great.

The water was cold, even though it was a warm day. The Southern Ocean loomed for thousands of miles beyond that beach. The water that finally hit those shores had once melted off some iceberg in Antarctica. It brought a crisp chill that hacked at your ankles.

I picked my way through the rocks, keeping to the small patches of soft sand that dotted the way. Eventually I was up to my waist and I dove under an oncoming wave. The cold rush washed over me. I broke the surface behind the waves. The buoy was closer now. I pushed on and swam out to meet it. It took a lot longer than I thought and, by the time I got there, I was panting from the exertion. The water was deeper than I had imagined too.

The wreck was a dark shape below. Who knew what lurked down there. I turned back to shore. The dog watched me. I was comforted I wasn't alone.

'Go on,' I heard it say. 'You're almost there.'

Its voice sounded full and close. I understood it better. No matter how far away I was from the dog, or how deep I'd go, it would always be by my side. Comforting me. Guiding me. I took a long, deep breath and filled my lungs with as much air as I could.

Underwater was a blur. Dark shapes materialised underneath. It was very deep and I struggled to push myself down. My lungs grew hot. I wanted to turn back. Just as I was about to retreat, a soft, green glint caught my eye.

I found the surface again, gasping for air. The dog still watched from shore, calmly waiting. I eagerly gulped more air and went back down. This time I went further.

Sunlight pierced the gloom. Reflections glimmered below. Something was down there. I pushed on, deeper and deeper. The air in my lungs began to fade. A green flash shone ahead. It was on my right, then my left. I was disoriented. I found something to hold onto, some blackened part of the ship, burnt from the fire and since encrusted with barnacles. I wanted to suck in some air but there was none to be had. The green glint was just ahead now. Tantalisingly close. I made one final lunge.

My air ran out. Water invaded my mouth. It attacked my nose. Spray tickled my lungs, provoking me to swallow it in. I was drowning.

I broke the surface, coughing like mad. Salt water surged out of me like a whale spout. Air was all around but I struggled to get it. My body gave out. I was going down again. Over the top of a rolling wave, I saw the dog was gone. It had left me to my fate. I was abandoned, about to disappear under the waves and join the lost souls on that wreck. I curled my lip and swore. I damned that dog and went under.

I think what saved me was rage; I was angry at the dog for leaving me. I grabbed hold of the buoy and my fingernails scraped into the crumbling polystyrene. It was enough to keep me from going back under.

I had the bottle. I would be rich. I could buy my parents one of those fancy new houses and we could eat roast dinners on white crockery and Eliza and me could just get the hell out of Middleford forever. The hell out.

But it was all for nothing. I was holding a lemonade bottle.

'Where were you, Monty?'

Eliza and me faced off in the street. She'd just spent the last two hours with my mother, no doubt talking about all my foibles and insecurities. My eyes fell to my shoes. I didn't realise it right then, but I now distrusted her.

'What's with the bottle?'

I still had the lemonade bottle gripped in my hand. I'd walked all the way back home with it. Even though it was worthless, some part of me had refused to let it go. I'd been on autopilot again. At least some dark recess of my brain had remembered I should get dressed. My shirt was on back-to-front and my shoes were on the wrong feet but at least I had my pants on.

'Found it,' I muttered.

Eliza looked at me curiously. She could tell there was more to this, but let it go. If I wanted to keep secrets from her that was perfectly fine, she wasn't going to ask me to tell her anything I didn't want to. That was the true mark of a stranger, I guess.

'We didn't talk about *you* if that's what you're worried about,' she said.

She left me there on the street holding the lemonade bottle, my shoes on the wrong feet.

My mother tried to coax one more cigarette into her ashtray. It had filled up hours ago. Still, she preferred to keep pushing more in than bother emptying it.

'That wasn't very good of you, Monty.'

What was this? Condemnation? Some futile, last gasp attempt at parenting? For as long as I could remember, we'd had a pact: she would never instruct me, never provide me guidance and, in return, all her shortcomings would be ignored. She would be allowed to fester inside that blue haze of tobacco. This arrangement wasn't my choosing. It just was. It was simply part of life, as involuntary as breathing. Her eyes focused on me, searching for something resembling shame I guess. I had none, only rising anger.

I suddenly flung the ashtray back at her and the dusty, grey butts spilled all down her front. She recoiled, covered in her own ashes. I don't know why I did it but I wanted to provoke some reaction from her. Anything. If I couldn't have approval, I'd gladly take disappointment. Show me your regrets, I thought. But don't just sit there.

She said nothing, and turned away to smoulder.

Chapter Nine

Alias: @The Full Monty
Date: Monday May 5, 2.45AM
I'm such an idiot. I pushed her away. I think I've lost her.

@Gutentag
So you are of losing. She will gain.

@The Full Monty
What do you mean? That neither of us can be happy?

@Gutentag
What is happy?

@The Full Monty
Having fun, I guess.

@Gutentag
What is happy?

@The Full Monty
A smile. Sunshine. Being together.

@Gutentag
What is happy?

@The Full Monty
I don't really know.

@Gutentag

Now we regard the truth.

Eliza sat outside Ms Finch's office on a long wooden bench reserved for detainees. That bench was probably the oldest relic in the school, hewn from the guts of a gum tree over a thousand years old. That bench was harder than any other material known to humanity. Many a sorry bum had sat on it over the years and every single one formed deep welts under the strain. By the time the Principal called the poor kid in, they would be pummelled into submissiveness, ready to confess to any crime. They'd happily agree to any punishment, anything but sit back on that bench. Eliza sat there with absolute ease.

'Where were you, Monty?'

'I went to the beach, that's all.'

'That wasn't all and you know it,' she said.

I didn't like the accusation. My blood quickened. My heart tightened. Defiance threatened. Normally, I would have stuck my tail between my legs if confronted by Eliza. But something had changed after she talked with my mother. I was angry, but I didn't want to let it show.

She caught my reluctance and smiled cagily. She still thought of me as some pathetic creature, I could see. She had played rescue with me. She knew I couldn't resist. I wanted to sit beside her so much.

'Next time, take me with you,' she said.

Relief flooded through me. My anger evaporated. My cheeks flushed crimson red. Tears welled up in the corners of my eyes and a liquid ball of snot involuntarily shot out of my nose and dripped to the floor. I was a mess.

Eliza regarded me without the slightest hint of disgust.

The Principal opened the door to call Eliza in. Ms Finch had one of those turned-up noses like a pig. You could always see directly up both nostrils, like someone was pointing the barrel of a gun directly in your face. Those nostrils were deep and cavernous. Hairy too. She had a serious amount of nasal hair. I guess we all do, it's just that you don't get a good look up most people's noses.

The teaching profession somehow attracted people with an unusual body part or an incredibly idiotic name. Take Mr Jones who had a mole the size of cockroach on the end of his chin. It wobbled around as he tried to explain functions. Very distracting. Then there was Mrs Smelling, Mr Grossman and Mr Goldsack. Really? Why would people like this choose to become a teacher? Was it a requirement to have something about you that would attract the instant ridicule of every student?

In Ms Finch's case, other than her unusual proboscis, there wasn't really much else to say about her. I guess that's the hunter instinct part of my own brain at work. That pig nose was the only point of difference she had to the rest of the world, but it was enough to remove her from it.

Eliza stood up from that bench with such grace that Ms Finch's jaw fell open in wonder. The numbing pain of that bench was nothing to Eliza. It was as if her childhood was spent enduring an even harder punishment. In comparison, that old relic was like sitting on a fluffy sofa. Eliza was completely at ease. At least, that's how she appeared. She floated inside the Principal's office, ready to receive punishment. I was ashamed, I was so caught up in myself I hadn't even asked what she'd done.

We looked out to the reef together. Strangely, it suddenly seemed smaller and less dangerous. I wondered if a passing fisherman decided to move the buoy in a few metres, or maybe the tide had gone out and we were standing closer to it. Whatever the reason, I suddenly felt foolish for nearly having drowned out there. Eliza stood there a long while contemplating what a complete idiot I was to almost drown myself over a lemonade bottle.

'You swam out there?'

'Yep.'

She didn't ask why. This wasn't some small mercy, saving me embarrassment. It wasn't even pity. I didn't realise it at the time but she already knew why, even though I didn't.

'With no bathers?'

'There's nobody around,' I told her.

'Turn around,' she ordered.

I looked at the sandstone cliff, my back to the sea. I could hear the curling waves kiss the shore. Above me, flocks of gulls cried for their lost children. I listened to the light and secretive sounds as Eliza undressed behind me.

A sudden heat raced through my body. Every part of me ached. I listened as her footsteps padded away through the sand. I heard the faintest intake of her breath as she felt the sudden chill of the ocean carve her ankles. My senses were a riot, fighting each other for precious brain space. The need to turn around overcame all logic. If this were the last image of Eliza Robertson I'd ever see, I wanted it to be this one. I turned but she was already waist deep in the ocean. I had missed my chance.

I turned back to look at the cliffs as she found deeper water. Then I heard her call for me. She floated in the deeper water, her head bobbing up with the small swell that ambled through. She wanted me to follow. I waited for her to turn aside but she just floated there, watching me patiently.

I undressed before her and placed my clothes neatly next to hers. I stared at her clothes, left discarded on the sand. A glimpse of white lace poked out from beneath her shirt. I longed to touch those clothes, to feel what it would be like to be close to her, to touch her residual warmth. I resisted the temptation. She was still watching me.

I walked towards her, cupping myself to hide the important bits. The cold was glorious. It stabbed at my nerve endings, reminding them of life. I swam out to meet her and we floated together in the ocean, treading water over the graves of the dead.

'How deep is it?'

'Deeper than you think,' I said.

She watched as I breathed in and out deeply, soaking my lungs with oxygen. I left her there on the surface and swam down. The wreck was a dark outline through the green haze. It grew larger and more ominous, yet more serene as I fell to meet it.

I gripped the rough barnacles and waited for her. My heart raced in anticipation. Eliza came down to meet me, backlit with sun.

She was more than me. I understood now that Eliza was fully a woman. Her every curve was rounded and bold, filled with the tension that only came with adulthood.

In comparison, I was yet to be formed. I had indications of where muscles might one day evolve or where hair might provide a thick layer of warmth against the cold. Yet these advances were still some time off for me. Compared to her, I was insipid and young. I swear if I was any thinner, I'd simply wash away with the tide.

I could see she was struggling. She paddled down but quickly found her limit and could go no further. I reached up to take her hand and drew her down to me.

Panic had set her eyes. The whites were vivid. Her pupils were deep black, wide and fearful. She reacted instinctually to my touch and embraced me with both arms and legs. She wrapped herself tightly around my body.

It came to me then. Down there, on the edge of all things, I was the stronger. She trembled against me. Her skin was velvet smooth, warm against the cold. She glided all over me, pressed against me. Her eyes were thick with terror.

Slowly her fear began to wane and she took in the sight of the shipwreck. I could feel her relax. The wonder of the place soothed her. It was peaceful, that underwater grave-yard. Her eyes were solemn. Her sadness, as dark as that wreck, washed away. For a moment she looked serene. We were happy, embraced deep in the shadows.

We broke the surface together. Eliza desperately gasped for air as we eased back into the world. Perhaps she wasn't used to this kind of thing like I was. She didn't have much energy left and I had to help her swim back to shore. I powered along with one arm, my other draped over her neck and shoulder. Above, those sorrowful gulls arced across the sky, still mourning their loss I guess.

We made it to the sand and dressed with our backs to each other. It was a pointless gesture. We had already seen everything but, back on dry land, we still required some level of modesty. We looked out to the ocean for a long while. I thought she'd berate me for holding her down there.

'Thanks, Monty.'

I guess it was just what she needed.

We walked back to Middleford in silence. Being with Eliza now was a meditative experience. It was a little intimidating to know just how much more she was than me. Still, I didn't care. If I closed my eyes, I could remember her. I could still feel her swimming against me. I wanted to go back and hold her under that ocean forever. We'd lie there for an eternity and never lose our breath. I'd never let her slip away.

I opened my eyes and found her watching me. A sudden pang of panic struck. Could she tell what I was thinking, standing there like an idiot, drool dripping out the corners of my mouth? Disappointment filled her eyes. She could see straight into me, I was sure.

'You got what you wanted?'

'No.'

'What do you want then?'

I hadn't a clue. Don't get me wrong, seeing Eliza naked was the best moment of my life. If I had died right then, suddenly sucked in all that salt water and drowned like a floundering rat, I wouldn't care less. I would've gone to my briny grave having seen what most teenage boys would give their right arm to see. Yet my foolish happiness wasn't about the silky sight of her. I had seen the unseen too.

'It wasn't just your body I saw,' I offered.

She looked at me sharply. Then, for the first time, it was her eyes that dropped away, eager to find safety in some far away place. The sound of her muffled sobs fell like soft rain. She felt something after all.

'Eliza?'

My hand reached out to her but she flinched before I even got close.

'Don't touch me!' she warned.

'Okay. I get it,' I reminded. 'There is no us, remember?'

Some changes are swift. They break over you like a tsunami and wipe away everything in its path. Other changes are gradual, and play out in such small increments you don't notice things are different until it's too late. I wish I could go back in time and live a moment all over again. With knowing eyes, I'd bend it backwards, force it uncut, and replay the way I'd like it to run. But which moment would I choose over any other? I guess that's the hardest thing: to know the right moment. It's the small things that get missed.

Alias: @The Full Monty
Date: Friday June 6, 4.22AM
I'm in a whirlwind that I can't escape!

@Gutentag
Is this what you of wanting? To exit this torrent?

@The Full Monty
No. I'm just saying it's a ride. Like a rollercoaster. I'm hanging on like mad, but I don't know where it'll end.

@Gutentag
Then why you buy this ticket?

@The Full Monty
Couldn't resist, I guess!

I waited at Middleford station, as per her orders. She was going to show me a secret, so she told me. I couldn't resist going. I had to know what she meant. It was early evening.

I waited for her as hordes of office workers piled off their trains after work, desperate for hot dinners and wide-screen TVs.

They probably all settled down to watch the same show, I thought. And maybe they were all having the exact same thing for dinner, after having watched the exact same cooking show the night before and all thinking they were the only ones who were inspired to make a rustic chicken pie. The effects fell like dominoes: the supermarkets would have sold out of chickens. Caught out, they'd buy twice as many the day after. But by then, people would move on to the next big thing, beef curry or something. And the supermarkets would be forced to throw out all those unsold chickens. Thousands of lives would have been wasted for nothing.

'Ready to go?' she asked.

Eliza appeared behind me, dressed like a teenage goddess. She suddenly looked much older. She wore a silky looking top, a tailored skirt, and her hair draped over her shoulders in perfect curls. She looked classy, sophisticated even, like a runway model stepping out with the social elite. In contrast I looked like a bum. I had on the same t-shirt I'd worn all week and my dirty pants and trainers looked like I'd just crawled out of a bin.

'Geez, good to see you put in an effort, Monty.'

'Sorry,' I said. 'I didn't realise.'

'Realise what? That when you go out, you make an effort?'

'Yeah. That.'

She rolled her eyes and we caught the train to the city. At that time of day, we were the only ones on board. The train at Middleford was a terminus. I always found that curious. The driver didn't need to turn the train around or anything. He just casually walked to the other end, put it in reverse, and drove backwards all the way to the city. No matter how hard I thought about it, I couldn't decide which way was forward, or which way was back.

I banged on his window until the driver opened the door. He looked annoyed and pointed to a sign above the cabin. It warned that it was an offence to interrupt the driver and I could be forced to pay a two hundred dollar fine.

'This is important,' I said. 'Which way is the front?'

'Just sit down and enjoy the ride,' he said, looking exasperated.

'I can't,' I insisted. 'Not until I know. Which way is forward?'

'Look mate, they go both ways. Forward and back. It's exactly the same.'

'Thanks,' I said, relieved.

I moved off to sit with Eliza who stared at me like I was completely nuts.

'We're not like trains,' I explained.

That didn't help. She was still looking at me like I was nuts.

'We can't go backwards,' I said.

'Right. Most people already know that, Monty.'

The train began its reverse journey all the way to the city. I amused myself by thinking we were travelling forwards and backwards simultaneously. We were heading to our inevitable conclusion, which we had already seen, and back to our beginning, where we'd already been. Only the ride in between mattered.

We sat opposite each other. Most people don't like looking at a person for very long. They find it rude or confronting, as if they're breaking some social taboo. I sometimes forgot rules like that. I stared at Eliza, unblinking.

'There's a window, Monty. Why don't you use it?'

'Huh?'

'Stop staring. You're giving me the creeps.'

'Oh. Sorry.'

I turned away and looked out the window. But it was dark out and there was nothing to distract me. I longed to see a man walking his dog. Or a couple sitting at a station. Or a bird on a wire. Anything. All I could see was her reflection. That's all I wanted to see, I guess.

The city was dark and loveless. Concrete and petrol fumes invaded my senses. Eliza seemed to know where she was going and led me through backstreets and alleyways. I hadn't been to the city much, maybe once or twice when our school went to an excursion.

One time, we had spent the day wandering around the Botanic Gardens looking for endangered plants. I didn't really get how a plant could be endangered. After all, couldn't you just plant more of them? It wasn't like an animal. You didn't have to wait for them to breed in a zoo or anything. If we wanted to, we could plant entire rainforests. Maybe that was the point? We just didn't want to. Our preferred habitat was bitumen and traffic lights and high-rise apartments. Maybe nothing else stood a chance? In the end the world would become one big city and people would go to museums to look at pictures of sunflowers.

The club that Eliza took me to was noisy. Music boomed from within and there was already a small line-up outside. Twenty-year-old girls in high heels giggled. Muscled guys in tight t-shirts paraded. At the door, a massive guy with arms as wide as a tree let people in one by one. He looked like some fierce Polynesian warrior, ready to go into battle at the slightest provocation. This guy put Tony Papadopoulos to shame. I looked to Eliza, a little fearful.

'I don't think this is a very good idea,' I said.

'It's alright, I know what I'm doing. Come on.'

Eliza led me around the back of the club to a small alleyway, filled with broken glass and the smell of dead rats. She pulled an old milk crate to the wall and climbed up to a small, high window.

'Give me a leg up,' she ordered.

I held on to her shoe and pushed her up to the window. She tugged it open and slipped inside. I waited in the dark for a second, and thought about being left alone in city. I feared abandonment. The thought of travelling back on the train alone terrified me. Her voice cut through the gloom and she extended a hand through the open window.

'Hurry up, will you?'

I took her hand, a little too eagerly, and pulled myself up over the crate and into the club. We had snuck in to land inside the toilets. Luckily nobody was inside that cubicle at the time. There were voices outside the loo. We weren't alone. Eliza didn't seem to care and led me straight out past a group of young women. They stared at us but didn't make a big deal of it. They just smiled and giggled as if they'd seen it all before.

The club was a dark pit of energy. Music thundered all around. The heavy bass boomed in my chest, commanding my heart to beat in time.

'Doof. Doof. Doof!' it summoned.

Over the top sang a high-pitched wail. It was relentless.

I thought of that mad cat and the sound of pure insanity. I lost all notions of time and space, up and down, forward and back. I was spinning out of control. Eliza grabbed my hand and led me towards the lights.

We descended to the dance floor and moved among a horde of people so thick I didn't know where their bodies ended and mine began. We became one with the throng. We surged and swayed. Dancing to the music was instinctual. I didn't think about it. I just did it. We held each other and danced like mad, lost amid the heat and the sweat.

I caught her eyes in the strobe lights. They flickered maniacally, like stuttering neon. Eliza was electric. She sparkled with life. I'd never seen her smile like that before. She beamed a wide, happy grin. Her face was joyous and light. She suddenly looked younger and I remembered the girl she used to be.

I saw her riding her bike up the street again, the one with the little pink tassels. She used to smile like that then: joyous and free, like nothing mattered. We were in the moment. That was all we ever needed.

We danced and danced and danced, for I don't know how long. It must have been hours because the people around us constantly changed and I thought I must have heard the same song at least three times.

We didn't try speaking to one another. There was no point. You couldn't hear a word you said, let along thought. And that was the best thing about it. On the dance floor, there were no thoughts. There were no distractions. There was only the music.

A great Polynesian hand gripped my shoulder. I buckled under the force of it, and my knees threatened to give. The security guard reached out with his other massive paw and snatched Eliza by her arm. He threw us out onto the street with about as much care as he'd take to swat a fly.

'Don't come back here, hey? You two kids could get in a lot of trouble.'

He spoke with a remarkably calm and sweet voice, like a little child's. He almost pleaded with us not to bother him. Two underage kids in a dance club was a problem. The cops would probably shut the place down if they found out. But his calm demeanour betrayed cold intent. He'd break my legs if he had to, I thought.

Eliza just laughed like all this was part of the fun and we ran down alleys and through empty parks. Eventually, we tired and returned to a steady walk.

'Do you do this often?' I asked.

'Not as much as I want to,' she said. 'Dad keeps a pretty close eye.'

'Thanks,' I said. 'Just what I needed.'

She smiled and we headed back to the station. It was close to midnight, and we had to hurry if we were to make the last train to Middleford.

I guess the club was Eliza's beach. Under the waves, there was nothing but emptiness. On the dance floor, you were enveloped by noise and light. Weirdly, they had a similar effect: both transported you to some other world. Both were free.

To save time, we cut through some dark part of the park lands. A bridge loomed over a cold river. Eliza ran ahead. That's when I heard his voice.

'You think you're alone. But you never are. And you never will be.'

It was a man. He was old, tucked up under that bridge inside a cardboard box. It was an odd sight. I know he was homeless, and he couldn't help it, but he looked strangely comical sitting in that box, like how little kids make cubby houses out of cardboard boxes left over after Christmas. He had fashioned a roof and a door out of spare sheets and was poking his head out like some angry gnome.

His face was etched in pain. Looking into his eyes drained all the joy out of me. I knew the feeling well. It came to me the day I turned fifteen.

'You must be the master,' he warned. 'Not the dog.'

He slammed his cardboard door shut and disappeared inside. I wanted to bang on that door, tear it open and take him by the scruff of the neck. I wanted to demand answers. I'd scream in his face until he told me everything he knew. I didn't get the chance.

'Geez, Monty. Come on! Hurry up!'

Eliza beckoned me, standing further up the river-bank. We only had minutes left before the last train to Middleford.

I saw something standing beside her, a dark shadow that quickly merged with the gloom. A sudden protective urge surged through me and I ran to her, searching about in the darkness.

'What is it?'

'Nothing. I thought I saw something, that's all. Are you okay?'

'I'm fine, Monty. We've got to go.'

She turned and ran up the grassy bank towards the station. I looked back to that cold riverbank and that poor creature in his box.

'Stay away from us,' I warned the darkness.

'Never,' said the night.

Chapter Ten

When I was about four or five we used to get the milk delivered. Our milkman was probably the last of his kind in Middleford. These days the only way to get milk was to visit one of those big fluorescent supermarket chains or the twenty-four-hour petrol station.

People who went in to those places were duped into upsizing: they'd go in just to buy milk and come out carrying four bars of chocolate for the price of three. I liked the old milkman. His name was Geoff. He never talked, just whistled old show tunes. Mum would leave the money under a rock the night before. The van drove up in the dark before dawn and, come morning, there'd be a carton of milk left on the driveway. He couldn't have made any money out of it, surely the price of fuel outweighed what he'd make in deliveries, but Geoff was a stubborn man. In keeping up something everyone else had abandoned years ago, he preserved a little piece of history. In the end, I think we were his only customers. He still came, determined to keep his identity alive.

We were being robbed of our milk.

Usually my mother's mystery intruders were an illusion. But when the milk didn't turn up, day after day, something was obviously wrong. Geoff's truck could still be heard rumbling past the house just before dawn but by the time I'd go out to fetch the milk it had disappeared. Geoff wasn't the kind to take the money and run. Plenty of times we'd forgotten to leave the money out and he'd still deliver the milk. My mother would then leave out extra the next night and we'd be square. This was different. Someone was stealing the milk.

Now, most people would watch for the thief and confront them, photograph them, call the police, that kind of thing. Not my mother. She took to urinating in a bucket.

It was drastic stuff. My mother filled up an old milk carton with her urine, glued the top back together and left it out the next night. The milk robber must have thought it was a bonus. Two cartons of milk there for the taking! I guess they got a real shock when they poured my mother's stale wee on their cereal.

Bizarrely it actually worked. We were never robbed of milk again. Yet there were consequences. Soon after, Geoff quit the delivery business. Apparently someone had complained to the local health department that it wasn't hygienic to leave milk out un-refrigerated in the night. We were forced to buy our milk in the supermarkets like everyone else.

Alias: @The Full Monty
Date: Tuesday July 1, 5.03AM
She is more than you can imagine.

@Gutentag
I am having the jealousy of you.

@The Full Monty
So you should. She's so amazing it hurts.

@Gutentag
Do you like this hurt?

@The Full Monty
I don't mean it like that. It's a figure of speech.

@Gutentag
I am to disagree. You like to hurt? I like to hurt.

@The Full Monty
Chill. Don't do anything. Okay?

@Gutentag
Too late.

I sat by myself at lunchtime in a dark recess of the school grounds so I wouldn't be seen. Most days, I didn't have anything to eat so I mimed eating a sandwich.

Miming eating was a great way to appear less conspicuous. People's hunter instincts looked for things out of the ordinary. When someone passed by, they would subconsciously sum you up out of the corner of their eye. All they would notice was some nondescript person predictably eating at lunchtime. The slow movement of food to mouth, even though there was no food, made sense to the part of their brain that was on the lookout for points of difference in the world. I faded into the background. Tim Smith would have been proud. Of course that only worked if someone wasn't looking for you.

'You don't even have a sandwich, you know.'

It was Becky McDormond. I continued miming, just to annoy her. She rolled her eyes and flicked her hair, flooding me with the scent of artificial strawberries. By her side was another girl. Becky McDormond had quickly replaced Amy.

Pippa Wilson had a face like a cartoon rabbit. She had a sweet little button nose and two enormous front teeth. Her eyes were deep brown and way too large for the rest of her face. Her auburn hair curled up behind her head in long pigtails, pinned back against her skull in an effort to make her look even more rabbit-like, I guess.

Pippa Wilson was the new apprentice, there to learn the dark arts from Becky. She hung on Becky's every word, begged for her attention, and basked in her presence. It was only through Becky's recognition that she gained credence. She now existed, because Becky had noticed her. All the other girls now took her seriously, more out of fear than respect. Of course, Becky didn't care about Pippa Wilson at all. She would have her uses.

I took another bite of my imaginary sandwich. They looked at me as if I was from another planet. I guess compared to them, I was. This infuriated Becky.

'Stop doing that. It's weird,' she pleaded.

Another bite had her looking to Pippa, exasperated. She handed Pippa a ten-dollar note and gave her orders.

'Go get him something to eat. And hurry up.'

'Sure thing, Becky!'

Pippa Wilson hopped away gleefully. She looked happy to be of service and zoomed off on her mission. Becky sat down close next to me. The strawberries were intense.

'You know when perfume was invented, don't you?' I asked.

She looked at me blankly.

'Eighteenth-century France,' I told her. 'Everyone thought the palace at Versailles was such a wonderful place but in actual fact it was a cesspit. People rarely washed and there were no toilets so everyone had to poo in the corner. That's why people loved perfume back then – to cover up the stink.'

'Are you telling me I stink?'

'No. I mean, when you cover up stuff, you have to ask, what are you really hiding?'

She stared at me blankly for a few seconds wondering, I guess, why she had bothered to talk to me in the first place. I wondered too.

'You've changed,' she said. 'The hair. Your face. You don't even have pimples anymore. What happened?'

'I washed,' I told her.

She didn't buy it. People didn't change without a reason. Mine was a subtle transformation, yet each day I washed, each day I combed my hair and brushed my teeth, I slowly encroached into the middle ground. I had rejoined the living, after staying so long out in the wilderness. Most people hadn't noticed. I was just so used to attracting minimal attention that these subtle differences went by unseen. But Becky McDormond had singled me out long before as a potential meal. She knew I was a fraud.

'Amy's in a new school,' she said. 'Heathmont High. Everyone there hates her. She had all her books stolen and she's been beaten up three times already. She's going to quit school and work in the supermarket.'

'We all need to buy milk,' I said.

As soon as I said this, I knew how insensitive it sounded. I didn't want to be mean about Amy. Becky fought the urge to slap me, I could tell. Pippa bounced back into our orbit carrying a hot chicken roll.

A fever gripped me. I'd never had a hot chicken roll. Those things were all the rage at the canteen. They cost a bomb and I'd never had anywhere near enough money for one, even if I could bring myself to eat something like that. It was a huge, foot long sub sandwich packed with hot roast chicken and creamy mayonnaise. Teenage boys gulped them down in droves while I resigned myself to an invisible sandwich.

I didn't mind. I was used to the way things were, but to have one placed in my hands was a shock. My stomach instantly lurched sideways, either out of hunger or disgust I wasn't sure. When you haven't eaten for long enough the hunger pains get all mixed up and turn back in on themselves. You start to become repulsed by the very thing you crave.

'Go on, then. Eat it,' Becky urged.

I took a bite. It was far richer than I imagined. I chewed the fat and licked the grease. It slipped down the back of my throat without effort. I gulped uneasily.

'There,' grinned Becky. 'That's better than that stupid imaginary sandwich, right?'

A little bit of chicken-flavoured vomit erupted out of my mouth. Mayonnaise spurted out of my nose. I managed to staunch the flow before it exploded everywhere but a little ball of sick now sat on my tongue like a hot lump of blubber. I had no option but to re-swallow.

'Euw! Did he just eat his own vomit?' Pippa winced, utterly horrified.

Becky fired her a look that silenced any criticism. They were there to offer charity and you don't complain about the sorry state of those less fortunate than you. Either that, or Becky wanted to keep me onside for some reason. Becky smiled cagily.

'Pippa and Amy used to be really good friends, you know.'

This was more an accusation than a mere statement of fact. Becky sat there looking smug. She had something. Information. Ammunition.

'Isn't that right, Pippa?'

That was her cue. The rabbit girl's entire reason for being was summed up in this one moment. I pitied her then. I could see she would be discarded the moment she fulfilled her duty. Her usefulness over, Becky would toss her aside. Her momentary rise would be short-lived. Afterwards, she'd become bitter and spiteful. Maybe she'd look for a weak underling of her own. I pondered what this other poor creature would look like. She'd be even more subjugated, even more timid, even more rabbit-like, but with terrible claws.

Pippa was halfway though explaining her relationship with Amy when my mind finally returned and I involuntarily squeezed the hot chicken roll.

A squirt of oil suddenly leapt out of the soft bun and flew past Pippa's head. It just missed her and she threatened to bolt, fearing I had taken to firing greasy missiles at her.

'See, this is what I was talking about,' said Becky. 'He can't concentrate. It's ADHD, or something. You just have to wait until he comes round.'

She talked to Pippa as if I wasn't there, explaining that I suffered from some sort of genetic disability or something.

'It's just a seizure,' she was saying. 'All you can do is make sure he's safe and wait it out. Oh, and if he turns blue call the ambulance.'

Becky nodded a silent command for Pippa to continue. This kind of thing was par for the course in talking to someone like me. Encouraged, Pippa went on.

'Amy lost her phone,' Pippa explained. 'The last time she saw it was in German class. With Eliza.'

That's all Becky needed. She slid forward and looked me straight in the eyes. Her hand reached out to perch on top of mine. Her grasp was soft and warm, and a single finger stroked the back of my hand seductively.

I'd never been touched like that before. My pulse quickened and she sensed the tension flowing through me. She knew I was on the hook. Her grip tightened.

'Amy didn't send the pictures,' she grinned.

'What do you mean?'

'Somebody took her phone. Those pictures weren't her.'

I tried to remember. I drifted back under those waves where she fell down to meet me. I could see her shape, back-lit with sun. Yes. It was true.

'Why would she do that to Amy?' Becky asked.

'I don't know,' I deflected. 'I mean, how do you know it was even her?'

'Oh, it was her. And you know why, Monty. Don't you?'

'No.'

'Eliza ruined her life, Monty. Do you understand?'

Becky moved off, having laid the seeds of doubt. Pippa bounded after her, hoping to catch any look of appreciation for her good efforts. I was left shaking, holding the remains of my chicken roll. It had gone cold. The grease had solidified into horrid white lumps. Sick caught in my throat.

The supermarket smelled of bleach and baker's yeast. Pleasant music softly played on tinny loud speakers. These tunes were upbeat and catchy, designed to make shoppers feel happy about spending more money. Most people entered supermarkets carrying the burdens of the outside world in with them. But by the time they got to aisle three everything was forgotten. The drama of their daily lives would evaporate and they now lived in a new world of discounts and two-for-one deals. It was all the sinister work of those catchy tunes, I thought. The shoppers became happy little zombies under their cheery spell. Previously unwanted items gleefully leapt off the shelves into their shopping baskets. In the carpark, these poor souls would suddenly come to their senses, wondering why they'd bought five packets of beef jerky.

Amy Fotheringham worked in the deli section and was slicing up a ham the size of football.

'Number twenty-three,' she called.

I didn't have a number. Whoever number twenty-three was had made a break for it between songs, suddenly realising they were vegetarian. Amy looked at me and made a big show of looking around for her lost customer.

'Number twenty-three!' she said again, more forcibly.

'I think I'm next,' I muttered.

Amy ignored me, pressed a button on the counter that made the numbers change on a little screen above her head.

I would have liked a little screen above my head. The red numbers that flicked from one to the next seemed important somehow. People took numbers like that very seriously. It proclaimed a sense of order in the world. It gave the impression there was a point to everything. A system was in play here. Some mysterious destiny was being shaped. You might not understand it, but you knew there was someone, somewhere, in control of things. The numbers changed. There was a sequence. It was predictable. Everyone liked those numbers. They made the world seem less chaotic.

If I had a little screen like that above my head, I could forget about the need for speech. Any question could be answered with a simple change of numbers. People would debate the hidden meaning of my numbers for years. They might suspect my responses were meaningless, but deep down they'd never really know. A simple series of numbers had gravitas. They implied meaning, even if there was none to be had.

'Number twenty-four!'

Amy almost screeched this in my face. I blinked and realised she had been waiting for me. I pulled out the ticket for number twenty-four from the little red dispenser on the counter. She obviously didn't need me to take a number, I was the only one there, but I guess she wanted to make a point. I was a stranger to her. A number.

'What do you want?'

Salami, ham and cured sausages were thickly arranged. There must have been about forty dead creatures in there, all sliced into neat little shapes. I fished about in my pockets and came up with the grand sum of nothing.

'Sorry,' I muttered. I showed her my empty, turned out pockets.

'Number twenty-five!' she shouted.

'I wanted to talk to you,' I said.

Amy gripped the back of the counter. Her fingernails were long and painted red. They had little fake gems set in the middle that tried to shine but couldn't quite do the job. Those long claws dug into a slice of bacon at the back of the counter. I thought how easily she could pluck out my eyes with one of those fingernails. She'd probably be happy to slice me up and display my remains with all the other unfortunate, dumb creatures of this world.

'Meet me out back in fifteen minutes,' she said and turned back to cut up her ham.

I sat on a pile of cardboard boxes, folded up ready for recycling or something. The boxes smelled of bananas and rockmelon and spices and dead fish. It was a heady mixture that made my brain spin a little. Still, I couldn't move away. It was a challenge, to discover all the smells hidden in those various boxes. Like some sort of nasal archaeology.

Amy sat down on a concrete step nearby. I wasn't sure how long she'd been there but she was taking out a cigarette, so I gathered not long. Amy smoked with a tense jaw. She was obviously new to this form of self-destruction.

'Well? What do you want?'

'I know it wasn't you,' I said.

She flinched and gripped herself tightly. Her stillness was intense. Her eyes searched mine. She couldn't read me like Eliza could, that much was obvious. I pitied her I think. Somehow I was responsible for this mess. She'd seen me standing outside Eliza's house and her simple threat to expose us resulted in her own destruction. It was death by social media. It was a pain she couldn't bear, so she ran away to the supermarket.

'I want to help,' I told her. 'I want to make things right.'

Amy began to cry. I sat next to her, unsure what to do. All I could offer was the solace of my presence. Once, she would have been content to watch me writhe in this kind of pain. But there she was, her anguish exposed. It made me ill to watch.

'You can't help,' she blubbered. 'There's no going back. This is it for me now.'

Amy gathered herself and went back to the supermarket. Maybe she'd live out her days in there, slicing up ham and packing shelves with toilet paper? Maybe she'd even run the place one day? Maybe she'd fall in love with the fruit and veg boy and they'd get married and have kids of their own and have all the fruit and veg they'd ever need? Or maybe she'd just end up alone, standing there forever with those little red numbers above her head?

Evening drew over Middleford. The air cooled, ready for day's descent into night. I liked dusk. Not quite day, not quite night. It was the half time, the time in between. Streetlights came on. Eyes struggled to adjust to the creeping shadows. I was one of those shadows.

I loitered in the street outside Eliza's house. I didn't care about Amy anymore. Besides, she was at work. Still, I didn't dare ring that doorbell and face her father. I could see by the lights inside they were ready for their evening meal. It would be deathly quiet in there. No television, no music, no sounds of laughter would break that silence. Eliza, up in her room, would be silent in her chamber. What she did on those long nights, I couldn't imagine. Even from out in the street, the silence was unbearable.

I angled off into her neighbour's property. They had a double carport with a flat roof. I floated up onto it like a cat. I sat a metre or two away from her bedroom window and tapped on the glass with a stick I found in the gutter. Eliza opened the window and peered into the gloom. In the half-light, she couldn't quite see who was sitting there. She was wary, certainly holding back a little fear, but what surprised me most was how in control she sounded. Eliza commanded the unknown.

'Who's there?'

'Me. Monty.'

She relaxed a little and stepped away from the window. I waited a few moments before I realised this was an invitation. The drop between the carport and her house wasn't enough to kill you if you fell, but certainly enough to hurt. The gap was less than a few metres, but it's funny how being up high makes it seem like twice as far. I took a deep breath, concentrated my will to survive, took a running leap and hit the sky. I flew, like a shadowy bat, and landed on a ledge under her bedroom window, stealthily, without a noise. My skinny frame hung to the ledge with ease and I flung myself inside the window. Eliza calmly sat at the end of her bed.

'What's wrong with the front door?'

'Nothing. I just ... thought they might ask me to dinner again.'

'What's the matter? Not hungry?'

She knew the answer to that already. She had knowledge and knowledge was power. She sat there quietly in her picture-perfect room.

'I spoke to Amy Fotheringham,' I told her.

A wry smile passed her lips.

'I know what you did,' I said flatly.

I waited for some glimmer of remorse. There was none.

'Is it true?'

'What do you want me to tell you, Monty? Was it me in that photo? Well, I guess we'll never know, will we?'

'I know,' I said.

'Geez, Monty. She saw you coming over here. I just did what I had to do.'

She was right, I guess. It was self-preservation. Amy would have gladly destroyed her. Eliza had just taken a pre-ventative strike, before any damage could be done. It was either Eliza in that supermarket, or Amy. With one click, Eliza ruined Amy's life.

'You enjoyed it, didn't you? Watching her suffer like that?'

'What if I did?' she grinned.

What if she did? She was not going to hide it. She'd accepted her nature long ago. It was now up to me to accept the darkness. I'd got her so wrong.

'I'm sorry,' I said. 'It was my fault.'

Her look softened and she shook her head in disdain, refusing my apology. A knock on the door startled us.

'Quick! Get in there,' she ordered.

I hurried into her bathroom. She closed the door on me and I stood in the dark, trying not to move. Blood gushed through my veins. The noise was a roaring loudspeaker in my ears. I was sure the sound would give me away. Wasn't there some Voodoo guy in Haiti who could stop his heartbeat, just by thinking about it? Now, that was control. I thought I'd give it a go and held my breath. I concentrated on my heart, willing it to stop, or at least slow down a bit. It didn't work. I just made myself dizzy.

'Eliza, dinner's ready.'

'Thanks Doreen,' Eliza replied. 'But I'm not hungry.'

I pictured the scene in the bedroom. Doreen would have the door open just enough to peer in tentatively. Eliza would be seated on the end of her bed, bolt upright with not a thing out of place. By the tension in her throat, I could hear Doreen was unnerved.

'But your father won't like that,' she whimpered.

'I don't care what he likes,' Eliza said calmly.

The door closed. A few seconds later, Eliza came into the bathroom to find me holding my breath. I gasped. I began to wobble. A floating gaseousness invaded my feet. I reached out for the shower curtain but missed and passed out. I woke to find myself upside down behind the toilet.

'Why are you such an idiot?' she asked.

'Just the way I am,' I replied.

I pushed myself up onto the loo and cupped my head in my hands, trying to regain some oxygen. My head slowly drifted back onto my shoulders, like a balloon deflating. She helped me up and I grabbed her arms for balance. She recoiled from my touch, as if I'd hurt her.

'You okay?' I asked.

'I'm fine. It's nothing,' she said.

She pulled her sleeves down over her arms, 'Do something for me?'

'Anything.'

'Take off your clothes.'

I stood there for an eternity before my brain kicked in with the obvious.

'Umm ... Why?'

'Because I said so.'

Eliza had already seen every part of me, but that time was different. At the beach, an entire wilderness – the deep, deep blue – had separated us, if ever so slightly. There, in that solitary room, I had nowhere to hide. Cold light shone into every nook and cranny. A harsh silence magnified every sound. My breath rose and fell in stuttering gasps. My body shook involuntarily like I had been tossed overboard on some boat lost in a malicious storm, hypothermic and near death. I took a breath, calmed my nerves, and obeyed. I always obeyed. Eliza watched as I took off my shirt, slipped out of my shoes and slowly dropped my pants. Her eyes betrayed nothing as I slid off my underwear. I stood there, buck naked, shivering under her careful gaze.

'Get into bed.'

My head threatened to float off to some far-away land of otherness. It took all my strength to hold it back, to keep myself there with Eliza. I begged my mind not to leave. Who knew where I could end up, if I allowed it to go? I could have been found wandering naked in the streets. Confused police would pick me up and charge me for endangering the public order. I'd rant and scream but my words would be jumbled, and they wouldn't understand. To them I'd look like a wild beast, gnashing my teeth. They'd have no choice but to call in some guy from the zoo with a tranquiliser gun to shoot me in the butt with a dart. I'd slowly fall to earth as the warm, honeyed dream took over and my brain would finally drip out of this world, popping like a bubble in slow motion. That would be it: no big bang, no fiery exoneration, just a quiet, soft pop in the night.

'Now would be good, Monty.'

I pulled back the sheets. Eliza's bed was made in perfect lines, pulled so taut it was like sliding inside a straitjacket. The sheets were cold and crisp and smelt of flowery laundry powder. I pictured Eliza between those sheets at night, staring up at her white-walled room, ensconced in that tight cocoon. She'd lay there, silent, her arms over her chest like a vampire. Eliza would never roll over, she would never toss and turn and fight against her dreams. She'd wake up in the same position and begin the day exactly where she left off. Everything about Eliza was precision and control.

'Now what?' I asked.

She caught the hopeful look in my eye and let out of sigh of derision.

'We wait.'

And so we did: ten, twenty, thirty excruciating minutes

ticked by. Eliza sat at the end of her bed and looked at me. I looked at her. Eventually Eliza tired of this game and her eyes began to drift. I was wrong. Eliza wasn't all precision and control after all. Her mind wandered too. Sure, maybe it didn't actually get up and leave like mine did, but she certainly thought of other things. What other things, I wondered. What delightful, dreadful things?

Eliza's attention drifted to the pile of my clothes at the end of her bed. She kicked at them and flipped over my underwear, as if inspecting something gross with the end of her shoe. Her nose curled up into a tight ball of revulsion as the scent of teenage boy assaulted her nostrils. I was embarrassed: I stank. I caught her glancing back towards her perfect, now ruined, bed. I realised Eliza would tear off those sheets and disinfect them in the washing machine as soon as I left. Why the hell did she ask me to lie there?

A thunderous rapping at the door jolted my senses. Eliza sat bolt upright, and turned to await her fate.

'Come in,' she said.

'Doreen's waiting for you to come down ...' boomed Derek as he entered, his sentence drifting away into a snake-like hiss as he discovered me: a boy, *that* hideous boy, in Eliza's bed. He looked down to see my clothes, including my underwear, on the floor. Derek's face threatened to ignite as a fierce red billowed up in his cheeks. Simmering, his eyes darted to meet Eliza's. She remained resolute under his accusing glare. On the face of it, Eliza was nothing but eternal calm. She defied him with her silence: dared him to accuse her.

'Get out,' he mumbled, 'Get dressed and get out.'

The door slammed shut with such force little chunks of plaster fell from the ceiling and drifted down over us like tiny, white snowflakes. I would have found it pretty, if I hadn't feared for my life.

'I better go.'

Eliza waited in the bathroom as I dressed. We walked down the stairs together and I passed the dining room to see Derek and Doreen sitting at the dinner table, waiting. Derek's beetroot-red face was buried in his hands in silent prayer, or silent curses, I wasn't sure which. Doreen simply stared, dumbstruck, as I continued to the front door.

After I was gone, I knew Eliza would take her usual place beside them at the dinner table. She would calmly say grace, diligently eat her meat and vegetables, report on her schoolwork then retire to her room for the night. And not a word would be mentioned of the naked boy in her room.

Chapter Eleven

Alias: @The Full Monty
Date: Thursday July 24, 4.20AM
How can you tell if you ever really know somebody?

@Gutentag
This is absurd question. Impossible this knowing.

@The Full Monty
You know me.

@Gutentag
I do of not.

@The Full Monty
Sure you do. You know me better than anyone. I tell you everything.

@Gutentag
Maybe I do not want to know.

@The Full Monty
Who are you?

Winter seemed to drag on in Middleford forever. The whole town seemed greyer, if that was even possible. I longed to go back to the beach, but it was just too cold now. If you went in the ocean at this time of year, you'd turn into an iceberg in seconds. I thought about floating off up the coast like that, frozen solid, with my head bobbing above the waves. I'd be a human icicle and go from port to port, visiting new lands, until I eventually hit the tropics and would melt onto a warm, sandy beach. There had to be a place like that somewhere, I hoped. An oasis.

I skulked into the school, practising my art of camouflage. I lurked from shadow to shadow, expertly avoiding attention. After I realised that I stank, I devoted myself fully to Eliza's washing regime. I had washed my face, brushed my teeth, shampooed and combed my hair. It wasn't in an effort to please anyone; Eliza just helped me to discover that's what most people did. I had even taken to washing my clothes.

Usually, the washing at our house would pile up until it reached critical mass, tip over into the hallway, and block our path to the toilet. Only then would the dirty clothes be noticed. My mother would reluctantly pick up an armful and run them through the washing machine, more in an effort to keep the toilet door clear than to have clean underwear.

I had what I thought was a stroke of genius and made a system. I called it the dirty clothes basket. It was a revelation. The dirty clothes went in and, when it was full, you'd wash them. Brilliant. I could have made a fortune out of this, I thought. I could become one of those billionaire teenagers whose only worry in life was all the people queuing up to claim they had the idea first. Of course other people did have the idea first. The dirty clothes basket had been around since people first had clothes. Still, I liked that little basket. It was simple. It had a clear function. More importantly, I had worked something out for myself.

Usually, I walked into the school expecting the worst but something had changed. When someone caught my eye, nothing happened. There was no outright revulsion, instead only straightforward recognition. Once my presence was noted, their gazes shifted back to whatever it was that they were doing at the time. I'd been ignored. I had been seen, then ignored. This was a massive achievement.

I went to the toilets and realised what had brought about the miraculous change. I peered at myself in the mirror. I looked good. My hair still looked neat from Eliza's haircut, and my zits had disappeared. My yellowed teeth now looked white from bushing and my clothes were fresh and clean. I appeared almost ... normal.

That was it! It wasn't recognition after all. People just didn't know who I was.

I walked back down the hall, taking in more glances than I'd done in years. Every single one turned out to be a non-event. People would look, note my existence, and turn away again. I was part of the horde.

In science class, Mr Rooney explained the concept of Brownian motion. One fantastic leap forward in our understanding of the universe was discovered by some guy with the extraordinary name of Mr Brown. A man with a name like that could never be a teacher, I thought. Anyway, the basic idea was to look at tiny specks of pollen darting about under a microscope. They bumped and jiggled among the chaos, as if they were alive. Apparently Mr Brown was a tad bit freaked out by this because everyone knows inanimate things are not actually alive.

I peered into my microscope and looked at the pollen bits under the light, focusing until the image was sharp.

The pollen certainly darted about, seemingly at random. They jiggled and bumped across life's little stage before me. It was like some kind of mad dance. Mr Rooney explained it remained a mystery until a guy by the name of Einstein realised the pollen bits were actually moved around by water molecules, proving the existence of atoms. The invisible stuff of our world was on show.

We were split up into groups of two for the assignment, which meant spending time with another student out of school. Usually when this sort of thing happened I was always last to be picked: this time, so was Tony Papadopoulos.

He fiddled with his microscope. His fat thumbs were too large to turn the dials properly and he still hadn't been able to see what all the fuss was about. His friends didn't do science, they were way too thick for that, and at that time of day were busy rounding up sheep.

The school had two sheep: Marilyn and Monroe. Jordan and Rhys looked after them in Agriculture Studies – which was code for trying not to get killed. Marilyn and Monroe were mean old beasts that only existed to teach kids the finer points of headbutting. Those sheep harboured a deep grudge. Perhaps it was their names. They were named as a joke by the teacher, Mr Hobbs, who by the way had a combover so extraordinary it stood up sideways in a good wind and flapped around like some kind of hairy sail. Marilyn and Monroe were actually male sheep. Or were. After it was discovered they were boys, not girls, Mr Hobbs had their boy bits removed. The poor guys were neutered. Mr Hobbs strapped a rubber band around their testicles until the life was squeezed out of them and they just fell off. Unlike their testicles, their names stuck. I think those sheep secretly despised their names. To this day, whenever anyone went in their pen, Marilyn and Monroe kept their backs to the wall, and headbutted anyone who came close.

Tony Papadopoulos was left unpaired. Nobody wanted to go near him. Everyone knew that being paired with Tony meant doing all the work. He consistently had the lowest scores in science. Nobody knew why he didn't just go play with the sheep. Oddly, Tony was enrolled in science, history and higher mathematics. He was flunking all three. Mr Rooney pointed to the two of us. I guess I was it.

I sat on a stool that Tony had spent the last two months colouring in with a blue pen. That was the sum total of his efforts in science, to colour in that stool. It was tattooed with swirls and patterns and intricate mazes that bent in on themselves. It was actually quite beautiful. I shuffled around so I could get a better look at it. Then it hit me. Tony was a genius. In those seemingly random doodles, I could see Tony had actually been listening to everything Mr Rooney had said for the last year. That stool wasn't just some kind of random daydream. Deep in those blue patterns were artistic impressions of Young's Double Slit experiment, the Doppler effect and even Newton's third law of motion, all intertwined in some sort of majestic dance.

I helped Tony with the dials on his microscope so he could see what everyone else could see. His face lit up with a twinkle of delight. He smiled like a fat little kid with a new toy. I could see the joy Mr Brown must have had all those years ago. It was the look of wonder. A moment of enlightenment as one small mystery of the universe was revealed. That scared the hell out of me. If Tony was capable of experiencing wonder, then he must think. He must feel. He must ponder things. Well, at least bits of moving pollen. I think the world was lucky Tony didn't make this discovery. Papadopoulosian motion doesn't have quite the same ring to it.

The journey to Tony's house was a silent affair. We were let out of school early to complete the assignment so Tony had the unusual experience of walking home. His face went red almost immediately and he puffed from the exertion. It was only two blocks. I didn't mention it, but I now knew his weakness. If Tony ever threatened me again, I'd simply outrun him.

Tony's house was one enormous concrete brick. It had metal shutters on all the windows to keep burglars out, and the Papadopouloses in. A concrete drive covered the entire front yard. Maybe there was grass there once, but it was now nothing but driveway. Nothing lived there but a solitary cactus in a small pot. It had a bright purple flower, obviously a trick to lure unsuspecting bees to their death. The front yard was secured by a high metal fence with pointy spears on top ready to impale anyone stupid enough not to use the gate.

The inside was filled with antique looking furniture. Everything screamed maximum expense. The lounge was filled with the biggest couch I'd ever seen in my life. Bigger still, was the TV. It was a giant plasma screen more suited to being inside a football stadium than someone's living room.

Tony's mother was loud. Actually, everything about her was loud. Her clothes were garish pink and her hair was coated in so much hairspray it looked almost solid, like a permanent fixture. She literally ran to meet Tony and grappled him in a crushing bear hug.

'My boy,' she screamed. 'Isn't he beautiful?'

She clenched his fat cheeks together, forcing him to pout like a baby then stuffed his mouth with a gigantic piece of salami.

'You must be hungry after your day. Sit. Sit! And who is this?'

She beamed at me as if I was Tony's best friend she'd been hearing all about but never set eyes on. Her expectation was frightening. I didn't know what to tell her.

I'm just the kid your son tried to murder, I thought.

Oh, that's wonderful, she'd say. *Do come in and tell me all about it!*

Tony looked at me out the corner of his eye. I caught the warning glare and decided to say the bare minimum.

'We're doing an assignment,' I offered.

'Well, you need energy if you're going to study!'

Tony's mother led us to the kitchen. It was a massive installation, designed to produce enough food for a military campaign. She disappeared inside a double door refrigerator so large they could have stuffed me in there behind the milk. Perhaps Tony would stuff me in there after I'd done the assignment for him. His mother appeared back out of the fridge, and promptly laid out a smorgasbord.

Tony ate like a machine. He churned through the cheese and the meat and the pickled vegetables and the olives and the strange little salted fish, leaving dust in his wake. I hadn't experienced this kind of food before. The smells tugged my body forward. I was eager for salt and sweet. Tony's mother took my reluctance as politeness and shoved a piece of soft cheese in my mouth.

'Don't be shy. You look like you haven't seen a good meal in years!'

She waited for me to chew, looking on in delight. I let the cheese ooze over my tongue. Usually, something high in fat like this would have sent me into immediate spasms of projectile vomit. Perhaps it was my recent encounters with roast meat and hot chicken rolls, but the cheese went down. Just.

'It's good. Thanks,' I said.

'Plenty more where that came from,' she beamed.

She caught Tony motoring his way through half a cured pig and suddenly, quite viciously, slapped him on the hand.

'Leave some for your friend, boy!'

It was a sudden streak of violence that shook me from my comfort zone. She had me fooled. From her joyful exuberance, I'd taken her for a delightful mother living her life solely to please her family. Sure, along the way she was filling her son's arteries with chunks of pig fat, but she was doing this out of love. I now saw the other side: she was a woman desperate for admiration.

The house suddenly made sense. The imposing façade, the imported walnut furniture, the gigantic entertainment room, her big hair: everything in the house had the same purpose. It was all to invite envy. Envy of what? I thought. I had no desire to live like that.

Tony sulked silently. He stopped chewing and started breathing hard. His face contorted and his breath quickened. Just as he was about to explode, he pushed the food away and bolted to his room. I was left sitting there with his mother and five kilos of ham.

His mother looked remorseful. I gathered this sort of thing was not unusual in their house. She didn't go after him or tell him she was sorry, she just quietly went about repacking the fridge.

I thought through my options: leave and fail the assignment; sit with his mother and fail the assignment; or follow Tony to his room, and most probably fail the assignment.

Tony's room was a cavernous space, more like a converted aircraft hangar than someone's bedroom. The house seemed to get larger the deeper you went in and Tony's room was no exception. He sat on his enormous bed staring at the floor. His room was filled with every toy you could imagine. His mother obviously had never thrown anything out. His shelves were testament to his privileged upbringing. I followed his life story on those shelves, from teddy bears to airplane models, to plastic guns to five kinds of gaming consoles.

Tony looked at me with an accusatory eye. I knew if any of this got out, I'd be dead meat. I sat at his desk and started going through the textbook. Tony took a chair beside me and I quietly coached him through two semesters worth of science in under an hour. He was impressed.

'How do you know all this stuff? I thought you were ... you know?'

'Stupid. Yeah, most people do,' I said.

He stared at me as if he'd just realised I was human, and not some feral rat he'd brought home by accident.

I was about to leave and had just made it out the front door when a white work van arrived, turning fast into the concrete drive. It pulled up just in front of me. The brakes squealed a little as it came to a halt. Obviously the driver wasn't used to having a visitor blocking the way.

It was Tony's father. He was a square man, almost as wide as he was tall. A thick beard masked his intentions. His powerful arms flexed as he slammed the door of the van. A gust of fish and petrol fumes followed him as he moved past. Tony's father was a fishmonger. He clocked me with a curious eye and questioned Tony who it was who had the gall to stand in his parking spot.

Tony lowered his eyes and I understood his father was just another thug. There's always a bigger fish, I guess.

I left Tony to his doting mother and his fishmonger father and wondered what their life would be like without all their things. Was that their problem? I wondered. Were they so caught up in having the best of everything that they forgot to say they loved each other? Were their ancestors in the old country happier because they were poor peasants? Or maybe I was just being self-right-eous. Who was I to judge these people? They lived their lives differently, according to their own standards. That was all.

Night fell into a moonless abyss. I stirred in my bed against the dark. It was syrupy, the more you peered into it. Shadows overtook the world. The night seemed endless and my head dissolved away. It left my body, headless, in that bed. I wondered what my decapitated remains would look like to an observer, whether there'd be a lot of blood and horrible gore poking out, or if the edge would be clean and beautiful, as if my head had just floated away like some kind of helium balloon.

'She's coming for you,' it said.

The dog coalesced from the nothingness. It slunk out of the shadows to appear beside me. I could barely see it in the dark but its eyes shone hotly. It fixed me with a stare that brought with it the red, metallic taste of fear.

'She wants to be with you,' said the dog.

It spoke with such a venomous streak I couldn't bring myself to believe. I knew this creature had a will of its own. It wasn't there to make my life easier. It didn't care for me. It didn't care for anything as far as I could tell. It acted only for itself.

'You don't know anything,' I hissed.

'You don't believe me?'

'No.'

'You don't think she wants you?'

'Who knows what she wants?'

'I do,' it said.

I almost saw it smile. That was impossible. I knew dogs were incapable of smiling. They just didn't have the facial dexterity to pull it off. They could only bare their teeth, which is never a good sign.

It disappeared back into the shadows to merge with the walls. I peered deeper into the night-time gloom, hoping to catch a glimpse of whatever universe the dog had descended into. I stirred from my bed and crossed the room as silently as I could, making only the slightest of creaks on those old floorboards.

The curtain ahead pulsed with movement. That was it, I thought: the portal to the dog's secret dominion. I pulled back the curtain ready to peer into that deadly nether realm. It would be the kind of place gods had rejected. It would be a universe unseen by the human eye, the only inhabitants either the sinful or the dead. I swept the curtain aside to reveal, instead, a wide vista of intense beauty.

'Geez! You scared me,' Eliza whispered.

We were face-to-face, inches from each other through the open window. I helped her inside, our thoughts invisible without light. Instead we relied on our other senses to understand one another. Words limited communication, really. Your body could always tell the deeper truth. She pressed her hands deep into mine. She dropped her forehead to mine. Her breath fell in step with mine. We stayed like that for I don't know how long. An eternity. A second. Both. I thought of nothing else. I was just there, with her. That is all I wanted to know. Her tears shook me to discomfort. I couldn't reconcile this with the person I knew. Crying just wasn't Eliza's style.

'You want a cigarette? I could get you one from the lounge,' I offered.

She sighed in relief, I guess more because I hadn't asked her what was wrong than the offer of one of my mother's cigarettes.

'No. Can I stay here for a while?'

'Of course. You can stay here forever,' I said.

I recoiled from my own idiocy. Stay there forever? Who was I kidding?

'Sorry, that sounded stupid. I didn't mean it like that,' I told her.

'Yeah you did,' she said. 'And it's okay, Monty. I kind of knew that already.'

We hopped into bed and descended under the covers to embrace. We just hugged in the dark, that's all. I thought of the dog. It was right. Eliza was with me. In my bed. I wanted to tell her how I felt, but I knew that was a waste of time. Words would shatter the moment. They would twist in on themselves and invite mistrust. Better to say nothing, I thought. Best to think nothing. That was seriously difficult though. Me? Think nothing?

The dog told me she wanted to be with me. But I knew it had reasons for telling me this. Perhaps it wanted me to try something? Perhaps that was its plan? It wanted me to ruin things, just as I did with the rose.

We stayed like that, embraced in my bed, for the rest of the night. Nothing happened. I didn't really want it to, I was just happy to be warm and connected. As the night went on, the strangest thing happened: I slept. We both slept. It was a world of warmth. We were secure, together. We were strong against the night.

Morning broke with the sorrowful cry of a magpie. I woke to find Eliza leaving through the window, disappearing into a halo of sunshine. She looked like some ancient queen surrounded by billowing silk robes as she slipped through those curtains. She turned back to me, I hoped to smile a sweet goodbye, but there was none. Her face was full of sorrow. Our night together had meant nothing to her, I could see. Any connection I felt was entirely one way. I had projected my own hopes and desires onto her. Those feelings were mine, and mine alone.

Mr Rooney droned on about conservation of energy to the class and was suddenly surprised when Tony Papadopoulos put his hand up to answer a question. He couldn't have been more surprised if a piece of furniture had put its leg up to answer. He looked utterly stunned, as if his entire world-view was suddenly shaken.

'Yes, Tony?' he asked tentatively.

'The total amount of energy in a system remains constant over time,' Tony said, sounding bored as if the question was so simple it was almost embarrassing for him to ask.

'Yes, that's correct Tony,' Mr Rooney said.

His gaze shifted to me and I caught his delighted smile. He turned back to the board and continued describing the maths. His shoulders lifted and he etched out the equations with renewed vigour. I pictured him running into the teachers' lounge during lunch. He'd finally done it! he'd exclaim. He had gotten through to his class. Even the thickest of the thick had finally understood his genius. He'd be on a high from this for weeks and would even give up drinking in the storeroom. The simple act of Tony Papadopoulos answering a question would make all the years of ridicule about his pungent breath worthwhile. His choice to become a teacher would be validated. Now he could retire, safe in the knowledge that he was a teacher. A real teacher, just like the ones in the movies that have all those preppy schoolboys hanging on their every word. He had fulfilled his purpose. Now he could rest. I wondered what he'd do next, after having completed his life's work? Perhaps he'd become one of those motivational speakers, peddling the keys to success, or maybe he'd follow his true passion of fixing up classic cars? Or maybe he'd just continue to be a teacher. After all, you only get a few chances in life.

Tony approached me in the hall. He glanced over his shoulder to check if his friends were around. They weren't. They must have been outside somewhere, happy with their sheep.

'You want to come over again after school?'

'Me?'

'Yeah. You.'

'Why?' I asked.

'If you don't want to, just say.'

'I don't know,' I told him.

To tell the truth, I really didn't want to go back there. To me, hanging out with Tony was a one-off. I had done my duty. We had studied together and that was it. I couldn't bear anything more. I looked at him, wondering if this was some kind of friendship proposal. While I was pondering this, Jordan and Rhys wandered up, thick with the smell of sheep dung.

A crushing weight suddenly rammed against my ribs and I spiralled to the floor. Tony stood over me, asserting the natural order of all things. I guess he took my hesitation for rejection, and this was his reaction. Fair enough, I thought. I didn't blame him.

Eliza hung out behind the sports shed at lunch, smoking cigarettes with all the other girls. Becky and Pippa were among the hangers-on, giggling as if they were all the best of friends. But the body language told another story. If you took the time to look, you could see the invisible daggers being thrown.

I watched. I kept my distance, not daring to be discovered. Only Eliza sensed I was there: her cat-like senses always on high alert. As I passed by she turned her back to me, making sure she avoided looking my way.

It was a blow more crushing than anything Tony could dish out. His punches were lightweight compared to this. The wind was squeezed out of me and my head quietly imploded.

'Walk up to her,' said the dog.

'I can't. The others are there.'

'Don't worry about them. Look at how far you've come,' it said.

The dog was right. I had made great progress. Still, it was a risk. Could I really just walk up to Eliza and say hi? Could I be that brazen? Maybe I could. Maybe I had the right? After all, she came to me. I should feel entitled to something, I guess.

'Do it now,' said the dog.

'I'm too weak. I can't,' I told it.

'You can and you will!'

Teeth suddenly flashed towards me. The bite was sudden and painful. The thing held me in its grip and ripped sideways, shaking its head viciously as if I were some easy meal. My arm flung out sideways with the attack. My shirt tore open. Blood splattered down my front. I yelled out in sudden pain.

I found myself lying prone on the ground, holding my torn arm, looking up into the bright sun. Eliza, Becky, Pippa, and the rest of their gang, stared down at me silently. Becky shot Pippa a knowing glance that seemed to infect the group like a virus.

'What are you doing here, Monty? Spying?' asked Becky.

'No,' I said. 'I just fell over.'

'Looking for someone then,' she asked. 'Who? One of us?'

All eyes darted towards Eliza. Giggles rose then descended into the muffled sounds of derision. It was happening. I was destroying Eliza, right before my eyes.

I ran, holding my bleeding arm. As I left, I looked back and saw the torn sleeve of my shirt stuck to a cyclone wire fence. I realised there was no bite. There was no attack at all. I had merely caught my arm on the fence, the rusted wire the dog's teeth. Doubt surged through me.

I found Eliza later by the art rooms. She was busy tipping out some large buckets of papier-mâché into the long stainless steel tub outside.

'You ever wondered where the drains go?' I asked.

'Nobody wonders that, Monty. Geez! Just for once, try not to be a total freak,' she said.

'I wanted to talk to you. About last night.'

'There was no last night.'

'You don't mean that,' I said.

'I can't do this anymore.'

'Why? Because of them? I thought you didn't care what they think.'

'Well, maybe I do.'

She tried her best but I could see she was lying. She didn't care about them at all, quite the opposite. For the first time, I could see into her. I was the one who could read minds.

'No, you don't,' I said. 'There's something else. I know you want to tell me. Otherwise, why would you come over last night?'

'Monty, you wouldn't understand.'

'I understand more than you think. I know who you are, Eliza.'

'You don't know anything about me, Monty!' she hissed. 'Not one single, damn thing!'

Chapter Twelve

Alias: @The Full Monty

Date: Friday August 1, 3.33AM

There are so many things I don't know. Like, I don't know what happens on the other side of the cosmos, or what happens in the middle of the sun, and I sure as hell don't know what's in her mind. But there's got to be a way to find out, right?

Hello?

Anybody there?

@Gutentag

I am of here. But a blink will send me towards night.

@The Full Monty

I know the feeling. I'm tired too.

@Gutentag

I am in your domain. You pull me down with you.

@The Full Monty

What did I do?

@Gutentag

This is the final time we speak.

@The Full Monty

Don't be like that. You're my only friend.

@Gutentag

I'm sorry. It's over, Monty.

@The Full Monty

Hey, your English is getting better ☺

Hello?

Please don't leave me.

'Morning, Monty!'

Pippa Wilson stared at me with her wide rabbit eyes, and flashed her wide rabbit teeth. She had me cornered by a recycling bin and was pressed in close to me. I could feel her quick breath pant in my face. She smelt of toothpaste and Weetbix. There were certainly no strawberries on Pippa Wilson.

'What do you want?'

'Oh, you know. I just saw you walking past, and I thought I'd say hi. So ... hi!'

'Is that it?'

She seemed nervous. I didn't get why at all. I looked around for Becky, to see if Pippa was under orders or something, but she seemed alone.

'I like your hair,' she blurted. 'I mean, it's growing back again now and it looks really cool. I always liked it long.'

A sudden pang of panic swept through me. She was flirting with me! Pippa Wilson smiled patiently, waiting for me to respond with some equally lame compliment about her pigtails. She teetered on the edge of hope, I could see. She had put herself out there. But why? For me? It didn't make sense.

'How did you go with the science assignment?' she asked.

'Huh?'

'With Tony? That must have been hard. He never gets anything.'

'You do science?' I asked.

'Well, yeah. I've only been sitting behind you all year.'

She looked disappointed I hadn't noticed. I'd spent so much of my life trying not to be seen that I didn't really notice other people, I supposed. Had she been trying to get my attention all this time, without me having the slightest idea? It was possible, I thought. She and I were cast from the same awkward gene pool. Where she had made the best of her looks, by trying to look like a pretty Viking girl in plaits, I had done nothing special until my recent attempts at personal hygiene. Apparently, that was good enough to gain some interest. Still, I had my doubts.

'I'm sorry,' I told her. 'I should take better notice.'

'It's okay. I understand,' she said. 'You're shy. Like me. But there's a lot more to me than meets the eye!'

She seemed to relax a little and I could see she was right. There was more to Pippa Wilson than I first thought. Sure, she was Becky's underling, aspiring to the life of the queen bee, but Pippa Wilson also had her own unique hopes and desires and fears and neuroses and other little bits and pieces that made her altogether her own person. I wanted to know more about her.

Guilt crept into the backs of my eyeballs. I thought of Eliza. The beach. Midnight in the dance club. Our dark embrace. We had shared so much. And yet there I was enjoying the attention of another girl. A gob of sick rose in my throat. I didn't know what to do.

'There's a party tonight,' Pippa said. 'At my place. Do you want to come?'

'A party?' I asked, looking dumbfounded.

'Well, yeah. You know, people get together, have some laughs. Maybe, I don't know ... have a little fun.'

She was teasing me a little. Her gentle sarcasm only drew me closer. I didn't mind. There was no malice. Pippa smiled at me playfully and the promise of a little fun was intriguing. I'd never had a little fun.

'Well?' she asked. 'You coming?'

Her hand slipped into mine and I felt her quick warmth. Her touch was soft and energetic and her little finger tickled the palm of my hand.

'You want to go? Then go,' Eliza said.

Eliza took the news of the party with her customary aloofness. She held her true thoughts close, hidden away. She looked down to me from her high tower, confident behind her defences.

'I've never been invited to a party before,' I told her.

'And why is that, Monty?'

'Because I'm a freak and nobody knows who I am,' I said.

She shook her head in frustration and sighed, as if I was a child who just didn't get it.

'Look, go to the party,' she said. 'Hang out with Pippa Wilson, if that's what you want.'

'That's not what I want,' I refuted.

Her cutting glare dissected me in two. She knew exactly what I wanted. She dared me to want it. She dared me to leave her, even after everything we'd shared. What did we share anyway? Everything was on her terms. Everything was some kind of one-way road to oblivion. I didn't know where we were going, or if we were already at the end.

'Why did you come over that night?' I asked.

'Go to the party,' she said. 'And do me a favour. Don't ever talk to me again.'

The end then, I thought.

The dog watched as I laid out a clean shirt. It was the only one I owned with a collar and long sleeves. It was bright orange with some weird off kilter pattern, but at least it was a proper shirt.

'Maybe you should try another one,' prompted the dog.

'What's wrong with it?' I asked.

'Besides ugly?'

I frowned. My father had passed this shirt down to me. It was the only thing I could ever remember him giving me. I wanted it to mean something, I guess. I hoped it had some power of manhood contained within it. Then again, maybe Dad just hated it too and wanted it out of his sight? Maybe the dog was right? It was just an ugly orange shirt. Still, I didn't want the dog making choices for me, not yet anyway. I put the orange shirt on, as much to spite it as declare my taste in fashion.

'Very well, but you'll have to work harder,' the dog said.

'For what?' I asked.

'You know what,' it grinned.

'I don't know if I can do this,' I said.

'She told you to go,' it reminded me. 'She doesn't want you anymore. Despite all my help, you've managed to ruin things.'

'Me?'

'Yes, you. And you alone. After all, it is your actions, not mine, that she has seen.'

True. I had damned myself to this fate.

The music was loud. Pippa Wilson lived in a sprawling three-level mansion that put Eliza's place to shame. It was simply huge, bigger than any place I'd seen before. The entranceway alone could swallow my entire house. I made my way in through the large double doors at the entrance, which were casually laid open to the street. I went to the party, orange shirt and all.

Music lured me towards the back of the house. Mixed among the beats, were the hoots and hollers of teenagers. Boys jeered each other. Girls offered delighted squeals.

Out back was a games room with a pool table, home theatre and a swimming pool complete with a bubbling hot spa. It was more like a fancy hotel than someone's house. I couldn't imagine what Pippa did when there was no party going on. Did she have to take a cab to get from one side of the house to the other? Who knew?

Pippa was among a group of girls from school, decorated in make-up and short skirts. She looked like a completely different person. Older even. Her little girl braids were gone and she had styled her hair into long curls. There was one notable omission to her party.

'Where's Becky?' I wondered.

'Who? Oh, she couldn't make it. Some family thing,' said Pippa. 'Why?'

'No reason,' I said. 'Just thought you two were really good friends.'

'Yeah, right. *Friends*,' she said dryly. 'Look, forget about her will you? Come in.'

She led me towards the others and hugged into me, dancing as we went. She skipped and frolicked, as if everything in the world was suddenly right.

'Hey! Someone get Monty a drink,' she called.

A beer was passed my way. I stood there looking at it, dumbfounded. I'd never had anything like that before. Pippa smiled.

'My dad leaves heaps of them in the fridge,' she said. 'He never notices if there's some missing. You don't have to drink it, if you don't want to.'

'It's okay. I can handle it,' I boasted.

I sipped the beer. It was cold and bitter. It made me gag a little and it warmed my insides with a blanketing glow. I didn't like the effect at all. I had enough trouble concentrating without something like that assaulting my senses. The other boys by the pool table chuckled knowingly and turned back to their game. Pippa giggled and took the beer.

'You can drink lemonade with me,' she said. 'We can go crazy on a sugar rush!'

She made her way over to the sound system, flicked through the playlist, and selected an eye-popping dance track. The boys in the corner groaned, preferring the harder guitar music they had on. But Pippa knew how to make them come around. She danced in the centre of the room like a wild thing and flung her hair around in wide swathes. She circled, drawing the boys in, and they began to dance too, mesmerised by her.

I had Pippa Wilson all wrong. She was not the demure little mouse, desperate to please. Out of school, Pippa Wilson was a force to be reckoned with. She was witty and soulful and in control of her own destiny. And man, she could dance.

I watched the dancing along with a couple of Pippa's friends. Until now, I had only known them as names on a morning roll call. Kristen and Allegra peered at me curiously over their sculpted mascara.

'Don't worry, it's happened to me before too,' said Kristen.

'What's happened?' I asked warily.

'Being told it's a dress-up party. And when you get there, you're the only one in costume.'

She caught my confused look. What costume? I thought.

'Your *shirt*,' she explained. 'It's totally hideous! Where'd you get it? Out of your dad's bottom drawer? Come on, what are you supposed to be, some guy from the eighties or something?'

'Yeah. Something like that,' I lied.

'I like it,' said Allegra. 'Kind of retro.'

They seemed to think I wouldn't actually come to a party dressed like that seriously. I was either playing a joke, or it was some kind of deliberate rebellion against fashion. I wanted to tell them I actually just liked my weird orange shirt because it reminded me of my dad. That clearly was not an option. So I did the next best thing: I said nothing. That actually worked. My cool silence made them think twice, I suppose. They suddenly looked uneasy, as if I knew something they didn't.

'First time?' quizzed Allegra.

Again, I didn't know what she was talking about, so I just gave her a silent nod. It had the desired effect. She stammered nervously and explained.

'At Pippa's house,' she elaborated. 'She puts on a great party, huh?'

'Yeah,' I covered. 'Not bad. How about you?'

'We're here a lot,' said Kristen. 'Pippa likes to have people over most weekends. Her dad's never around much. She likes to have some company, I guess.'

'She lives here just with her dad?' I asked.

'Yeah,' said Allegra. 'He works a lot of nights and stuff. When he is home, he's always stuck in his office. She's got the run of the place really. Cool, huh?'

I thought it was pretty sad actually. I imagined Pippa coming home from school alone in that giant house, talking to herself for company. How was your day dear? she'd ask herself. Oh, good. Got an A in Biology. Wow. That's fantastic, she praised herself. You're really going to do great things, I just know. Did I ever tell you how much I love you? Yes, all the time. Well, I do. I love you. And I love you too, she'd tell herself, as she'd sit down to her usual night of toast and television. Poor Pippa. No wonder she invited everyone over on a Saturday night. Anything, just to avoid that chasm of silence.

'Come on, Monty. Don't just stand there!' called Pippa.

She spun around in the middle of that great hall and her arms flung out wide like an Olympic ice-skater. She looked so free and happy out there. How could I have not known about her? I wondered. How could I have passed her by? How could I have sat in the same classes, walked the same halls, and not even noticed her until these last few weeks? Then it hit me: Pippa Wilson was just like me. Perhaps she'd been practising her own art of camouflage all these years and had expertly hidden in the shadows? Perhaps she, too, had a friend like Tim Smith when she was younger? Tina Smith, maybe?

I ventured out to meet her and we spun together like a pair of whirling dervishes caught in a tornado. Time seemed to drift and my head began to lift, bubble-like, off my body. It was happening again, the out of body experience. I watched myself from above. Down below, my body danced along with Pippa and her friends. I did a reasonable job of not falling over, I guess. Dancing was a trance. I loved it, right from that first time with Eliza in the club. It was freedom personified. The body took control. The mind slipped. Time fell away, turning all gooey and slow. Everything was good. Nothing else mattered.

But my thoughts solidified. Pippa and her friends merged into one, fluid organism. The lights dimmed and the music pumped louder. Arms and legs gyrated all around. We were one creature, moving to the beat. Out of that storm of flesh and blood stepped Eliza. She emerged from the dancers and moved towards me. Her lips were full, and her eyes sad.

'Why did you leave me?' asked Eliza.

'I didn't leave you. You left me,' I said.

'You're right. I'm sorry,' she said. 'But you forced me to go.'

'I just want you to be honest.'

'I can't,' she said. 'Don't you understand? I thought you knew. I thought you could see me, that you could read my thoughts.'

'I can't,' I admitted. 'You're a mystery.'

'And so are you, Monty.'

Eliza smiled and disappeared.

Suddenly, there was blue all around. I was underwater, back under the waves. The music fell away and I was transported, to some other realm. I searched around to take hold of the shipwreck, but it was gone. There was nothing to take hold of. Air burned hot in my lungs. Bubbles escaped. Ahead, a clear white light beckoned. I floated towards it and reached out. I wondered, was this life? Was this bright light the end of all things? It was beautiful. I touched it. It was hard and dome-like and felt oddly industrial. My mind came back into focus and I realised I'd just found some underwater lighting. I was in a swimming pool.

I rose up, gasping for air and looked about. I was in Pippa's swimming pool. How I'd fallen in there, I had no idea. I paddled around, lost, as my confusion ebbed away. Pippa swam up behind me and wrapped her arms over mine.

'Pippa? Where is everyone?'

'Oh. Around,' she said. 'Crashed in the bedrooms. Some went home. It's pretty late.'

She gave me a tender smile. My head ached. I'd only had one sip of beer, so it couldn't have been that. Still, my gut roiled and a rise of vomit readied to purge.

'Are you okay?'

'Yeah. I'm fine,' I lied. 'I'm just a bit cold, I guess. How'd we end up in the pool?'

She laughed and recounted our entire evening. The story made no sense to me at all. Apparently, we'd had a great time. I was a party animal. Everyone was so surprised at how much fun I was. We had danced on tables and thrown food at each other and went generally out of control. After all that dancing, I had simply jumped in the pool. I had no recollection of this at all.

'And you were so sweet,' she said. 'You told me I was a mystery.'

'I said that?' I asked. 'To you?'

'Well, yeah. It's the nicest thing anyone's ever said to me, Monty.'

She swam closer and pulled me towards her. I realised I was swimming in my underwear, and so was she. She pressed herself against me. Her lips kissed mine and I dissolved under her spell. I was making out with Pippa Wilson. I didn't resist. She was gentle and honest. She didn't make me feel bad for wanting her. She didn't make me feel like an unworthy fool. It should have been a moment of change for me. I could have had something good with Pippa Wilson. It might not have been as deep and all consuming like Eliza, but at least it would have been real. She wouldn't reject me for no reason. She would be caring, like real people are meant to be.

I began to cry. Sobs burst out of me like stuttering fire-crackers. I couldn't go on. All I could think about was Eliza. The dancing. The water. My every thought was for her. Regret shone its harsh light upon me. We stopped kissing and Pippa looked at me, all confused. Her make-up ran down her cheeks from the water and she smiled curiously, baring those enormous teeth. She suddenly appeared so bizarrely rabbit-like that I couldn't help but laugh, and cry, and laugh at the same time. She knew then that I was totally insane. Her brief attraction to me was over and she cautiously paddled away.

'You better go,' she said.

'Yeah,' I agreed. 'It's getting late. See you tomorrow?'

'No, Monty. You won't.'

She hurried out of the pool and into the house. Kristen and Allegra met her inside, along with Becky McDormond. I hadn't seen her arrive, but that was no surprise; I'd spent the whole night dancing on autopilot. Becky handed her a towel and seemed to ask a lot of questions. They conversed silently. Pippa kept her head low in remorse. They all looked my way. I knew this meant trouble.

'How was the party?' asked the dog.

'Why'd you tell me to go?'

'I told you no such thing. Eliza told you to go. She didn't want you, remember?'

'I don't want to do this anymore,' I told the dog.

'I know,' it said.

We sat together in my darkened room for what seemed a lifetime. Finally it walked up to me and pressed its dark fur against my hand. It was the first time I'd actually touched it, and my hand reflexively recoiled. Not because it wasn't soft or anything, just that, up until now, I wasn't actually sure if it was really there. But it was real. It was warm and alive and its body rose and fell as it breathed. It eased its sad head into my lap to comfort me. I had lost everything. Now there was only the dog.

'There is a way,' it said.

'For what?'

'For the pain to go.'

'What do you mean?' I asked.

'Come to my world. Leave this place, this torture. Come live with me where there is nothing.'

'Nothing?'

'Nothing that will hurt you. Never, ever again.'

It sounded nice. A place with no pain. A place where I didn't mess things up, where I could just float and be free. Forever.

'What about Eliza?'

'What of her?'

'I love her,' I said.

'You don't love anything,' it told me and disappeared.

I was alone. Even that one exit had been denied me. It made me want it all the more.

Chapter Thirteen

It turns out my family is distantly related to a British lord who lives, to this day, in an actual castle and owns about a hundred square miles of green, lush, English farmland. This guy, in turn, is distantly related to the royal family and is about 114th in line to the throne. All this, according to my mother, is the solid truth. If, by a terrible series of events, all those other people in line to the throne were to die, then I'd become King of England. My mother has empirical proof of all the genetic twists and turns, the swings and roundabouts and multiple dead-ends that would result in my coronation if such a catastrophe were to occur. She was firm on this. She'd done all the genealogy, apparently. Of course, all this had nothing to do with me; she just wanted to prove that she was important, that she occupied a rightful place in this world. Of course, if it were true, she would be crowned before I was.

For years she had painstakingly researched files in the library, sent overseas for strange people's birth certificates, and spent many hours putting the epic puzzle together. It took up four volumes and when spread out on the kitchen table looked eerily similar to something a serial killer might put together on his next victim.

'Here! This red line takes us to the Earl of Cornwall,' she'd rant. 'And this red line here brings us back to the Spencers in 1863! See what I mean! You see?'

My father and I didn't. He would politely excuse himself to tinker about in the shed while I would be stuck at the table to have the entire encyclopedic set read out to me in overzealous tones. It made no sense to me at all. It wasn't that I didn't share a passing interest; it was just so incredibly boring. I mean, really boring. I'd rather eat a bowl of my own nostril hairs than listen to three hours of family history.

The only thing that barely interested me was the idea that people used to marry their cousins. And not just one or two oddballs from the backwaters: a lot of them got married, all the time. The further you'd go back, the more common this incestuous practice seemed. I began to see a pattern, at odds to how my mother saw things. Where she saw honourable arranged marriages, I saw a disastrous clash of incompatible genes. Our family lineage was strewn with twisted misconceptions, mistakes built upon mistakes, and I was the net result. I was literally created from centuries of faulty DNA. No wonder I didn't stand a chance.

I woke up the next day and felt disgusting. My head throbbed and my memory dripped away elusively. Worst of all, the texture of my tongue resembled something like a hundred-year-old carpet. I shuffled into the kitchen and gulped water straight from the sink like some lost desert wanderer, finally finding oasis.

My mother watched me out the corner of her eye, peering through her cigarette haze.

'You came in late.'

I grunted and wiped my mouth with the dirty tea towel. She looked at me harshly but her gaze softened into some kind of flat resignation. She drifted away with her smoke.

'I don't know who you are anymore Monty,' she exhaled.

I was incredulous. Infuriated even. What the hell did she mean by that? She didn't know who I was? When did she ever take the time to *get* to know me? And then she had the gall to accuse me of holding back the truth all these years. This was her home, I thought. She ran life here exactly the way she wanted. If she wanted to know me, all she had to do was ask.

'You want some breakfast?' she offered.

'Since when did you make breakfast?' I asked belligerently.

'You look like you need something,' she said. 'After your big night.'

'It wasn't like that.'

'Really?'

'Yeah. Really. I had one sip, that's all. You don't believe me?'

'There's plenty I don't believe.'

She exhaled, deep and soulful, calming herself against the situation. I stood by the sink and wanted to dive down that drain. I'd escape that house, my mother, Middleford and the whole damned lot. I'd flow out with all the waste-water into that wide blue ocean. Damn. Not the ocean again.

'You're only fifteen. What's your father going to say?' she admonished.

'Him? He never says anything.'

I leaned in to peer through her smoky, blue haze. I wanted her to see me up close, so she could finally see me for real. I was no phantasm. I was no ghost. I was there. I was a living, breathing person. Her son.

'Maybe you're right,' I intoned. 'You don't know who I am. That's just the way it is. You and me, we're strangers. We're nothing.'

She gulped uneasily. It was the strangest thing: I could see she feared me. My own mother feared me, despised me even, as if I were some foul creature she'd accidentally made from the sickly mud of her womb. She gazed at me with a mix of regret and horror. She wanted to exorcise me, I could see. She'd created a monster, and now she was stuck with it.

The video went viral.

In just a few hours it went from one inbox to twenty, to sixty, to four hundred, to over five thousand and counting. Lots of little thumbs up. Everyone seemed to like it. People from all across the globe had commented and shared it. It was even trending above some video of a Korean cat that couldn't be bothered catching a mouse because it was so fat from eating noodles. It had wormed its way into many lives. Even though I still only had three friends on SpeedStream, this video went all the way to New Zealand and back just to find its way home to me.

There I was, in the pool with Pippa. We were making out. And the whole time I was bawling my eyes out like a spoilt toddler who dropped an ice cream. The girl in the video keeps trying to kiss spoilt-toddler Monty, to seduce him, and all he does is cry like a baby. I suppose everyone likes a good comedy. It attracted a lost of posts:

Alias: @Fearless22
Date: Saturday August 2, 12.55PM
What a doofus! Share to everyone you know
#CryBabyPool.

@CrazyCowMan
If I had a chick like #CryBabyPool, man I wouldn't be crying!

@Anon-e-mouse

I love the look on his face at 2.35. #CryBabyPool looks like he's just crapped himself!

#CryBabyPool is such a total jerk!
Yeah, what a moron.
Waste of space.
Can't handle it.
Loser.
Must be gay.
She's so hot.
Yeah. A bit funny looking, but still hot.
Who is this guy?
I want to beat him up so bad.
Yeah, slap him.
No way! Kick him in the head.
Then steal his girl.
He's not good enough for her.
Get ME in that pool.
I'll show her how it's done.
Come on, baby.
He should just end it, man.
Yeah, do it.
End it.
I would.
Go on.
Die.

Thousands of posts like this, all the same. I read them all. In all but a few, I was seen as the stupid fool who, for whatever reason, couldn't get things together. I was pathetic. I missed my one good chance. And for that, I did not deserve to exist. They were scathing. I thought I had a pretty thick skin, but the abuse was relentless. If everyone thought of me like that, perhaps they were right? I thought. Perhaps they saw the real me? Maybe this was all I was? A blathering cry baby who didn't know how to live life.

I didn't know what to do. I waited for the dog, but it didn't come. I wished I hadn't cut down the roses. I would have gladly spent the day in there, tucked away under those protective barbs. Anyone trying to get me would have to fight through those formidable defences. I would have stayed in there until I couldn't move. Eventually the postman would smell something bad and come looking and see my remains tucked inside, curled up in the foetal position. They would have to send in the fire brigade to cut me out but all they'd find would be an empty shell. Everything inside of me would have turned to dust. I'd leave nothing behind but a thin, papier-mâché version of myself. As they dragged out my frail corpse, I'd disappear into a shower of grey dust, never to be seen again.

I suspected Becky was somehow instrumental in all this, but there was no way to prove it. Whether my night with Pippa was some kind of set-up or not didn't matter. My actions were there for all to see. Was that what I really wanted? I wondered. Did I go there willingly, knowing this would happen? I had openly slain any connection I had with my mother. Did I want to do the same to Eliza? Did I want to hurt her? Could she even be hurt? So many questions.

Eliza waited by the bus stop. She didn't look up as I approached. She looked so beautiful I could have died right there on the spot.

'I'm sorry,' I said.

'What for?'

She gauged me with the coldest of looks. I knew she'd seen it. Everyone had.

'It looked like you were having fun.'

'No,' I told her.

'You didn't like it?'

'It wasn't what I wanted.'

'Liar,' she said coolly.

'So what does this mean?' I asked tentatively.

She regarded me, devoid of all emotion, and made things eternally clear.

'It means the end, Monty.'

The rest of the day was a blur. School was a tide of derision. Kids teased and mocked. They gave me whatever was my due. I tried to take it all in my stride and walk through the wall of contempt with my head in a cloud. But it still got to me. I was jostled at every corner. I was harassed in every class. I had nowhere to hide. All eyes searched for me. My camouflage skills meant nothing. I was laid bare before them all. The pressure was intense. Fight or flight kicked in. I had to run. But where? I thought of Amy Fotheringham; the supermarket beckoned.

Even the teachers had seen it. I was taken to Ms Finch's office and lectured on my rights and responsibilities. She went through a checklist for online bullying, designed by some well-meaning departmental psychologist. I muttered the right answers and she ticked all the right boxes. She wanted to know if I understood the consequences. She told me it wasn't going to easy, because the operator was an overseas company, but there was a way for the video to be pulled. She took pity on me, I guess, and helped me fill in the right forms and call the right numbers. After one long, agonising hour, the video was deleted, along with the scorn of a generation.

I left her office and sat on that long, hard bench, eager for its punishment. Sure, Ms Finch had done all she could, and I appreciated her for it, but it wasn't going to be enough. Yeah, kids from Sweden to Montreal would forget all about that bawling guy in the pool and go back to watching Korean cats, but school was another thing. I'd never be like Tim Smith again.

My thoughts lingered on conspiracy. My mind began to twist under the weight of paranoia. It had to be the only explanation. It was all planned, not in an effort to assault me, but Eliza. They had meant to flush her out in the open. They wanted to strike at her heart, to push her jealousy. They assumed she would react. Seeing me with another girl would crush her, they thought. She would cry at school and all would be revealed. Eliza loved Monty, the lowest of the low. Her fall from grace would be complete and her heir would seize the throne. Yet none of them counted on how cold Eliza's heart would be.

Eliza stood among them, holding court as if nothing happened. The sun shone. Girls giggled. They shared stories and complemented each other's clothes. Eliza smiled, unaffected. Becky, Kristen and Allegra could only watch in quiet awe. She was stronger than any of them. They couldn't touch her. She was immune. I noticed their group didn't contain Pippa.

'Ms Finch told me you pulled it down?' she asked.

Pippa had found me between classes. The bell sounded and the hall was empty of life, except for us. A momentary reprieve.

'Yeah,' I said. 'She was really good about it.'

'Did she call your parents?'

'Yep.'

'What'd they say?'

'Nothing. But that's not unusual,' I said.

'I wish my dad was like that. He's totally gone off. Says I've disappointed him.'

She began to tear up at the thought. She was moments away from dissolving under the pressure, I could see. I watched her silently. I suspected her collusion. She had done all this on Becky's orders, I was sure.

'He's going to send me to a private school. He thinks I need to learn some boundaries. So I guess we won't see each other anymore?' she asked.

'That's what you wanted, remember?'

'I know. I didn't mean it to turn out this way. I'm sorry.'

'Did Becky tell you to invite me?' I asked.

'What?'

'Did she tell you to ask me over? Did she tell you to ... you know. In the pool.'

Her face froze in shock as if I'd just slapped her clean across the cheek. I knew I'd gone too far. Pippa burst into tears, deep and sorrowful. She hid her little rabbit face in her hands and began to shake all over. I could do nothing but stand and watch. Part of me wanted to hold her and tell her I was sorry but, mostly, I was detached and cold. I knew then what it was like to be Eliza. I took no solace in Pippa's pain. It just didn't exist.

I had heard about this kind of psychological disorder before. Plenty of people had become detached from the world, in order to deal with it. It was called compartmentalisation. If you were unlucky enough to experience a true horror, like seeing your entire family hacked to death with a meat axe or being tortured for ten years in your mad uncle's basement, then compartmentalising was a wonderful survival strategy. All you had to do was put all the pain away in a small, sealed-off section of your brain. All the horror was locked away in a vault, unable ever to be heard again. It would still always be there, and would call to you in the dead of night, but you'd have control over it. It was exorcised from you, no longer part of you. Your every debilitating torment would be rendered meaningless. Sounds good, right? Except to do this would force you to become a cold, wreck of a human being, unable to connect to another living soul. But if you hadn't imprisoned these emotions, they would drive you as crazy as that mad uncle in his basement. It was the perfect deceit.

So as I watched Pippa, I felt as cold and devoid of emotion as Eliza. Empathy meant nothing to me anymore. I understood she was crying but that suddenly had no connection to me. Her pain was an abstract concept, like a bunch of numbers. Her emotions became a simple set of information. She was in a negative mind state. How low she would go could even be calculated on a graph, I thought. One vector would chart the scale of her agony and the other, time. As time went on, her pain would subside. She would forget me. She would move on, go to a new school, and form a new identity. But the graph was a lie. I had no idea of the hidden dips and vortices that could trap you. If you found yourself in one of those downward spirals, it was almost impossible to rise above it.

Weirdly, as Pippa cried, what caught my attention was the sight of her little pigtails bobbing up and down in time with her tears. They looked like happy little puppy dog tails wagging away, full of joy. The thought made me smile. She looked up and was horrified to catch me grinning stupidly at her.

'You don't care how I feel at all, do you?' she spat.

'What? No, I was thinking about something else.'

'You're not the only one affected by this Monty,' she said. 'We had a good time. I thought you were nice.'

She thought I was nice? I could feel the vault begin to crack open. I held the pain back. I feared I would drown under its torrent.

'I was wrong,' she said. 'You're worse than the lot of them!'

She hurried away, her pigtails drooping mournfully behind her.

That was the last I ever spoke to Pippa Wilson, the little rabbit girl who kissed me while I cried. She left Middleford and went to some girls' school in the city where they all dressed in shirts and ties and shiny black leather shoes. Those girls would confide in each other, telling cautionary tales about all the horrible boys they'd left behind. Pippa would keep her story in the vault, I knew. She'd remain secretive and shy, unable to tell her new friends she was the girl in the CryBabyPool video. No matter what, the effects of that night would trickle down for both of us through the years. Time would not heal us. I still thought of her, and what I could have done differently. But maybe nothing would change the fact I was now a cruel and selfish human being.

Alias: @The Full Monty
Date: Monday August 4, 8.45AM
There's someone who knows the truth.

Hello?

You there?

Okay, be like that. But I'm going to find him. He's going to show me the dark. And I will be his master ☹

A sudden jolt of the train as it changed tracks woke me. Out the window, sprawling identikit houses gave way to vast industrial estates. The sun fell into deep, orange streaks signalling the end of the day. Above the factories and their rows of smokestacks, the failing light mixed with exhaust fumes to create beautiful eddies of auburn-coloured steam.

The city station was a windy, lonely place that smelled of diesel and ozone and the humid stink of a thousand office workers. Those harried suits shuffled to their seats, trying desperately not to look one another in the eye. That was another survival strategy, I guess. Train stations were always an odd mix of everyday office workers and the mentally deranged. All those accountants and secretaries and personal assistants knew they were mixing with bad company, but didn't have much choice; running the risk of confronting one of life's many weirdoes was the price they paid for cheap public transport. I looked around and nobody dared look me in the eye. Maybe I was one of the weirdoes?

The hovel was empty. All that remained of the man in the box was a smear of brown, I don't know what, on the path under the bridge. His cardboard house was gone. It was as if he had never been there.

A gust of cold wind ripped through the grey concrete walls of the city and funnelled straight into me, tearing at the skin beneath my shirt. I wondered how anyone could live on the city streets and survive. The homeless must be made of sterner stuff, I thought.

I kept looking. I had to find this man. He had seen the dog.

Kids flew vertically in the sky above the skate park nearby. The park had a good view of the bridge so I thought this was as good a place as any to start my search. They wore baggy jeans and weathered t-shirts that looked as if they'd never seen the insides of a washing machine. Compared to me, these guys were hardcore grunge. Maybe before Eliza sat me down to wash, I would have looked just like one of them. Not now.

I watched a skinny looking guy on a skateboard fly horizontally above a twenty-metre sheer drop to the bottom of the skate bowl. He landed with practised ease on the concrete slope and slung himself up the other side to come to rest among a couple of other guys. They were all heavily tattooed and had piercings through every nose and ear lobe they could find. They were all well into their twenties, thirties even. Their faces were gaunt, skull-like sneers. Stubble and sweat hung from them. They stank of smoke and old grass clippings.

'I need to find someone,' I asked.

The oldest one, the flying skateboard artist, stepped towards me threateningly. Two large, black rings squeezed open his earlobes. The holes were enormous. You could see right through them, like something you'd see on a member of an African desert tribe. It took all my energy not to ponder what it would be like to poke my finger in that terrible wound.

'An old man,' I continued. 'The one who lived in the box.'

Ear lobe guy looked across at the brown smear left by the old man and winced. They obviously had history.

'Him? He's a waste of space,' he muttered.

'Just tell me where I can find him.'

The guy looked towards his two mates, amazed by my gall. As he turned his ear lobes swung around like ropes suspended from a tree. It was too much, and I began to drift into thoughts about low-flying pigeons and how they would get caught in there and accidentally hang themselves on his ears. Delightful punk jewellery, I thought. Maybe this guy would start a new trend and, in a few months' time, all of his friends would be wearing dead pigeons too. Adorned with death, they'd rebel at life.

'Try Misery Mission.'

'Huh?'

'The hostel. He usually hangs out there during the day.'

'Thanks,' I said and began to move off.

'Hey! Why the hell do you care?' he called.

'I don't,' I told him. 'I just need to find him before he dies.'

The guy looked at me, stunned by my frankness. He turned to the others and shook his head in disdain.

'Freak,' he jeered.

Yes, I was the freak here. Ear lobe guy had nothing on me.

The hostel was a red brick monstrosity with one door out the front and no sign. It was placed opposite a green city square that performed the twin civic duties of roundabout and park for the homeless. A procession of threadbare horrors walked in and out of that building. Some carried old shopping bags. Others had nothing more than a large overcoat to carry their life's possessions. All bore the same dispassionate look for the world, as if they had grown tired of it years ago. Nobody spoke. They ignored each other and disappeared into back alleys and dark crevices to merge with the cold, grey of the city.

I ventured inside. The main doors opened to a glass cubicle and a long hall with a succession of doors off the sides. A sign told me that check-in was strictly at six and all rooms were to be given on a first come, first served basis. Anyone fortunate enough to get a room for the night would have to be out that front door again by nine in the morning, no excuses, or the police would be called. The list of rules went on. I was busy studying them when I heard a woman remonstrating through the glass.

'Honestly, I can't make it this weekend. I know, I'm always busy. I'll come visit you on Wednesday. Okay, how's Thursday morning then? Look next weekend I've got Sunday off. Well, alright. If you don't want to see me either, just say so. No. I didn't mean it like that. Of course I want to see you. I do.'

She spied me through the glass and looked almost relieved to have an excuse to hang up the phone.

'Someone's waiting. I've got to go. No. I'll call you back when I get a chance. Yes, goodbye Mother.'

She hung up, breathed a deep sigh of relief, and smiled at me pleasantly. She looked way too old to be having parent trouble. I wondered how old this cantankerous mother of hers would be. Maybe she lived in the same home as Dolly? Maybe she wanted to see her daughter so much, and called her every hour at work to badger her, because she was afraid of some old greyhound that had been sniffing outside her front door? Even annoying people have their reasons.

'You're not here for a room I take it?'

'No.'

'You part of the church?'

'No.'

'Didn't think so. No tie. So what then? School project?'

'I need to find someone.'

She regarded me more seriously now. Her hackles went up and she went into a weary explanation about how family members couldn't be told if their loved ones were booked in to the hostel.

'Client confidentiality you understand?' she said. 'Everyone has a right to privacy. It doesn't matter if he's your father, your uncle, your long-lost grandfather, whatever. Our clients deserve respect. Besides, even if I wanted to, legally I can't tell you anything.'

'I don't know who he is. In fact, I don't care.'

'You've lost me.'

'I just need to speak to him. Then he'll never see me again.'

She paused, looking curious. Her face set sternly and she leaned in to whisper gravely.

'Has someone hurt you?'

'Not recently.'

'One of the men here?'

'No.'

'Because if they have, you can tell me. I'm a social worker.

Damn it, I'm not meant to put leading questions to you. Forget what I said, let's start over.'

'Nobody's hurt me,' I said. 'You can forget your questions. I just want to talk to a man. He lives in a box.'

She pressed her lips together and I could see she knew immediately who I was talking about. Recognition flashed red across her cheeks.

'You know who he is,' I said.

'Look, as I said . . .'

'Legally you can't tell me, I know. Just point the way.'

'You shouldn't go looking for a man like that. It's not safe.'

'He won't hurt me,' I told her.

She gazed at me quizzically and caught my solid assurance. Yes, when it came to the old man in the box, he was the hunted, I the hunter.

'You got a mother?' she asked.

I nodded warily. She pushed the phone through a large slit in the glass.

'Call her. Tell her where you are. She's probably worried sick about you.'

'What? Like your mother,' I defended.

'You don't know my mother,' she retorted.

'And you don't know mine.'

A glaze of mist rose in her eyes. Her perception of me swung, distorted through that glass. I was no longer a lost child to save. A future client maybe? Certainly I already held the same empty look as the old men she counselled day after day. She looked shocked to see it start so young. She pitied me I think.

'Listen to me,' she said. 'It doesn't matter what's happened, or what you think will happen. Your family is important. It's the one thing that binds you. Everything begins with family. Do you understand?'

I knew she wanted some recognition, some indication that she'd solved my problems for me. She honestly cared for people, that much was obvious. She cared for everybody it seemed, even some lost urchin off the street. But why? I wondered. Was her need to help driven by her own lack of family? She wanted others to have what she couldn't.

'Yes,' I lied. 'I'll call her soon as I'm done.'

She relaxed into a soft, benevolent smile. It had become so easy to tell people what they wanted to hear, I thought. She pointed out the door.

'He was too late for a room tonight,' she said. 'He'll be down at the other end of the square. Good luck.'

He spotted me straight away, before I even got close. The old man in the box sniffed the air, as if he saw the world through his sense of smell. He wasn't like other people, caught up in the world and its day-to-day obstacles; the old man in the box meditated on life with an appreciative eye on everything. He saw both sides of the stream. His face curled into a snarl as I approached, warning me off like I was a rival come to usurp his territory.

I snarled back.

He dropped his gaze first and retreated to his box, circling round and round until he found a comfortable spot. The old always bow to the young eventually, I thought. We sat in the park together for what seemed an eternity, watching the cars go round and round the square. People with jobs and husbands and wives and children and bills to pay and holidays to arrange raced past on their incessant digressions.

All this, I realised, the world and its many passions, were

also illusions: another play put on by a deeper force for our entertainment. Even if the play had sad moments, or a terrible sequence of tragedies, that only helped make it all the better. Comedy and tragedy were twins on the same coin, as were the two worlds. They were inseparable.

'You see it now,' he grumbled from inside his box. 'It's them who stray from the path.'

He was first to speak. So I had taken his crown. I was now the alpha.

'You have also strayed,' I told him.

He looked fearful of me. From the sideways angle of his nose and his missing front teeth, I understood this man had seen plenty of beatings in his life. I knew he would do as I did. He'd lie down and take the blows while his mind drifted away. He'd watch on from afar and hope for release, but that day had never come. Eventually he'd return to the blood and the flesh, resentful. Physical pain held no fear for him. He feared me in an entirely other realm.

'You see the dog,' I said.

He remained silent, but I could almost hear his thoughts rambling away. He wanted to lie to me, to defend all accusations, but he knew that was pointless. His mind was open, like an old movie projector. He tried his best to exorcise me from his mind, but he was too weak. He was too old. He succumbed to my will and showed me images of his youth, his dead parents, his first car, his first love, his last, and then his wife. He showed me a career and success and a house and tailored suits and holidays and a life just like those driving around us on that roundabout. He showed me cancer and a child and a terrible, demon-filled night when his world came crashing down around him and his mind was lost forever.

And in every scene of this passion play was the dog.

'Will you kill me?' he asked.

'No.'

'I can't do it myself. I've tried. But I can't. I'm too weak.'

'Yes, you are weak Martin,' I told him.

'How do you know my name?'

'You've shown me everything,' I said.

I had what I wanted. Giving him the gift of salvation wasn't my place. He would have to find that for himself. The weird thing was he wasn't responsible for any of the bad things that happened in his life. They were all merely a set of unfortunate events that were either going to happen, or not happen. There was no reason, no blame behind any of it. There was no such thing as fate. It was meaningless: a random set of atoms bouncing off one another and that was all. He had prescribed a hidden meaning to his life and come to the conclusion that he was to blame. And the dog had watched, always waiting, biding its time.

No, I thought. If Martin wanted absolution he would return to his wife in his own time, by his own free will. Either that or the play would soon be over. He would enact the final tragedy, and the curtain would be drawn.

Perhaps then the dog might show some emotion, might smile or cry at the story that had been told. Or would it still feel nothing? I wondered. Would it merely turn the pages to another story and watch another curtain being drawn, to while away the eons?

I left Martin alone in the park. I don't know what became of him. The dog certainly knew, and would be more than willing to tell me, if I asked. But how could you trust a talking dog?

Chapter Fourteen

Tony sat in science and flicked snot at me. He mined his nose for ammunition, rolled it into little sticky balls and machine-gunned them, rapid fire, at my head. I ignored the first five or six, but on the seventh I had enough.

'You got a problem?' I asked.

'Yeah. You,' he grumbled.

Tony wasn't used to being confronted, unless it came from his father. He stared me down with the cold intent of a predator.

'You were meant to help me study,' he said. 'I failed the test. Because of you.'

'No. I was meant to do a project with you. Which I did,' I explained. 'Passing the test was up to you.'

He shook his head and stood up. He towered over me but I stood my ground.

'There a problem here?' asked Mr Rooney.

The class jeered and goaded Tony to punch my lights out right then and there. Tony blamed me for all his short-comings in science, but the rest of the school still paid me out on a daily basis. After the video with Pippa Wilson, I would not be forgotten for a long time. I no longer had the luxury of merging into the background. I was sought out by all. Even the first-year kids had taken to me. I was routinely slammed into walls, I had paint thrown in my face, and I'd even been tripped down the stairs. All this I had endured but I drew the line at Tony's snot.

'No problem sir,' Tony sneered.

I could see the wheels turning behind his eyes. Tony had a plan.

In the weeks after the video, humiliation became a daily chore. I told myself that people would get bored of singling me out soon enough, but that day hadn't come. The thing with Tony was building up to something, too. I could hear the whispers and the jeers behind me as I walked the corridors. Someone filled up my locker with sheep poo. Another kid, I don't even know his name, poured twenty litres of craft glue into my school bag. All my textbooks were destroyed, along with about half of my work for the semester. I had no option but to write it all out again. Ms Finch lectured the school on prank behavior. She asked everyone to put themselves in the position of the person being pranked. How would they feel if that happened to them? she asked. Everyone knew she was talking about me. Their eyes drifted my way, but none of their compassion. I was under siege. My head bulged under the pressure of it all. I wanted to explode.

Eliza kept her distance. I saw her occasionally in the halls or by the bus stop, but she always simply turned away. I didn't blame her. All this was my fault. She was in the girls' loo washing her hands when I walked in.

'Stop avoiding me,' I ordered.

'I'm not avoiding you.'

'Then what do you call it? You've been acting all weird.'

'Hey. You're the one in the girls' loo!'

'Why did you tell me to go?'

'You wanted to go. You wanted her, remember?'

She was right. Damn it. I didn't want her to be right.

'I don't know why I told you to go to the party, okay Monty? It could have been good for you. A chance to grow up a bit.'

'Is that what you think – that I'm just a little kid?' I asked.

'No. I didn't mean it like that.'

'Come to the beach with me?' I asked hopefully.

She shook her head and walked out. After she'd gone, some girls from year eight walked in and screamed, running out to find a teacher, to tell them of the horrid pervert they'd found loitering in the girls' toilets. That night I sat alone and waited for the dog. It withheld itself from me, making me want it all the more. I paced my room, lost. Even Gutentag had deserted me.

Alias: @The Full Monty
Date: Thursday August 28, 2.12AM
Hello?

Come on. I know you're there. Respond.

I know you are reading this.

I'm so alone.

Something had to give. It was either going to be me, or them. I was like a caged animal, destined for the slaughterhouse. I decided if I was going down, I'd take some of them with me. I was going to fight back. So I took to exercise. I discovered that by eating properly and doing some physical exertion, things changed. I began to grow.

Now, most normal people would find this utterly obvious, but I had never really thought about what it took to grow. Back in primary school, we were given wheat seeds and some cotton wool. We all had to soak the cotton wool in water and, sure enough, after a few days we were delighted to see little green shoots spring up out of their fluffy white beds.

But then came the hard part. Those little seedlings needed more. Only the kids who were wise enough to replant them in some soil kept their seedlings alive. The rest of us kept our green shoots stunted in their cotton wool. Without the proper nutrients, life withers and fades.

I was no different. I had purposely restricted my own access to nutrients. Food, exercise, human interaction; I had limited all three in an effort to seize control. Yet now I was doing just the opposite. Eating well didn't come easy, and neither did the exercise; I simply wasn't used to moving. My muscles had withered like an old man with the palsy and my first attempt at working out left me gasping on the floor of the shed. My father had some rusty old weights out there, left over from his youth. He must have experienced the same desire to bulk up. Sometime, long ago, a teenage version of my father had bench pressed those weights in the hope that muscles would solve all his problems. As far I could see, my father didn't have a problem with muscles. His work at the motor shop meant that he was always lifting heavy things. He was literally bulging with them. Even the muscles under his eyebrows flexed furiously, like angry caterpillars on steroids. I swear he could probably lift more weight with his eyebrows than I could with my entire body.

I lay down on the cold concrete floor and heaved those weights into the sky. My arms threatened to explode and send that heavy bar down to my throat. Perhaps I'd be found there years later, I thought, like a piece of petri-fied wood under that old barbell. Oh, that's where Monty went, people would say. I thought he just left school and got a job in a pencil factory. No, I wouldn't end it like that, I thought. I fought against the tide of gravity and set that ten-kilogram weight safely down.

Working out became my daily ritual. Days turned into weeks. After so many years of neglect, I sprouted like a spring sapling. I slowly added kilos, along with some muscles. Eventually, I could lift more weight than I ever dreamed possible. The exercise helped me sleep too. To go with this, I now had a ravenous desire for eggs. One morning, I passed the mirror to realise I was ripped. Okay, maybe not exactly ripped, but I did have the beginnings of some actual muscle: little bulges of hope sprang from my otherwise puny arms.

I always thought it was some old wives' tale, that kids literally grew overnight. But there I was in front of my mirror, looking as if I'd caught up fours years of growth in as many weeks. I was still paper-thin but where I was once skin and bone, I now had an underlying cover of hard muscle. I was wiry and lithe. To go along with this sudden explosion of masculinity, I had hair. Firm curls hung off me. They'd no longer blow off in a stiff breeze. My chin became shaggy and my armpits grew in confidence. They were manly and smelled of freshly baked yeast buns.

The flood of energy was relentless. The eggs and the weights made me hungry for more eggs and more weights. I couldn't get enough. Adrenaline charged through me, like a young bull trapped in a field. I needed to get out. I needed to see things. I don't know what things, just things. I wanted to take on the world. I wanted to rage at the machine. I wanted Tony to pick a fight with me one more time.

The day began like any other. I watched from up the street as Eliza took the bus. I walked to school the long way and came in late, so I didn't have to meet anyone before class.

I did my work, kept my head down, and suffered the usual lunchtime taunts. It's often on the boring days that your life gets turned upside down, and is changed forever.

I was king-hit from behind on my way home from school. I didn't see it coming. Tony karate kicked me across my back. I fell and hit my head. Snowflakes invaded my vision. Concussion threatened to spirit me away. I could feel the old urge to float off with it, to relax in the fluffy white nothingness. I fought it though, and for the first time in my life I tried to remain where I was. A hot mix of egg yolk and testosterone surged through my muscles. My fist clenched. I swung around and let it fly.

The punch I threw at Tony Papadopoulos is commonly known as a haymaker. It was a wild swing that arced out in the longest possible route towards the intended victim. It would be a devastating punch if it landed, but it was so uncontrolled that it gave Tony plenty of time to get a look at it, think about it, make a cup of tea, watch a game of football, step aside and defend it then land a crushing blow of his own to my gut. Which he did.

I was a winded snow angel, gasping for air. Tony, Jordan and Rhys flogged me, laughing the whole time. I hit back. I got some good punches in. My new physique held up for a while but I was outgunned. It was three against one. They held me down and pummelled my back with their knees until I gave in. Then they each took turns to urinate on me. Hot piss splashed all over my face, soaking my hair. I spluttered against the putrid, yellow tide, desperately trying not to swallow any. They laughed and aimed at my mouth. I had no choice but to taste their fetid curses on my tongue. I cried. I was small and helpless, like a mouse caught in a trap by its tail, doomed to die a slow death. As their wee finally petered out, I thought that was going to be it. Tony had made his point. They'd had their fun. They'd leave me to dry off in the sun. But then Tony did something unexpected.

In science we had studied exothermic reactions. Mr Rooney led the class out to the shelter shed and placed down a cute little ceramic flowerpot. This was a teacher-only experiment, he warned. We all stood back as he added two seemingly innocuous powders together to produce something truly terrifying. Iron oxide and aluminium were completely harmless on their own. Put them together even and they happily coexist. But increase the temperature, like by adding a really hot spark, and they explode. These twin elements fuse and merge; atoms reorder themselves and become something entirely new. Along the way huge amounts of energy are released. We all shielded our eyes that day as the little flowerpot blew up in cloud of smoke. All that was left behind was a little ball of molten iron, bubbling away in the bottom. That's what Tony Papadopoulos put in my back pants pocket.

In the days before, somebody had broken in to the chemical storeroom. Mr Rooney couldn't tell if anything had been stolen; he just put a new lock on the door and left it at that. It had been Tony. He'd taken just a few grams of these chemicals. Jordan and Rhys had no idea what he was doing. Neither did I, until it was too late.

My bum literally exploded. A red, hot fireball tore through my back pants pocket. My pants were on fire. I was on fire. A ball of molten iron filled my pants. I screamed and ran around like mad, trailing smoke and ash. I tore off my pants and my jocks. The pain was incredible. The reaction was short-lived, but it was so hot it left a burning hole in the cheek of my bum, big as a dollar coin. The smell of charred flesh hung in the air. Jordan and Rhys looked on, shell-shocked. One of them threw his water bottle over me. It didn't work. The pain was intense. My mind had enough of this world and disappeared.

I can't exactly remember how it all went from there. It was like a dream. I remember Tony and Jordan arguing. An ambulance came. They were gone by then. The ride to the hospital was loud. The siren reminded me of a dying cat, moaning in the night. The paramedics gave me a little green straw to suck on and all the pain drifted away. I woke up in a clean white bed with Dad sitting at the end on a plastic chair. His face was creased into a sharp point, like a dagger poised to strike. His shoulders were tensed. His thick, meaty hands gripped the steel rail at the end of my bed. He curled his lip into a fierce line. I thought of those laughs. I thought of that reeking torrent and the hot, searing pain. Dad's look frightened me and I cowered.

'Tell me their names.'

'Who?' I asked.

'The boys who did this,' he said.

'No.'

'Monty, this is serious.'

'I'll handle it.'

'I called the police,' he said. 'I want to press charges.'

'I didn't get a look at them,' I told him. 'I'm sorry.'

Dad furrowed his enormous eyebrows together in frustration. He walked out and talked to someone beyond the curtains surrounding my bed. I couldn't hear what they were saying, but I guessed it was the police. I could hear my mother crying.

I lay on my side in the bed, with my bum all bandaged up like a wounded soldier. Nurses tended to me. They changed my bandages and wiped the weeping sores. I needed a skin graft. The surgery took weeks to recover from. They literally shaved the skin off my other butt cheek with a massive stainless steel cheese grater thing and glued the fresh skin to the wound. It hurt like hell. My arse was a red-raw disaster zone. After weeks of lying on my front, aching pain and dealing with a dangerous infection, I finally took my first few tentative steps, like a toddler walking for the first time. I thought I knew agony but I had no idea. Mum and Dad visited me, but there were long times in between where I'd just ponder what I'd do to Tony Papadopoulos. Muscles weren't going to be enough, I thought. I needed a better retribution.

I woke to see Eliza. I don't know how long she had been there but when I opened my eyes she was staring right at me. She was silent as night. I blinked and she was gone.

A phantom, perhaps.

Days drifted by. The nurses were great. They never once pitied me, never once told me they were sorry for me. I guess they'd seen much worse in their time, like kids with cancer and mashed up car accident victims. They always remained upbeat and businesslike. They just got on with the job, wiped the festering sores on my bum, and moved on to the next kid in need. Eventually my pain subsided. My skin healed. Walking became easier, if I didn't stretch too far. Dad came to pick me up, and on the way home told me the news.

'You'll need a uniform. Heathmont High wear blue and

yellow. It's pretty casual. Just t-shirts and shorts mainly. It's a bit of a drive, but I can take you before work.'

'I'm changing schools?'

'You can't go back to Middleford,' he said. 'Not after this.'

'I want to go back.'

'You're not going Monty. That's it.'

Mum and Dad bought me the uniforms. They enrolled me in the new school. They had a special program in science, so I'd fit right in, they told me. Dad continually quizzed me about the names, but I kept quiet. My butt eventually healed. The scabs were enormous. The skin graft left me with two matching scars on each butt cheek. I looked like a walking Rorschach test. I stared at my butt in the mirror, to see what I could make of those dark, symmetrical shapes. The blots coalesced and changed form. Then it all made sense. The dog was tattooed on one side, and I was on the other. I was the dog and it was me. We were perfectly reflected on my butt.

'He can't get away with this,' said the dog.

'No. He can't.'

'You can't fight him. He's too strong.'

'I know.'

'There's something else you can do, though.'

'Yes?'

'Go now. While they are busy. Be quick. Nobody will know it's you.'

I found the old spearfishing rubber deep in the back shed. I had thrown it in there and vowed never to use it again after I'd killed that bird on a wire. But vows can be broken, I guess. I set the rubber back into the gun and went to pay Tony Papadopoulos a visit.

From the perspective of an uninvited guest, Tony's house looked like a fortress of concrete and high bars, with metal shutters on all the windows. I guess when you fill your house with the most expensive gear you can buy, you have to make it secure. I wasn't out to steal anything though. I lay in wait out front and watched.

Night fell and the smells coming from inside Tony's house were intoxicating. I knew the Papadopouloses were sitting down to a hefty indulgence. It seemed to go on for hours. Finally, lights came on in the lounge room. I guessed they were finished gorging themselves and were sitting down to watch some TV. Tony came out to the street carrying a bag of garbage. I watched silently, lying in stealth. Tony had no idea how close he was to the end, as he lifted the lid of the wheelie bin to discard the remnants of his night's meal.

The spear flew like a dart.

Tony froze, shocked, as the garbage bag he was holding split open, blasting rubbish all over him. Meat fat and cheese and half eaten pickles splattered all over his front. The spear went right through the bag, cut it open, and ended up stuck in the neighbour's timber fence. Tony stared at me, wide-eyed in fear, as I lowered the spearfishing gun.

'Next one's got your name on it,' I said.

Tony wilted. Urine soaked his pants. His breath cut short. He dropped the garbage bag and ran back into the house, screaming his head off. I could hear his cries from the street.

'Mummy! Daddy! Mummy! He tried to kill me!'

I didn't have much time. Tony's father would be out looking for trouble. I quickly pulled the spear from the fence and shuffled away to disappear into the night. I merged with the darkness to listen in Machiavellian glee. Tony's father roared at the empty street.

'Show yourself! Come on! How dare you!' he screamed.

He hollered at the night, desperate for his revenge. Yet, for all his fury, he could not see me. I had taken to the shadows and was beyond him. I calmly watched as he paced back and forth up his driveway like some beast marking the edge of his territory. He didn't dare venture out any further, I could see. Soon enough, his pride gave out and he returned to the house, slamming the door behind him in a final act of bravery. They were all weak in the end.

I hid the spearfishing gun in the train tunnel on the way home. The only evidence was a small dent in a timber fence, which would be hard to find, and almost impossible to determine what really had made it. All that remained was a spilled bag of rubbish and Tony's testimony. It was his word against mine.

Two police officers sat with my mother for around an hour. The oldest one was fat and grew a moustache straight out of the seventies, which was odd because he would have only been about twenty-five. Perhaps he'd grown up watching old TV shows and thought having a large gut and a gigantic moustache was what it took to be a cop. The other one was younger, maybe straight out of cop academy, and looked no older than some of the kids at school. She was thin and angular and her police-issue utility belt hung off her hips like a gigantic weight. I imagined her ultimate demise, not from fighting criminals, but by being suddenly crushed one morning under that ridiculously heavy belt. They both wore guns too. I was metres away from their guns. Something in me wanted to reach out to touch them.

They looked so light and plastic, nothing like the shiny metal guns from the movies. I wanted to feel how light they were. I wanted to feel the recoil as I triggered off a round, aiming it straight at Tony's head.

'Show us the shed Monty,' fat moustache guy ordered.

I led them out back and turned the light on in the shed, allowing them to freely look around.

'Like I told you, I was in my room all night,' I lied. 'I don't know what Tony's talking about.'

They dutifully ignored my testimony. I sensed cops spent almost everyday being lied to by some lowlife or other. I needed to give them some element of truth, just enough to deflect suspicion.

'Look, Tony is angry with me because he failed a test. I was meant to help him and I didn't. Now he wants to get back at me, I guess.'

The younger cop's eyes searched mine for any hint of duplicity. Her cop training wasn't up to the task. She looked as if she believed me straight up.

'Your father says you've had some trouble?' fat moustache guy quizzed.

'That? Yeah. Like I said, I don't know who did it. Just a prank, I guess.'

'Is that what this was? A prank?'

'No.'

'Someone could have been killed.'

'So you say.'

'There's nothing here,' younger cop reported.

Moustache guy nodded and approached me swiftly, pushing his round gut into me threateningly. This was all he had left to intimidate people with, I guess. That and his moustache.

'We'll let this go with a warning. If we hear anything further, action will be taken. Is that understood?'

I desperately wanted to look him in the eye and stare him down. I knew I could do it. I knew I had developed the coldness required. But that would give me away. I needed to feign submissiveness. He needed to see me cower before him.

'Yes sir,' I said.

I bit my lip, forced myself to tremble, and held my gaze on the floor. He sniffed the air around me, trying to discern any hint of deception. Eventually he decided I was frightened enough and left, followed by his eager young protégé.

'Well done Monty,' said the dog.

'I don't need your praise,' I told it.

'True. You don't.'

'Don't act like you've got some plan.'

'It's not *my* plan. I simply allow you to see, that is all.'

'See what exactly?' I asked. 'Will you do to me what you did to Martin?'

'It was unfortunate you met. I did not mean for that to happen.'

'You destroyed him.'

'He destroyed himself.'

'And you watched?'

'Yes.'

'You did nothing. You could have stopped him. You could have helped.'

'And what would that do? How would my intervention change anything?'

'He could have been happy.'

'No, he couldn't.'

'People loved him.'

'No, they didn't. He was alone,' said the dog. 'We are all alone.'

The dog and I looked out of the shed, the night framed against the spill of an incandescent bulb. Rogue insects began their suicide missions against the light. It was a stupid, futile exercise. They couldn't resist its magical charm, driven by some uncontrollable genetic urge. Moths to a flame. It always ended the same way. The dead bodies fell to the floor, discarded remains to be crushed underfoot. A waste. Nobody missed them. Nobody cared. They were simply an inconvenience.

'You missed me, didn't you?' asked the dog.

'No.'

'Liar.'

The day came for me to go to my new school. I decided I wasn't going and refused to put on the yellow and blue uniform. I rejected my new life, new friends, moving on: it all seemed too hard. Everything seemed too hard. I stopped lifting the weights. I stopped eating properly. Sleep became a stranger once again. I only wanted one thing.

'You've grown,' said Eliza.

I found her by the train tunnel. She'd come out of it so suddenly, materialising from the gloom, that it gave me a shock.

'Shouldn't you be in school?' I asked.

'Shouldn't you?'

'I thought you weren't talking to me anymore,' I said more as a statement of fact than a question.

'Things change,' she said.

She looked out across Middleford, almost wistfully. I

thought of offering her an out, like they do in the movies. I'd say something really cool. I'd hit the nail on the head and sum up everything that was wrong in our lives in a neat little speech that would leave her crying and wanting me forever. It would all be about how this place was holding us back and how all the people here were just selfish and didn't understand us. We were important. It was all about us. If we could just escape from all of this and be together, we would be happy. We didn't need Middleford. We didn't need friends or family, just each other. Come on baby, I'd say. Let's steal a car and get out of here. We'll be rogues. We'll travel the world on forged identities. We'll be the world's most wanted. And we'll be happy, because we'll have each other.

'Did it hurt?' she asked.

'The burns? Yeah. They said I was pretty lucky. It just missed an artery. I could have bled out in the street.'

'That would have been something,' she said.

'Yeah, something.'

She peered at me and I could see she understood my pain. Her eyes swelled, ready to shed tears. She felt for me after all. She wasn't cold and dead inside. That really threw me. Maybe I had Eliza all wrong.

'Show me,' she said.

'What? Now?'

'Yeah. I want to see.'

'Okay. But I'm warning you, it's not pretty.'

'Your butt or the burns?' she asked sarcastically.

It was a half-hearted attempt at lightening up the situation. We smiled earnestly at one another, knowing the true gravity of what had happened. I dropped my pants, turning around so she could witness the damage. She was suitably appalled.

'Geez, Monty.'

'It's okay. I deserved it,' I said.

'No, you didn't. No one deserves that.'

She gazed back into the tunnel and ruminated on Tony Papadopoulos.

'You're better than me,' she said. 'I would have shot him in the leg.'

'I'm sorry,' I quickly said. 'For everything. For Pippa. I only went because I thought you hated me. It was a mistake.'

'Yeah. Well, we all make mistakes,' she sighed.

'You ever want to go? I mean, get out of here?'

'What do you mean?'

'Just asking.'

'Why? You offering?'

'What if I was?'

She gave me a stern look. This wasn't something to offer lightly. It was a once-in-a-lifetime chance that people like us took and never looked back. If we were to do this, nothing in Middleford would make us return. We'd go where desire took us. World's most wanted and all that.

'Don't ask me that, Monty. Not if you don't mean it.'

Eliza pulled her sleeves down and crossed her arms. It was the kind of subconscious gesture people made when they wanted to protect themselves, like I was some kind of threat.

'I do mean it,' I said. 'That's what you want, isn't it? To just disappear?'

Her tears were a shock to me. They gushed down her cheeks so suddenly I thought she had accidentally stepped on something sharp. For a second, I didn't think they were real: they'd come on so quickly. Then I realised the obvious, she'd held this back for a very long time.

'I can't, Monty. I just can't.'

I understood why. I had betrayed her. She wasn't going to give me that chance again.

Chapter Fifteen

Back in the seventies, when my dad was as young as me, the nerdy types at NASA decided to send up a little greeting card inside the Voyager spaceships. The ships were the height of technology at the time, and had the computing power of a toaster. These tiny little calling cards flew out of the solar system and are, by now, the furthest things our civilisation has ever thrown away. Inside each one was a golden record, complete with instructions on how to play it, in case sometime in the next couple of billion years some aliens came across our little time capsule and just happened to have access to a record player. If they did work out how to play it, they'd get some pictures and sounds of all the wonderful things on Earth: the animals, the people, the land, the sounds of waves, even whale songs.

Along with these wonders were directions to Earth. Some people apparently thought this was a really stupid idea. Maybe the aliens would love to visit Earth, and eat us for afternoon tea. But most people thought it would take aliens so long to get here, millions of years probably, that it wouldn't be much of a threat. Besides, by that time, we might have evolved into something completely different, or become extinct.

So what was this golden record all about? It summed up an entire species into a neat little package of images and sounds. That was it? That little golden record was all we'd bequeath to the universe, declaring that we, humanity, had ever existed? What's the difference between that, I thought, and some teenage kid scrawling out his name on the side of a train? We had made our mark. That was it. The rest of it was all white noise. It made me think: what would my mark be? I couldn't think of a single thing.

Dolly was dying. She had passed away about three times overnight but each time, just as the sheet was pulled over her head, she'd suddenly take another huge gulp of air and miraculously rise again. Every time she took her last breath, and floated away into the aether, some strange force of nature abruptly recalled her back into existence. Stubborn until the end was Dolly. Apparently she was pretty annoyed by this.

'Where am I?' she asked. 'Heaven? It looks just like the retirement village! Why am I still old? And why is the food still horrible? I should be young, eating fresh watermelons and kissing Karl all over for the first time.'

Karl was her husband, my grandfather. He died when I was little. I never knew him, never got to bounce on his knee, or laugh at his old-man jokes, or wonder at the length of his bushy eyebrows. To me, Karl was only a figure in an old photograph. The only thing I really knew about him was an anecdote about some fishing accident. Apparently his tinnie got stranded out in the gulf and he had to swim for his life. Ever the miser, he managed to tow his bucket load of fish with him all the way to shore. Sharks circled, but Karl didn't give up his bucket of fish. Waves threatened, but Karl didn't give up his bucket of fish. Exhaustion and hypothermia set in but, you got it, Karl didn't give up his bucket of fish. Stubborn, just like Dolly, was Karl. He risked life and limb but at least the family had fish and chips for dinner.

'If this is heaven, then show me hell,' pleaded Dolly. 'Maybe they'll have better food!'

My mother and father looked at each other, bewildered, and talked to the doctor.

'You think it's just an infection?' my mother asked.

'Yes,' the doctor said. 'The infection spread to her lungs. She was touch and go last night. But her attitude this morning is encouraging. She's displaying a lot of energy.'

Energy. That summed up Dolly. She was the type of grandmother who could knit you a woolly jumper and bake a batch of scones at the same time. Dolly had left us with specific instructions not to allow medical intervention in case of her demise. They could make sure she was comfortable and in no pain, but we weren't meant to put her on life support or anything. So she stayed in her room in the retirement village, hallucinating, as she drifted in and out of life. The whole time, that greyhound sat out front, sniffing at the door.

'Go on, get!' I snapped at the stupid creature.

It didn't seem to understand I was angry at it and just kept sniffing at Dolly's door. I gave it a kick in the guts and it yelped and ran off, tail tucked under its legs. It wasn't like the black dog. This one felt pain. Still, it knew things we didn't.

'You're wrong,' I yelled after it. 'She's going to be fine.'

It didn't speak to me. It didn't seem to understand me at all. That greyhound simply cowered and limped off. I'd keep it at bay. Dolly deserved that at least. I went to her room while my mother and father talked to the doctor. I gave Dolly a sip of orange cordial. She seemed to like it. She always liked sweets.

'Tell him to get out,' she hissed.

She was looking behind me, towards the window. I turned around but there was no one there.

'Who?' I asked.

'Him. The man in the black hat.'

'What's he want?'

'Me. He wants me, of course. Tell him to get out of here! I'm not going with him.'

I moved to the window and gestured towards an empty section of wall.

'Here?' I asked.

'Yes. There. He's standing right in front of you!'

I fixed the empty space with a cold stare and whispered in this imaginary man's ear.

Dolly watched me intently, and I saw her face ease into relief. She began to cry, soft and birdlike.

'Is he gone?' I asked.

'Yes,' she said. 'He went back through that door. Lock it for me. Don't let him back in.'

There was no door of course, just and empty section of wall beside her bookshelves. Still, I reached out and turned the invisible knob until her reaction told me I'd found the secret portal and had it locked.

'Have you seen this man before?' I asked.

'Sometimes. He never says anything. Just stands there and holds out a hand for me. I don't like him. It's his eyes.'

'Does he have a dog with him?' I asked.

'In heaven?' she squawked. 'They don't let dogs in heaven!'

'Maybe they don't,' I said. 'More cordial?'

'Thank you Silas,' she said.

'I'm Monty,' I told her.

'Don't be ridiculous. You're Silas.'

'No. I'm your grandson.'

'Yes. My grandson. Silas,' she said and grinned at me over her cordial.

I was confused. She only had one grandson.

'You're such a nice boy,' she said. 'It's so good to see you all grown up. You proved them wrong, didn't you?' she beamed. 'I knew they shouldn't have given up on you. Poor Silas.'

I caught my mother outside in the garden, sitting with some other old lady, one of Dolly's concerned neighbours I guess. They were sharing cigarettes.

'She's not long for this world,' my mother rasped.

'Who's Silas?'

My mother pinched her cigarette so hard it split in two. Hot ashes fell to her feet. All she held was the decapitated stub.

'What did she say to you?'

'She thought I was her grandson. Silas.'

'You shouldn't listen to her. She's not in her right mind.'

'No, I think she knows what she's talking about.'

'She's not in her right, mind. Monty. That's all there is to it.'

Her deflection was thick with the dismissive tone adults held in special reserve for their children. It was the sound of indifference. She regarded me with contempt. I was too simple and childish to understand the world around me. I should just run along and play.

'Why should I believe your word over hers?' I asked. 'You're lying.'

My mother ignored me, relit the charred stub of her cigarette and inhaled. The old woman by her side watched me talk back to my mother with clear distaste.

'You shouldn't speak to your mother like that,' the old woman said.

She shot me a condescending smile and placed a comforting hand on my mother's arm. But who was she to judge? She didn't know me at all. She was just some passer-by in this sorry tale. They puffed their smokes in unison, looking down on all those around them.

'It'd be quicker if you just walked in front of a bus,' I told the old woman. 'Spare us all the waiting.'

'Monty!' My mother shouted.

I left the two of them there to stare after me, enraged by my gall. They could rage all they liked. It might do them good. They could blame that horrid teenager for all their problems. I could be their vessel, filled up with venom, so they could pretend to be pure. All I needed was to find someone to nail me to a cross.

Yeah, bad thoughts, I guess. I was in a downward spiral. I had no idea how to lift myself from it. I was too far gone now. The only way out was to dig deeper.

The public records office was at the back of Middleford town hall, down a long corridor framed with a succession of teak doors. I counted twelve identical offices running off that corridor, each one exactly the same as the one before it, save for a tiny plaque showing the occupier's name: Mr Raymond Hawkins, Town Planning; Mrs Felicity Bradshaw, Communications Officer; Mr Henry Coombs, Social Services.

How nice, I thought, to have a little sign that gave your name and occupation to everyone who passed you by. There was no doubting their role in the scheme of things. There it was, in black and white written on the door. These people had a function. They had a duty to serve. They could look back upon retirement, and take stock of their little sign. There. I did it, they'd say proudly. I planned all those towns, officiated all those communications, and serviced my society. I left the world a better place. Or maybe they'd look at their little sign and wonder what it all meant. Had they just wasted their entire lives because a little sign told them what to do?

Mrs Jennifer Nolan, of public records, looked like a shrivelled cactus. Her skin was off-colour and pockmarked with dark circles, like craters on the moon. Her glasses were enormous, and they magnified her eyes to about twice their normal size. When she peered up at you, you had the distinct impression she was suddenly closer than she actually was, as if she had sneaked up on you and was about to devour you whole.

'Yes?'

'I want to find somebody.'

'Name?'

'Silas Ferguson.'

She turned her enormous eyes to her computer and typed the name out with one finger, so slowly that the clock ticking above her head seemed to drone on for hours.

'That'll be thirty-nine, ninety-five,' she muttered.

'Huh?'

'For the birth certificate. If that's what you want?'

'You got a death certificate too?'

She typed some more. Entire days seemed to drift by. Clouds raced above us in fast motion. The world spun on its axis, to finally come to rest.

'No. Not yet, anyway,' she grinned as if she was the keeper of all things. 'That'll be thirty-nine, ninety-five,' she repeated drearily.

'Look, I don't need a print out,' I said. 'Can I just see?'

She sighed reluctantly and turned her screen around.

There it was. The names. The dates. Written in black and white. Silas Ferguson, son of William and Miranda Ferguson. He was four years older than me. Dolly was telling the truth. I had a brother.

It was weird. I had no idea I had a brother, yet the news made me feel guilty, as if it was my fault I didn't remember him. Had I been so caught up in my own problems that I hadn't even noticed him? Or did he just get sick of my family and leave, never to return? Whatever the truth was, he had been kept secret.

I went back to the retirement village to find Dad loitering in the entrance hall. He stood by a vending machine and repeatedly pressed the same buttons over and over, as if the damned contraption hadn't got the message. Cruel things, vending machines, designed by cruel people. It slowly, excruciatingly, deposited a packet of chips in the bottom drawer and my dad had to force himself up to his elbow to retrieve it. He was madly scrambling for it when he looked up to see me.

'Where's Silas?' I asked.

Dad dropped his chips. Resignation flooded his face and he turned for the door.

'Follow me.'

We drove in silence across Middleford to park out the front of a dingy looking red brick home, bang in the middle of suburbia. A white mini-van was parked outside, and the windows had metal shutters locked into place. The garden was dead and the letterbox was wired onto a fence post, as if someone had ripped it off and this temporary fix had slowly become permanent.

Dad waited as I knocked on the door. The doorbell, too, had been ripped off the wall and a stout middle-aged man with a long beard and tattoos answered. He looked at me quizzically through the security mesh door, until he saw my dad alongside me. His easy recognition told me Dad was a regular visitor.

Silas sat at the end of a long table. He looked a lot like me, only older, and thinner, if that was possible. He didn't look up when I stood before him, or indicate that he recognised my presence at all.

I saw myself reflected in him. The genetic resemblance was astounding. Some siblings, even though they may be separated by years, look like twins, their DNA matching so closely that they look almost identical. Silas and me were like that. Looking at him was like looking at myself in a time machine, transported four years into the future.

Drool dripped from his mouth and he screamed loudly, then smashed himself across his head with a clenched fist.

Okay, so there were a few differences. I could see that Silas liked to hit that same spot repeatedly, because there was a large lump of scar tissue just visible under his hair, as though part of his brain had oozed out and solidified like lava gone cold. He stank of stale urine and faeces and I could see the top of his sanitary pad poking up from under his tracksuit pants.

In front of him was some sort of game made out of a homemade wooden ramp. Silas held a tennis ball and raised it to the top of the ramp and let it fall. It rolled down to the bottom and he shrieked. There was no joy in his shriek, well none that I could hear. It wasn't frustration either. It was the sound of acknowledgement. His shriek was matter-of-fact. Another roll had been performed. And another now waited. He rolled that ball again and again. This was his lot in life. He owed his existence to that ball and ramp.

'He was born like this?' I asked.

'Yeah,' Dad explained. 'Your mother and I took care of him until he was four. By then, it came too much. We just didn't have the skills. He's better off here.'

'He's better off, or *you're* better off?' I asked.

'You don't understand, Monty. He can't help it, but he can be ... violent. Not just to himself. But to anyone,' said Dad.

'When I was born? You put him away when I was born?'

'I had to protect you,' said Dad.

His eyebrows furrowed together fiercely and I understood that there was more to it. Dad may have wanted to protect me, the new baby in the house, but my mother had not.

'What about Mum? She didn't want to put him here, did she?'

'No.'

'But you did it anyway? You brought him here?'

'Yes.'

'No wonder she hates me.'

'She doesn't hate you, Monty.'

Silas shrieked and let the ball roll down the ramp. It fell to the floor this time and bounced away against the wall. I retrieved it and handed it back to him. He wouldn't take it from me. He refused even to look at me. Only after I placed it back on the ramp did he take it and set it off on another futile journey.

'Why didn't you tell me about him?' I asked my mother.

She ignored me, as if I was nothing but a shadow. Perhaps I was. Perhaps she thought of me as a ghost, only there to haunt her pain.

'You should have told me,' I said.

'And what good would that have done?' she asked.

We sat there for a time in the kitchen. She had the phone on the table, awaiting the call. She'd spend the night there, I knew. She wouldn't sleep. She wouldn't leave that phone. She'd fill up her ashtray and, come morning, would know one way or the other if her mother was still alive.

'They gave her morphine. At least if it happens, she'll go in peace,' she muttered.

'There is no peace,' I told her. 'There is only here, and the shadow.'

'Don't talk like that. I don't believe you,' she stammered.

'Dolly's afraid,' I said. 'She doesn't want to die.'

'Monty, go away from me. I don't want you near me right now. You hear?'

Her eyes swelled puffy and red, ready to burst forth. Something in me enjoyed watching her suffer. I was toying with her, making her squirm for my own stupid benefit.

I understood now that she lived with the guilt of giving up Silas, and every time she looked at me, she saw his face staring back at her. I was his reflection. No wonder she had turned away from me. Yet I wasn't him. I was her other son. I had needed her once. And she had deserted me. Whatever schism fractured her mind after she gave up Silas wasn't my fault. I knew it was wrong, but I despised her weakness. I hated her for it.

I stood on the cliff above the shipwreck. Despairing gulls circled, filling the air with their soft cries. The cliff held shattered nests; the chicks were all gone now, either grown up and far away, or long dead and turned to dust. Far below us, ice-cold waves rolled into shore after their thousand-kilometre journey from the Southern Ocean, finally coming to rest. The reef looked black and foreboding. White water crashed against rocky outcrops, sending up hisses of angry foam. I wondered how far down the drop would be. How long it would take to strike those rocks. One step, one breath, and I could take to the wing, grasp a momentary flight, and enact my fall from grace. The dog sat beside me on the cliff, looking out to sea.

'Was that you in the room?' I asked. 'With Dolly?'

'You'd take the word of a dying woman over mine?' asked the dog.

'I'd take anyone's word over yours. Tell me, honestly, if you can.'

'It wasn't me.'

'It wasn't you, or it wasn't some *form* of you?' I asked.

'It wasn't me.'

'Do you know the man in the black hat?'

'Did you see any man?' asked the dog.

'No.'

'Then it wasn't there.'

'Are you there?' I asked.

'You see me, don't you?'

'Yes.'

'Then I am here.'

'Did you know about my brother?' I asked.

'Of course,' said the dog.

The creature fixed me with a cold stare. Its dark eyes

bored into me, but I didn't look away. I wasn't going to be the pursued any longer. What would you do, dog, if I took you under the waves? I wondered. Would you put up a fight? Would you struggle for breath? Would you cling to life, fight to remain alive? Or would you succumb to me, and the dark?

'I am the dark,' said the dog.

'Yes. I know.'

'You mother never loved you,' it said.

'I know.'

'She is broken,' said the dog. 'She could not bring herself to love you, for this would require her to acknowledge him, and her rejection. She despises you because she despises herself. You never stood a chance. These are the wrongs she has done you, Monty.'

'Yes. I know.'

'And yet you have a choice. Do you know what that is?'

'I do.'

'What would you do, Monty, if I took you under the waves?' asked the dog.

I remained silent as Earth drifted through space. The sun bestowed its warmth. The gulls sang their songs of doom.

'Not today dog,' I said.

I stared the creature down. I knew the moment I turned away, it would be gone. I held it within my grasp, within my sphere. It was mine, while I had it in sight.

It almost grinned, mocking my empty assertion.

'You have no control over me,' grinned the dog. 'Don't think that you do. I'll pass on my condolences to your mother.'

I blinked and it was gone.

I turned and ran. My mother was in danger.

The street was empty and so was the house. No car in the front yard. No lights on inside. I bolted in through the front door and called out for her. Nothing.

'Dog!' I screamed.

'Dog!' I hollered. 'What have you done with her? Where is she? Dog!'

The world was silent, only the slight creaking of the house broke the stillness. There was nothing left but a cold ashtray and an upturned chair. I cried for her then, my mother, the woman who'd spent her life regretting my existence. I didn't hate her, far from it. Even though she was incapable of any form of honest connection, it was her I dreamed for. Her touch. Her understanding was all it would take. Only then could I exorcise the shadow. And the dog.

I sat alone for two hours. Eventually, the phone rang. It was Dad. He told me a cab was coming around to pick me up. My head reeled. My dad had never paid for a cab in his life. It had to be bad.

The mental hospital was strange. It was nothing like what you'd read about in books. Asylums were meant to look like eighteenth-century prisons: all stone turrets and bars on the windows and even surrounded by a moat. This was classy. It looked like some kind of designer hotel behind a grand hedge. A gravel driveway circled up to reception. Those little stones muttered a wonderful crunching sound as the cab tyres rolled over them, as if they secretly enjoyed the pain of being crushed.

The woman at reception beamed a soothing smile. She was young and pretty and dressed in a neat blue cardigan. I was expecting some strict matron in a white lab coat maybe, but not her.

'Your father's waiting for you up the hall. Outside room twelve,' she said.

I stood before her, my mouth agape like some kind of comatose patient. I thought she might throw me in there with the rest of the nut cases so I quickly shut my trap. My teeth clanked together loudly. She smiled uneasily as if I'd just tried to bite her.

'Mint?' she asked tentatively.

'Okay. Thanks.'

I sucked on the mint and found my father sitting in the hall on a floral chair, underneath a matching floral print on the wall. The whole place look as if it had been styled to ease tension, to give as little offence to the senses as possible. Nothing was out of the ordinary. And that's exactly what made it so grating on the nerves. It was *too* ordinary.

'How is she?' I asked.

'She's asleep. But not hurt, if that's what you mean.'

'What happened?'

He shook his head and gazed solemnly at the floor. He'd better not be thinking of car parts, I thought. I'd take his skull and scream into it. Feel something! I'd holler. Anything! Just don't sit there and think of car parts!

'Some things don't make sense,' he said. 'She's been under a lot of pressure.'

'I need to speak to her,' I told him.

'You can't. She's out to it. The doctors gave her sedatives.'

'But she's okay? You said she wasn't hurt?'

'I only stepped out for a minute. To get milk. Some bread. When I came back, she was talking to someone. Asking them to take her away.'

'What did she see, Dad?' I asked. 'A dog?'

He looked up at me, suddenly aghast. Fear gripped him.

She'd seen it then. She had made the transition. She could now view both sides of the stream.

Watching my father cry was debilitating. It crushed me. The man who I thought was so strong and bereft of all emotion dropped his head and cried like a baby. He howled, long and hard and gripped my leg with his bear-like fist. I cried with him and patted his back. It was a strange feeling, to console your own father. He began to look weak. I saw his bewilderment at the world around him. My father was confused and lost, just like the rest of us.

He gathered himself and we drove home without a word.

Chapter Sixteen

I watched Eliza's house. I watched as she left for school. I watched as she arrived home. At night, I saw the light come on in her room. I watched everything from our front porch. I had set up an old chair for my observations. Eventually, the scars on my bum hurt from sitting too much so I took to wandering up and down like a caged animal in a zoo. When Dad went to work in the morning I was there and, when he came home at night, I was still there. He'd given me some time to sort things out, after quitting school and everything, but that wasn't going to last much longer.

'Ms Finch called this morning. She asked about you,' he said.

'What did you say?'

'I said we've been going through a rough patch.'

'So that's what this is?' I asked sarcastically. 'A rough patch?'

'Don't get smart with me, Monty,' he chided.

I caught his disappointment. Dad wasn't going to take my belligerence like my mother. He never once raised a hand to me, but I knew Dad grew up in a time when it was okay to smack your kid across the ear for less. The man was a gentle giant and rarely lost his temper. Still, I didn't want to press him. He could snap me like a twig if he wanted to.

'Sorry,' I offered.

'You need to go to school, Monty. What are you going to do? Sit here all your life?'

'What difference does it make?' I asked.

'I told you, don't get smart.'

'I'm not. I'm really asking. What does it matter?'

Dad regarded me with sadness. He looked lost, as though I was a riddle he could never solve. Helpless, he ignored me and went to work.

The house missed her. Something felt wrong with it, as if the walls had become addicted to their daily nicotine fix and were shuddering from withdrawal. The whole place creaked and groaned in her absence. The pipes made their grievance known with loud rattles and thumps whenever you turned on a tap, and the floorboards uttered painful sobs whenever you stepped on them. It was as if the house was moaning in protest, desperate for her to return.

I came out to begin my day of watching and found Dad setting down a trailer-load of paint cans on the front porch. He stood there with a knowing grin, man-sweat already beading on that thick, meaty brow of his.

'What's all this?' I asked.

'Paint.'

'Yeah, I can see that. Why?'

'The house,' he said.

Dad was nothing if not matter-of-fact. I had to fill the gaps in his explanation.

'Shouldn't we be at the hospital?' I asked.

He wrinkled his brow together so his eyebrows came close to touching. I'd always thought of them like two furry caterpillars, forever kept apart by one centimetre of bare skin. No matter how hard they'd tried over the years, they'd never made it to touching, despite their obvious yearnings for one another. Some things just aren't meant to be together, I guess.

'There's nothing we can do there, Monty. She's in good hands,' he said.

The stupid thing about Mum's episode, as Dad called it, was that it had all been for nothing. Dolly wasn't in mortal danger at all. She eventually made a miraculous recovery and the whole thing was put down to a bad ham sandwich; the retirement village had inadvertently given her food poisoning. There was a newsletter all about it, along with a sincere apology. Apparently, the kitchen had strict protocols on food service and everything in the fridge was marked with a use-by date. On this one occasion, however, somebody mistook the number three for the number eight, meaning Dolly got to eat a rotten ham sandwich. Her hallucinations were all because of a fever and she woke up the next day, perfectly fit and healthy. That greyhound had made a mistake. Or perhaps it wasn't Dolly it was scratching for? I wondered. Either way, my mother ended up in a mental institution out of sheer bad luck. That and some bad ham.

Dad tossed me some overalls. Now, some tribes teach their sons how to hunt, or initiate them into manhood by cutting open their chests and rubbing hot ashes into them to see if they cry. My dad was going to teach me to paint. Following Dad's orders was pretty easy. He communicated his instructions with three types of grunt. The first kind of grunt was friendly and meant I should put something down where he was indicating. The second was more urgent and meant I should hurry up or I'd ruin everything. The third kind of grunt was seriously harsh. I only heard that one when I dropped a ladder and almost knocked him on the head. No surprises there.

We worked most of the day and at lunchtime Dad drove

me down to the shops and bought me a meat pie and an iced coffee. This was the usual kind of meal Dad and his mates at the auto shop bought. The iced coffee was rich and milky, but had enough caffeine in it to give you a rush. Mixed with a sloppy meat pie it made me feel a little queasy but, after all the hard work, it actually worked. My body was keen for maximum energy, and this was a meal meant for working men.

'Thanks,' I said.

'You look like you needed it. Hardly see you eat anything,' he muttered.

He chomped into his pie and ate half of it in one bite. Dad could seriously win a pie-eating competition, I thought. The man was built to eat meat pies. What a life he could have lived. He could've taken home trophies, been on the news, even won an oversized novelty cheque, if only he'd taken up eating pies competitively. We could have been famous. I would have been known as the son of the pie man. Maybe I would have lived another life too? Maybe I would have been different, growing up in his humungous shadow. But maybe, no matter what choices my dad made in life, I would have turned out exactly the same.

Painting turned out to be a nightmare. With an old house like ours, you had to spend hours sanding back all the old paint first. It was seriously hard work and my arms ached like crazy. Still, by the end of the first day, we'd taken the house pretty much back to bare timber. It looked like something out of an old cowboy movie. Raw. I kind of liked it like that but Dad popped the first tin of paint. By the fading light, we slapped on the first coat of gleaming white.

I went to bed tired and with aching arms, wondering how the house looked. It was too dark to take in our efforts. As evening drew in, Dad quietly took off to the hospital and left me on my lonesome.

I waited for the dog. It didn't come. I was too tired. My body screamed for sleep, but I resisted. I wanted to confront the dog. It had sent my mother away. It didn't come. I couldn't keep my eyes open any longer. My eyes finally fell as a warm, bear-like hand smoothed my hair.

'She's going to be okay, Monty. Just give her a little time,' said my dad.

I drifted into a deep, dreamless sleep. Until then, I didn't know what it felt like to be safe.

The morning sun dazzled as Dad flung back the curtains in my room.

'Breakfast,' he muttered and walked out.

'Yeah. Good morning to you too,' I said and fell out of bed.

I stretched, still sore from the previous day's work. But my muscles felt good, stronger somehow. Dad had bacon and eggs and strong coffee on the table. The food was good. As I finished my bacon, Dad slapped down another pile of it out the pan.

'Eat up. You'll need your strength,' he said.

'I can't. I'm too full.'

'Eat. I don't want you lazing around on the job.'

'Alright,' I groaned and re-filled my plate.

Dad watched me eat and smiled. He had a plan for me, my old man.

The house looked amazing. Even with just a base coat of white, it had taken on a new lease of life. It shone in the morning sun. Dad passed me a pair of old sunglasses from his car so we could admire our efforts.

'Wow. It looks great,' I said.

'Not bad. It'll look even better with a second coat.'

I pondered my father. Why do some people, when they discover their sister has cancer, decide to run clear around the country to raise money for charity? Or why do some people, when they find out their wife is dying of a breast tumour, decide to paddle to New Zealand in an upturned bathtub? What was the point of that? I wondered. It wasn't like their efforts were going to change anything; by the time this money could be used, it would all be too late for their loved ones. Surely their sisters and wives would prefer them to be by their side, not running through the desert or paddling around in the middle of the ocean? People couldn't fix things like that. They were just doing it for themselves, I thought, to feel useful. These acts of compassion were nothing more than a way to hide from the truth: we were all helpless in the face of fate.

'Why now, Dad?' I asked.

'Don't think about it, Monty. Just do it.'

'Yeah, but why now? After everything ...'

'Monty,' Dad interrupted. 'Just shut up and paint the house. Understand?'

'Yeah. I understand.'

We worked in muted silence, communicating only by grunts. The simplicity was meditative. Dad had one thing right: if I didn't think about it, time passed quickly. Eventually, he gave me a wall of my own to paint and a nod of approval when I'd finished. After two days of solid work, the house looked like it could have featured in some trendy magazine. The weatherboards were now straight and white and Dad even re-nailed and sanded the front porch, bringing it all back into line. The old, snarling face of our house now gleamed with a cheerful looking smile.

I still wanted answers. Why did he wait for my mother to be committed to paint the house? Despite my desperation, I couldn't bring myself to ask him. He stood looking at it from the street, and a strange smile crept on his face. Did he want to surprise her when she got home? A darker thought crossed my mind; perhaps he didn't expect her home at all?

'Shouldn't we go visit Mum?' I asked.

He glowered, as if admonishing me for having such thoughts.

'I'll go check on her later,' he said. 'You don't need to worry about all that. She'll come round.'

He disappeared into the shed to clean up his paint-brushes.

I tried to stay awake in case the dog came but exhaustion overtook me. Night used to be my time. Often, I'd lie awake the whole night and maybe get ten minutes of sleep here, five minutes there. My thoughts had free rein over the world. I could fly free, a discombobulated head in pure nothingness. This was harder now. My body needed rest. My mind eased. Thoughts quickly fell away to morning.

'I want to see her, Dad,' I said at breakfast.

'Maybe tomorrow,' he muttered as he sopped up his fried egg with a slice of bread.

'She doesn't want to see me, does she?'

He looked up and wiped a little egg from the thick stubble on his chin.

'Monty, it's more complicated than you think.'

'She blames me, doesn't she?' I asked. 'For Silas.'

'She blames herself, Monty. That's what guilt does to people.'

This was, by far, the most thoughtful thing my father had ever said. I nearly burst out crying in relief to hear him utter it. Yet he seemed strangely embarrassed by the thought and quickly cleaned up the plates, keeping his back to me so I couldn't see his face.

'You're going to be sixteen soon, right?' he asked.

'Not 'til next year. February, if you've forgotten.'

'Yeah, I know,' he said. 'The fourteenth.'

He knew. It was so simple when you had all the facts. My parents couldn't bring themselves to recognise birthdays. It just reminded them of their loss. Silas was a permanent shadow.

'You'll want your licence then,' he grunted.

He looked at me as if this was an accusation, like I'd been hounding him for months about getting my driver's licence. The thought hadn't even crossed my mind. Then a wink flashed across his face. This wasn't an accusation. It was an invitation.

We drove out of Middleford to a paddock miles beyond the reach of civilisation. Dad drove the car up a dirt track that opened up to a wide field. There was nothing in it but dirt tracks and dead grass.

'Righto. This'll do. Your turn,' he said.

He got out of the car and rounded it to open my door. I just sat there, stupefied. He looked down at me, a little annoyed that I hadn't grasped his meaning.

'Slide over, Monty.'

I swallowed a ball of terror and slid over into the driver's seat. I had to pull myself up over the handbrake to get there, and nearly tore the seat out of my pants, but I eventually deposited myself behind the wheel.

The wheel felt cold and powerful in my hands, as if I was in possession of a loaded weapon. I hadn't even started the engine yet.

'Go on then, start it,' he said. 'Turn the key then quickly let it go.'

I did as he instructed, and his satisfied grunt told me I'd done it just right as the car growled into life. It was an entirely new sensation, to start a car on your own. As a passenger, you don't even notice when a car starts. It's totally boring. All you're thinking about is getting to where you're going. But the act of having control was something else. It was power. I had exercised my will over something else. It was freedom.

'Go on, then,' he said. 'Put it in drive.'

He caught my confused look and clarified his instructions.

'The big D,' Monty, he explained. 'Pull the gear lever down to the big, D. Handbrake off, then gently squeeze the . . .'

Suddenly, we were off. I didn't know to start with my foot on the brake, so we lurched away with a loud clunk as the car thundered into gear. His annoyed grunt told me I'd made a mistake, but not a vital one. Next time, I would do better. The car rolled along in idle and I steered with my elbows locked, so all we did was follow the dirt track, going about five kilometres an hour. I could have got out and walked faster.

'Now, hit the accelerator a bit,' he said. 'The pedal on the right.'

I looked down at my feet and felt for the pedals. Taking my eyes off the track wasn't a smart thing to do and we began to drift a bit. We angled into the paddock as I hit the accelerator. Now, a real car is nothing like a computer game, where the accelerator is either on or off. When you hit the gas in a real car, you can feather it a little, or gun it hard. It was stupid of me. I hit pedal to the metal.

Dad let out a holler of shock, louder and more urgent than any of his warning grunts. This meant we were in serious trouble. And we were. The car literally leapt up in my hands as the engine went into overdrive. The thing boomed in our ears. It was like riding on the back of some mad beast sprinting at full speed. All my feelings of power evaporated. I no longer had control over this creature. It had control over me.

We sped across the paddock. Clods of soil flung up from the tyres, covering the car. Grass flew around the windows and I screamed out in shock. Then something crazy happened: Dad was laughing. He was roaring with laughter, louder even than the roar of the car.

'That's it boy, give it some more!' he shouted. 'There's nothing to hit out here!'

He looked so alive I almost didn't recognise him. I fought through my fear and held on to the wheel, steering us to who knows where. We flew across the paddock like a metallic demon. I began to smile, enjoying the sheer rush of it. His confidence gave me false hope, I guess. Or maybe it was just bravado, and secretly he feared for his life, I wasn't sure. A fence came into view.

'Righto. Back off now,' he said. 'Brake, Monty.'

I didn't brake. I didn't back off. It wasn't that I didn't realise which pedal was which. I guess I was just in some kind of catatonic state. Fear can do that to you. The truth was, it didn't even seem real, like I was watching a play or a movie about someone else's life. Whether they went through that fence or not, lived or died, would have no real effect on my own life. We were separated through some imaginary fourth wall. All that mattered was the drama along the way, the colour and movement. It was just something to keep you interested until the lights went on and you realised it was over.

Dad acted swiftly and threw the car into neutral and slammed on the handbrake. The engine suddenly screamed out in agony. The back wheels locked up and Dad reached over to hold the wheel straight so we didn't end up in a spin. We slid over the dirt and pulled up metres in front of the fence.

'Guess I'm not ready,' I apologised.

Dad looked at me harshly, studiously. I never felt him look at me so deeply before. His fear gave way to anger. Then pity, I guess.

'Why do you do that, Monty? Why do you act like nothing matters?'

I had no answer. I did what most stupid teenagers do when confronted by their parents: I simply shrugged and remained silent.

He gave an exasperated shake of the head and helped me turn the car around.

'Let's try it again,' he said. 'Slower this time.'

Dad didn't give up on me. He didn't scream and shout and order me out from behind the wheel. He simply told me to do it again. He didn't say it outright, but this was his way of telling me not to give up.

I took to driving relatively quickly after that, and

discovered I had a skill almost equal to my dad's in controlling a vehicle. The only difference between us, I guess, was the propensity for my mind to wander off at crucial moments. But the near miss with the fence had taught me to focus. Driving forced me to concentrate on this world. It forced me to keep my mind on the task at hand. I loved it.

We swapped places again by the main road. He looked across to me and I saw something in him I'd never seen before. Pride. We'd connected. It wasn't just the car, or the act of driving; he had given me a glimpse into his world. He showed me I had the power to make my own decisions. I never wanted a car so much in all my life.

'This girl you keep watching?' he asked.

'Eliza.'

'It's over between you and her?'

'Yeah.'

'Then it's over, Monty. It's not good for you to keep watching.'

'Is that why you got me to paint the house?' I asked.

He smiled and continued driving us down the highway. Sunshine made the thick hairs on the backs of his fingers glow. He gripped the wheel with muscular ease. The car would never dare bolt out from under him.

'Exams are coming up,' he said. 'If you don't go back now, you'll have to repeat next year.'

'I know. I can't go back. Don't make me.'

'Hey. No one's going to make you do anything you don't want to do. Got that?'

'Yeah. Got it.'

'Tell you what,' he said. 'Come work for us down the shop. Just over the summer break. If you don't like it, you can always go back. Earn enough to buy something cheap. I'll make sure it's decent.'

'My own car?' I asked.

'Nothing too fast,' he grinned.

We drove home in silence, listening to Dad's favourite country and western music on the radio. The wind blew through the open windows and filled the car with the warm, fresh scent of spring. Dad took the long way home, through winding roads and country scenery. We swept past lazy sheep in their meadows, cows, and even the odd alpaca. Dad drove with one arm leisurely out the window. I imagined myself doing just that in a few months' time.

I had the sudden urge to see all there was of the world. I'd start with Australia, head up the coast all the way north until the roads ran out and there was nothing but jungle ahead, then I'd turn west and circumnavigate the whole country right back down to the Southern Ocean. After that, I'd fly to other countries, getting work picking fruit or whatever and always I'd buy a cheap, decent car. I'd know what to look for after my time working in the auto shop, and I'd always pick up something that would get me around, no trouble. I'd even make a few bucks on it when the time would come to sell it. I'd travel the world this way, touring. The States, Asia, Europe, even Africa; I'd see it all. I'd drive every car known to mankind. You could say I was hooked.

The auto shop smelled of grease and instant coffee. The other men who worked with Dad were all cut from the same frame as him; all genetically gifted with massive shoulders and thick, square hands. Their fingers were like lines of fat sausages. They didn't speak much either. Just like Dad, they communicated in grunts and showed their affection to me by ruffling my hair with their greasy, blackened hands.

Old Bob owned the shop. He was a wizened crow of a man and stank of Brylcreem and onion farts. You never knew when he'd let one loose. You'd be standing next to him, checking out an engine, and he'd let slip the most hideous fart imaginable. The sound would go on for minutes. I swear it was like there was some kind of angry animal growling away down there. He only did this in the shop though, and had to control himself when dealing with customers. I found out later Dad had already arranged for me to work there during the holidays. Old Bob heard the stories about what happened to me at school, and with my mother and everything. He must have taken pity on me, I guess. He didn't need an apprentice, so I was just given clean-up duties. They called me the dogsbody.

I worked hard and quickly had the place swept up, with all the tyres and radiator hoses arranged in neat rows. There wasn't much else to do and Old Bob quickly got sick of me standing around, looking useless, so he gave me my first oil change.

The work was simple. There was an order to things. Old Bob farted and guided me through the process and clicked his tongue in approval after I was done. Later, he thought he'd keep me busy and tossed me a workshop manual. I speed-read it cover to cover over lunch. By the time Old Bob got back from the shops with his steak and onion pie, I'd changed the car's brake pads and given it a radiator flush as well. He didn't want me getting too cocky and told me to just stick with the oil changes, even though I'd saved him some time.

My first pay packet was a gift from heaven. I didn't earn much compared to the qualified mechanics like Dad and Old Bob, so they just paid me cash out of the till. The envelope bulged with twenties and fivers and some coins too. I'd never really had any money of my own before so I just stared at it.

'Don't blow it all at once,' said Dad. 'I can hold on to it if you want. To make sure you save it.'

'Alright. I'll just keep twenty.'

Dad smiled and ruffled my hair proudly. I knew how filthy his hands were from all the grease, but I didn't care. Affection coursed through me. I had made him proud. I had done something worthwhile. I had made my mark on the world, however small, even if it was just changing someone's oil. My father's acknowledgement was a rush of excitement. Until then, I had no idea how much I needed it.

I could see what he was doing; Dad was keeping me busy. He stole me away from that porch, distracted me from Eliza and the school. He'd forced me to move forward. Everything was in the past now. I could choose for it to affect me, or not. He was right and I was happier for it. Still, when silence returned, so did the past.

Middleford House, or the asylum as I preferred to call it, was busy with excitement. Piano music tinkled from a room out the rear. Someone was singing old timey show tunes. It was happy stuff, written to get your toe tapping and your troubles forgotten. My mother was at the front, absent-mindedly leafing through the choir booklet. She didn't sing along. Actually, none of the patients sang along. They all just stared at the old gal playing the piano with a passionless gaze. The woman banged away at those tuneless keys with more gusto. Trying to frighten them off, I thought. She looked fearful of them. Any minute their medications would wear off and they'd attack. The more silent they were, the louder she played, warding off danger. Unpredictable folk, the insane.

I grabbed a choir booklet and started singing. I had no idea what the song was about, I didn't care, I just sang. I had never tried singing before. I now knew I had a terrible voice. It suited my purposes I suppose; everyone turned around.

My mother took one look at me and quietly walked out.

I raced after her down the corridor. She quickened her step to get to her door. I ran to cut off her exit.

'Why don't you want to see me?' I asked.

She pondered this for a moment, as if weighing up telling me the truth, or lies.

'It hurts me to see you. That's why,' she said.

The truth then.

Chapter Seventeen

Alias: @The Full Monty
Date: Monday December 1, 10.00AM
I know how to get out now. You just have to keep going. You just keep working. Don't think about it. Just do it. So what if things don't make sense? So what if you feel pain?

Tears are salty to remind you that you're still alive ☺

Hello? Come on, you can't ignore that one.

Fine, have it your way. This is my last post to you.
I'm out.

I missed Gutentag. His posts were annoying, and I swear he probably spoke English fluently, but he was a friend. He heard my innermost thoughts. I didn't even tell those to the dog, not willingly anyway. Talking with Gutentag was probably the most honest I'd ever been. For whatever reason, he'd grown tired of me and disappeared. I deleted my account. I had to take my own advice, I guess. It was time to move on.

Summer break arrived and kids finished school for the year. I saw them around more often, dressed in shorts and t-shirts for the holidays. Some of them came into the shop with their parents. A lot of families were going on holidays and we were flat out servicing cars ready for road trips. Some of them recognised me and sniggered, but most didn't know who I was. To them, I was just some young mechanic, dressed in blue overalls and covered in grease.

My past had gradually drifted away. Yet I couldn't allow everything to go.

When Dad was busy, I secretly crept out to the porch to watch her. The light in her room was the only thing I had left of Eliza. I wanted to fly into it. I wanted her to look up and see me, buzzing around in her room. I had undergone a metamorphosis. I had left my ugly-grub stage behind and was now a wonderful, colourful butterfly. She'd be enthralled at my majestic beauty, my new strength and power. Yet, no matter how hard I'd try, we'd be unable to communicate. My voice would be strange and insect-like and all she'd hear were weird buzzing sounds. I still love you, I'd holler, I miss you, buzz, buzz, buzz! Annoyed, she'd take a great roll of newspaper and swat me into oblivion. I'd spin away and find myself pulled towards the light. It was a force I could no longer resist. I'd fly into it and burn away, cremated before her. Nothing would be left of me but dust. I was a moth to a flame.

Silas rolled his ball down the wooden slope and grunted acknowledgement. Another roll had been performed. Another now waited to be done. I visited him most nights now after work. I'd take off before Dad had time to wash up and walk home. The detour to Silas's place was a little out of the way, but I guess I needed the exercise. The guy with the beard and tattoos, Erik, was so omnipresent in the house I thought he actually lived there.

'Nah, mate. Got a wife and two kids. Divorced, mind you. Have to put in the extra shifts to pay child support,' he said.

Erik worked his guts out in the house. He did all the cooking and the cleaning and wiped their bums and changed their gigantic nappies without complaint. He told me it was just a job, and that he'd had worse. I wondered what in the world could be worse than that, but he wouldn't go into it. He looked sad and angry at the thought of it. His tattoos were of skulls and topless girls and guns and coffins. I wondered if he'd been in jail, and this was the only work he could get. His broken teeth grinned cheerily through that wiry beard. He seemed happy enough.

'Do you like working here?' I asked.

'Beats a lot things,' he said.

'Like what?'

'You don't want to know.'

'Yeah. I do.'

Erik continued to smile, but his good cheer began to falter. His yellowed teeth disappeared back into that bushy thicket and his eyes drifted away sadly. His knuckles, inked with love and hate, clenched involuntarily.

'Did you kill someone?' I asked.

'What? No.'

'Someone close to you then? They died?'

'Why are you asking me this?'

'I want to know.'

'No, you don't,' he said. 'You just want to see me suffer. I know your type. I'm not giving you the satisfaction, so stop asking.'

'I'm sorry,' I said. 'I didn't mean to offend you.'

'Really? Look, make yourself useful and clear the table. I need to get these blokes fed.'

Erik held his cards close. He wasn't going to let me pry into his history. And he didn't want to know mine. I respected that. I never found out what it was that forced him to work there. He had lived a hard life, harder than I could ever imagine. Whatever disaster had befallen him, he'd accepted it long ago.

Two other men lived in the house with Silas; each had about the same cognitive ability. Erik termed them severely challenged, whatever that meant. They were seriously bizarre. One guy, Huong, squawked all the time and perched on the back of the couch with his arms tucked up under him like a chicken. Erik affectionately called him the Birdman. He was thin and wiry and grinned like a maniac. His favourite activity was pressing the TV remote buttons. He constantly flicked from station to station, not watching anything for more than a second before seemingly tiring of it and looking for something more interesting. Of course, he just liked the action of turning over the stations. He had control over something, I guess.

The other guy, Keith, was enormously fat and didn't do anything other than eat. And I mean, eat. He had some kind of strange disorder that caused him to eat practically anything he could get his hands on. Dishwashing detergent, soap, toothpaste, socks, fluff off the floor, bottle tops, bleach, plastic wrappers, you name it, he'd eat it. Food too of course, he loved real food, but when there was none to be had, he'd try to satisfy himself by gnawing on the furniture. Erik said he was a human goat. He explained that it was actually a really serious condition and he could easily poison himself. The guy had been in hospital far too many times to get his stomach pumped. He sat on the couch eyeing off Birdman's remote control.

Silas ignored everything and just rolled his tennis ball. I continued to visit him, not to talk or anything, that was beyond him. I'd just sit and watch.

Dad was right about one thing; Silas was unpredictable.

For no reason, he'd yell and smash himself over the head, or try to smash anyone who was close enough at the time. Erik knew not to get too close and so did Birdman and Keith, but I forgot the warnings and scored a couple of punches to the side of my head. Silas didn't seem to get pleasure out of it. He didn't even seem to recognise the fact that he'd hit me. You couldn't get angry or blame him. There was no plan behind it, no animosity. It was just something that happened. I continued to watch. After a few weeks of this, Erik became irritated.

'You're never going to get anything out of him, you know.'

'I know,' I said.

'He's never going to know you're there. He doesn't feel anything for you.'

'I know. That's not why I'm here.'

Erik looked at me suspiciously. I think he'd worked that one out already. I never brought Silas a gift or anything. I never once tried to help him get into his pyjamas, or feed him his stewed apple. I especially never offered to wipe his butt. I left all the work up to Erik. The only thing I did, was sit and watch.

'Do you think he's happy?' I asked.

'Look mate, I just work here,' he said. 'You'd be better off asking the professionals.'

'I want your opinion. You know him better than anyone. Do you think he's happy?'

Erik looked at Silas for a long time, pondering all the moments they'd spent together.

'I don't think he even understands what happiness means,' he finally said. 'He just is.'

He just is. Those three simple words were profound. He lives. He exists. He rolls the ball. He sees it fall. He uses energy. He moves from one state to another. He moves through time. He has direction. Purpose. He has reason for being.

Silas, with the mental capacity of a toddler, had worked out something I hadn't even come close to grasping. Every living being needed action. Existence required movement. If you denied this simple fact, you just stopped working. You'd fall into the darkness. That was when the dog would become your friend.

I took my brother's lead and worked. I didn't think about anything else, I just worked. Gradually, I understood the simplicity of my father's world. We'd drive to the shop in the mornings and now it was I who muttered those mechanical mysticisms.

'Nissan Navara, tie rod ends. Volvo V40, high tension leads,' I'd say.

Dad listened and quietly nodded in appreciation. I saw now what he saw. All around us was a visual world of schematics. There was order among the chaos. By making something new again, we were fighting against the ravages of time's arrow. We took something back from the brink. Okay, maybe I was overthinking it a little, but we certainly saved more than one car from the scrap heap. I had a purpose. I had action. Direction. I was like Silas and his ball.

It was late when the light went off in her room. I watched from the front porch. At the other end of our street, Eliza was getting ready to sleep in that cold crypt. I recalled the time when she'd cut my hair, the night she lured me into her bed. I wanted to go back and tell her everything I'd learned since then. We didn't need the school, her friends, any of it. All we'd need was each other. We could have got out, before everything had been destroyed.

'You're not going to let this go, are you?' asked Dad.

'I don't know how.'

'It's alright. We all feel that way once.'

'Even you and Mum?'

'Even me and your mother. We still do.'

I didn't understand that at all. How could he love her? I mean I knew he did once. But now? How could he after she had ignored him, and me, for all these years? She destroyed herself in front of him and he still stood by her. I thought of Martin and his wife. Loyalty and guilt can be ugly little twins.

'Why, Dad? Because you feel guilty?' I asked.

'No, Monty. She wasn't always this way, you know. She'll come round.'

I couldn't believe that, like my father. He had to trust her, I suppose. Me? I had only my own experiences to draw from. I never knew her like he did; the woman she once was simply never existed for me.

'Get some sleep,' he said. 'I've got a surprise for you in the morning.'

The car rumbled in to the auction rooms, hardly visible through a thick cloud of smoke. People gagged and held their noses in disgust. Dad glanced over at me and winked. It was perfect.

The ute had blown a head gasket, probably because the owner never got it serviced on time and allowed it to over-heat. It wasn't going to be an easy fix. I hadn't performed something as technical as rebuilding an engine before, but

I knew from my reading what to do. With a little help from Dad, I was confident I could have it up running.

Dad had picked it out as a winner. It was almost new, except for the engine. The sound was sickening. It rattled and spat, threatening to explode any second. It was a bomb. Dad explained to me about the car auctions. They were full of buyers from car yards, who were on the hunt for a quick sell. They'd never bid on something with obvious problems. He also liked the car because it was a ute and when I got my licence, I could use it to pick up parts for the shop.

I liked it because the rear tray had a canopy, a fibreglass hood with windows on the back. My dreams filled that space in the back. When I had my licence and enough cash in my pockets, I could toss a mattress in the back and get the hell out of Middleford. I pictured myself cruising up the east coast, lazily driving with one arm out the window. I'd live off fish and chips and get work in auto shops along the way. I'd buy some camping gear and see all the National Parks and, at night, I'd make a campfire then tuck up warm in the back of the ute. I'd be a transient creature, only staying in one place long enough to feel the warmth of the soil, breathe the air, and move on. I'd live. I'd exist. I'd use energy. I'd move from one state to another. I'd always seek a new direction. I'd have purpose. I'd have a reason for being.

The auctioneer asked for first bids and the car promptly died. A horrible sound rattled under the bonnet and the smoke finally stopped. We were the only bidders.

Old Bob thought the car was a waste of money, until he heard how much I'd paid for it. I'd got a serious bargain. Even if we'd just sold it for parts, I'd make some good money on it. But I had better plans. Old Bob let me keep it in the back of the shop while I earned enough to buy the parts. Dad and I would fix it up in our own time.

I was close. All I needed was a few months. But time can be disingenuous. Just when you think you've got everything sorted, it throws a spanner in the works.

Middleford mall was small by city standards, but had the ubiquitous collection of fashion shops and juice bars. Both seemed to sell everything in hyper-colour pink. I looked out of place in the mall.

'Nice outfit,' said Eliza.

She was looking at my greasy overalls and blackened fingernails. I didn't care. I had become what's known as a tradie, I guess. I didn't shy away from it. The work was honest. I stood tall in my filth. I had managed to run into Eliza, on purpose, on her way out. Like most kids from school, she spent most of the holidays hanging out there. Eliza looked different somehow, smaller and less confronting, I guess, like she'd lost something. She even seemed nervous.

'You want to grab a coffee?' I asked. 'There's a cool little café that's opened up. Got all junk from Paris and stuff hanging from the ceilings.'

She looked at me in wonder, or possibly hope.

'Yeah, okay.'

The little Parisian café was a couple of streets away from the auto shop. I had stumbled across it after being sent for meat pies and iced coffees for the crew. When I returned with espressos and French pastries, they teased me for the rest of the week. Still, they ate everything. Secretly, I think they loved the change. I could see them dream of walking the cobblestoned streets of Paris as they chewed their pastries. For one small moment, they were transported far away from the stark suburbs, to a world of impressionist painters and joie de vivre.

A little iron bell tinkled our arrival as we opened the door. Marion, the woman who ran the place, knew me well by now. She gave me a courteous nod as we sat down and brought my usual order over, times two. After my accidental purchase for the boys, I had come back here everyday to sip espresso and gaze at the pictures of the Eiffel Tower and Notre Dame. I'd go to Paris one day, I thought. After I'd seen this country first, of course. I'd cross Europe on foot so I could get to know the people. I'd pick up French, Spanish, and maybe even a little Portuguese. I'd live off fresh baguettes and hoon around on one of those mopeds. They looked like fun. And I'd have a girl with me. I'd always have a girl with me.

'Since when do you drink coffee?' Eliza asked.

'Got a taste for it. This place does it really well. Good, huh?'

I liked the rush of caffeine and had quickly become addicted to it. I suppose I had the personality to go to extremes, even with coffee. I looked at Eliza and my tongue failed me. There was so much I wanted to say, but our shared past suddenly seemed distant. It was unreal. She looked like a completely different person, come to me from another time.

'I heard about your mother,' she said. 'It must have been hard?'

'Yeah.'

'When's she coming home?'

'I don't know.'

'She probably just needs some time.'

'No. It's not that,' I said. 'I mean, I don't know if she *wants* to come home.'

We sipped our coffee. We listened to the sounds of French folk music on the tinny speakers. I'd heard this song almost every day by now. The song was passionate, almost too agonising to listen to. Something about having no regrets, Marion had told me. No regrets, I thought, as I caught Eliza's eye. We could have been in Paris for all we knew, except for the view of Middleford out the window.

'I bought a car,' I told her.

She looked at me, dumbfounded.

'Dad and me are going to fix it up. By the time we're finished with it, it's going to be the hottest thing around. But I've got to be careful. Dad thinks I'm a speed freak.'

'You don't even have a licence yet, Monty.'

'I will. Soon. By the time I'm sixteen, I'll have it all ready to go.'

She sipped her coffee, and looked at me thoughtfully. Warily even.

'Come with me,' I blurted.

'Where?'

'Anywhere. We'll have to wait until I can get my P's but after that, I can drive solo. Let's get out of here. Away from everything. You and me. We'll go round Australia. I'll get work along the way. We'll go wherever we want. The Great Barrier Reef, Kakadu, Uluru, the world. We can go to Paris, for real.'

'You want to take me on a holiday?'

'I want to live. I don't just want to ... waste away here.'

'And what does that make me? I just go along with your plans?'

'There's no plan. No one in control. We just do what we want.'

'You can't just do what you want, Monty.'

'Yeah, you can.'

'No, you can't. Life isn't that simple.'

She didn't want to come then, I thought. Fine. Stay here and live the rest of your life working the checkout and paying off your flat screen TV. I didn't want any of it. I was going to get out, away from Middleford. There had to be more out there. Eliza pulled her sleeves and crossed her arms. There it was again; I was a threat. I finished my coffee and paid up. I looked back to her by the door.

'See you then,' I said.

'Yeah. Okay. See you.'

I crossed the street in the dark. Maybe it was curiosity, or my indignation at yet another rejection, but I stayed to watch her from across the street. Through the café window, she looked like some beautiful heroine out of a French movie. She cried over her coffee. She looked so forlorn. I knew then it was me who had rejected her, that night with Pippa. Eliza was right; you can't just do what you want. Consequences always come back to haunt you.

Chapter Eighteen

Dad woke me up from another night devoid of the dog. He told me the eggs were ready, as usual. I put on my overalls and gulped down my coffee, ready for another day's work. As we came out of the house, I stopped by the car. The world had turned while I slept.

Red and blue lights cut the morning air.

A police car and an ambulance were parked outside Eliza's house. I ran like crazy down the street to see what the hell was going on. Thoughts raced through my mind. It would have been Derek, who had tried to fix the hot water service by himself, but stupidly had forgotten to turn off the gas and the whole thing had exploded, decapitating him instantly. Or it would have been Doreen, who had tripped over the iron and sent the steaming hotplate onto her face, forever burning a brown triangle with little dots onto her forehead.

I watched as two paramedics wheeled Eliza's body, covered in a green sheet, into the back of the ambulance. They were not in a rush. There was no point. They slowly pulled out into the street and drove her away.

Two officers chatted quietly to Derek and Doreen. Her father watched the ambulance drive off, stoically keeping a silent perspective. Doreen broke down into heartfelt sobs and fell to her knees on the front lawn. She looked up at me and wailed in horror.

I hadn't noticed it until then, but I was bawling my eyes out. I hadn't made a sound. I just cried silently and hard. My whole body shook from the damage. Derek walked inside without a word. Doreen and I watched each other writhe in mortal agony. How could this be true?

Eliza was dead.

Dad helped me to the car. It was the first time I could remember him giving me a hug. It was warm and enormous. His shoulders were thick and powerful, like he could protect you from all the dangers in the world. But he couldn't, not now. Time had seen to that.

We waited for about half the day at the hospital. Dad didn't mention work. I guess he must have called in and told them what happened. Old Bob must have been up to his armpits in jobs. He wouldn't put up a fuss though. He'd get it all done, no matter what.

Doreen finally came out to the waiting room. She took my hands and peered into my eyes. Her tears had dried away. So had mine. She'd cried them all out, I guess. There was nothing much left but the coldness of grief.

'Why'd she do it?' I asked.

'I was going to ask you the same thing,' she said, her voice throaty with decay.

'How?'

'Monty, please. I can't say.'

'I need to know. How did it happen?'

Doreen covered her mouth as if willing it not to speak. But her body seemed to gain the upper hand and took control. She told me that when Eliza had gone to bed the night before, everything seemed normal. She'd done her homework, all her chores, and had laid out her clothes for the next day. Then she took a bath. They didn't hear a sound. Doreen found her in the morning, with her life drained away. From that moment on, she couldn't really remember anything else. Her perception of the world changed. Things happened too fast, as if time had sped up. Everything was a mystery to her again. She didn't understand her own reality anymore, the worth of it all.

'I'm sorry, Monty. I'm so sorry,' she offered.

'Sorry doesn't bring her back,' I said coldly.

She let out a little gasp. How could I have been so cruel? She'd just lost her daughter. I knew the truth though; Doreen had been afraid of her all along. She didn't understand Eliza. Then again, who was I to judge? I had been with Eliza just hours before that final act. And I had walked out on her.

'We want the funeral to be small. Just family,' she said. 'But you're welcome to come. I think that's only right.'

She turned away from me, unable to look me in the eye.

Dad stayed with me all day. He didn't let me out of his sight. Even when I went to the bathroom, he came in with me. He stood by me. Eventually, I got annoyed and told him to leave me alone.

'Can't do that Monty,' he said.

'You can't watch me forever.'

'We'll see.'

He didn't trust me, I guess. But he knew I was right; as time went on, he'd eventually have to leave me alone. And then he'd have to hope like hell nothing would happen. He'd just have to wait and see what fate would bring him. Or what it would take away.

Dad made dinner of sausages and mashed potato but neither of us ate. We stared at the plates of food and went to bed. He moved his bed closer to the hall so he could hear me in case I got up during the night.

'Goodnight. Better keep the doors open,' he mumbled.

'Okay.'

'I'll see you in the morning,' he said.

Hope stung his voice. His throat cracked a little, upending it into a question. Was he really that fearful of what the night would bring? I thought of telling him not to worry. After all, we didn't have a bath.

I didn't sleep. The night cooled the house and all the old ghosts settled, lost along with the heat of day. I thought of her in my bed, curled up warm against me, the night she came through my window. I opened the window again for her, willing her to step through those curtains. But she didn't come. She was gone.

'It's time, Monty.'

The dog sat in the hall. Its infectious eyes boring into mine.

'Come with me,' it said. 'Let's go outside. Just for a little while. It'll be alright.'

'I can't,' I said. 'My dad wants to see me in the morning.'

'I can take you to her,' said the dog.

'Leave me alone,' I groaned.

'I can never leave you alone,' Monty. 'I'm part of you. I am you.'

'Go away! She wouldn't want me to go with you.'

'Of course she would,' said the dog. 'After all, she is with me now.'

'You took her?'

'She came to me, as you must come to me now.'

I was too tired to resist. A cold emptiness was all I had left. I acquiesced and slinked out of bed, still in my jocks. I knew the floorboards would give me away to my dad, snoring there with his head by the door. The dog sat inches away from him. He could have reached out and punched it away into another world. He could have protected me, but he was asleep, drifting away into a dream of his own. I slipped out my window and into the night.

I followed the dog through Middleford, only wearing my jocks. The summer night was cool but I didn't care. We drifted like ghosts down my street, past Eliza's house, past Amy Fotheringham's place, past the school and the mall and the auto shop. All of Middleford slept. Inside rows of houses, rows of people were tucked up safe in their beds. Outside, the rest of the world was keenly awake. The night never slept. Cruel things lay in wait ready to pounce.

Time seemed to slow. The traffic lights didn't seem to change. There was nobody around for them to signal anyway, so they just stayed put. I followed the dog into the tunnel, and disappeared into that dark maw. Part of me knew its plan then. Part of me understood how obvious it all was. The conscious part of my brain was howling in protest. It ordered me to turn around and run back to Dad, slide into his bed and tell him everything about Eliza and the dog. Talk to him! the reasonable part of me demanded. He'll understand. He'll know what to do. He's right back there at the house, with his head by the hallway, snoring. Go back and wake him the hell up!

But those calls seemed far off, from some other time and

some other place. They were echoes of someone else's life, muttered in some long dead language. I struggled to listen to those words, to understand them. The strange protests faded away, replaced by emptiness.

The tunnel was pitch black. Still, I could just make out the shape of the dog waiting inside. I went in deeper and my eyes began to adjust. Starlight trickled in from the openings at either end. The colours ran rich. Whole other galaxies circled beyond, through those twin portals. I stood in the nothingness between all things. I could peer over the horizon. The dog was right, there was something else out there. I had been wrong to mistrust it. Eliza would be standing there waiting for me. She was inches away. All I had to do was reach out and take her hand.

I reached into the refuge in the wall and pulled out the spearfishing gun. It had been there since I'd stashed it after scaring Tony. I felt the long, cold steel of the spear. I could be with her again, I thought.

I turned away. I was too weak. I knew then why Martin had begged me to decide his fate. We were both cowards. Poor Martin. Poor Monty.

'I can't. I'm too weak. I'm sorry,' I told the black dog.

'That's okay,' said the dog. 'Would you like some help?'

'Yes, please.'

A beacon of light split the gloom. An epic rumble ground me down. A force greater than my own bore down upon me and I was grateful. I dropped to my knees, slicing them open on the rocks. The tracks shook. My ears thundered. A warning siren screeched. My body was devoid of energy. I had nothing left. She was moments away.

I looked up to see the dog grinning at me. There was

hunger there. This is what it wanted, to feast upon me. I touched the hot stick of blood on my knees and remembered which world I was in. Energy surged back through me. I still had some fight left. I scrambled to the refuge, seconds before the train screamed by.

'Breakfast,' called Dad.

I came in to the kitchen wearing my overalls, ready for work, and sat down to Dad's eggs. He wasn't dressed yet and watched me intently from across the table.

'You don't have to go to work, Monty.'

'Yeah, I do. I've got a car to pay off.'

'Not today, you don't.'

I wiped up the rest of my breakfast with some bread and gulped down the coffee. I drank it a little too fast and scolded the back of my throat. I gasped in pain and ran to the kitchen sink to lap some cold water. Dad just sat there and watched. I feared he knew where I'd been in the dead of night. I hoped he didn't know.

I reactivated my Speedstream account to find news of Eliza's death had exploded online. Hundreds of posts snowballed. Everyone seemed to think they were just like her. They identified with her somehow, I guess. Kids she didn't even know posted heartfelt goodbyes, as if they'd been the best of friends. If it could happen to someone like Eliza, they said, it could happen to any one of them. Typical, I thought, still thinking of themselves. Eliza quickly became a symbol, more than a person. Leading the charge was Becky.

Alias: @Beckstar101
Date: Thursday December 11, 4.55PM
I can't believe she's gone. Will never forget U
#Eliza4ever.

@AllegraCool
Me too. She was the best! Love #Eliza4ever always.
Please share.

@KristalK
#Eliza4ever My best friend for all time.

Miss you girl #Eliza4ever.
OMG I just saw #Eliza4ever the day before!
Me too.
You wouldn't know. #Eliza4ever looked happy.
Yeah, totally normal.
I didn't see this coming.
If it can happen to #Eliza4ever it can happen to us too.
I know how #Eliza4ever feels.
I get that way too.
Me too.
We're all just like #Eliza4ever. Speak out!
Does anyone know when the #Eliza4ever funeral is?
#Eliza4ever family keeping it quiet.
They don't want any fuss!!!
More like a secret.
Not fair! #Eliza4ever was our friend too!
We deserve to say goodbye.
I agree. What can we do?
Tell them we have to go!
Post your protest here #SayGoodbye.
One hundred followers now.

Keep up the good work #SayGoodbye.
They have to give in soon.
We should be there #SayGoodbye.
It's our funeral too.

And a thousand more posts just like these. They thought they owned her. Eliza's death was nothing compared to their need for shared grievance. Their hollow empathy infuriated me. They turned Eliza into a commodity. She was their possession. None of the posts asked the simple question. Why?

I asked myself this a thousand times. I watched the curtain in my room sway in the breeze. Any minute she'd step through and tell me her secrets. I'd finally understand the mystery. But the more I thought about it, the more I already knew why. The answer was bleak.

Derek and Doreen managed to keep the location of the funeral secret, even in the face of a growing online backlash. The posts began to turn negative, as they almost always do. People didn't like being left out; it made them feel less important about themselves, I guess. When someone had the courage to back the family's position, they were attacked.

Alias: @SunnyGirl
Date: Friday December 12, 6.45PM
If the family want to keep #SayGoodbye to themselves, let them. We should respect their wishes.

@Beckstar101
Get off here SunnyGirl. You don't belong #SayGoodbye is ours!

@Fearless22

I agree! Keep #SayGoodbye for everyone!

Who does she think she is?
Have you seen her photo?
She's so fat.
Ugly too.
And stupid.
Should top herself too.
Then see how many of us come to your funeral!
Follow here #GoHomeSunnyGirl

The chapel was small, a generic-looking room designed to accommodate multiple funerals in the one day. It was a simple, efficient-looking place. Everything in it spoke of orderly transition. Nothing seemed permanent, except for the worn-out furniture. I wondered who was next after Eliza. Maybe some old woman whose family had been shocked to read the will and discover she'd only left them a couple of starving cats? Or maybe it would be some middle-aged accountant, who died alone after completing his final tax return? There, I did it! he'd exclaim. My life's work is finally finished. I balanced all those books. Uh, oh. I'm dead.

Whoever was next, I knew it would be quick. They'd be mourned and the coffin moved out so the next dearly departed could take their place at the altar. As Dad and I entered, I realised I was the only kid from school to attend. The online protest went on right up until the morning of the funeral then suddenly petered out. Most people had given up and were now posting about some Hollywood movie star who'd gone missing during a film shoot in the Grand Canyon. Well-wishes and tributes flooded in. Eliza, and everything she symbolised, turned to electronic dust. The world had turned. She no longer trended. Everyone forgot her so quickly it made my gut churn. I wanted to scream. I wanted to cry.

Doreen had obviously neglected to inform Derek that I was coming. He kept glancing at over me during the service, as if I was some intruder. A priest stood by Eliza's casket at the front.

I couldn't take my eyes off the coffin. Eliza's body was in there, just inside. She was so close, under all that polished timber, surrounded in satin silk. Her flesh and blood was cold but I wanted to race up and pull back that lid and take her in my arms. I wanted to cry into her hair one last time. Dad patted me gently on my elbow. He was there for me.

The ceremony was religious. The priest spoke about the realm beyond and God's greater plan. We weren't to question His motives, he told us, but to accept the mystery of life. Whatever the reason for Eliza's passing, she was with Him now. She was in peace. She lived on.

The power of his words struck me like a hammer. I'd vaguely heard all this stuff before, but never really understood it. I was consumed by loss. Confronted with her death, I desperately wanted to believe every word. She would be in a better place. Yes. She would live on. She was in peace. It was all part of God's greater plan. But it was a lie, I thought. The dog had shown me the world in which she now lived, and it was a cold and desolate place.

There was no burial. Eliza was going to be cremated at some later time. They simply ended the service and her casket rolled away through a little door in the wall. They all turned their backs on her and went to get a cup of tea and a sandwich. I didn't move.

'Come on, Monty. Time to go,' said Dad.

'Just a minute,' I said.

'Right. I'll go get a cuppa. See you in a tic.'

I walked over to that little hole in the wall. It was like one of those conveyor belts you see at airports for people's luggage. Was that how we'd treated her, like a piece of baggage to be offloaded? I peered through to see if I could catch a glimpse of some baggage handler on the other side, pulling her body out of the casket so it could be reused for the old cat lady. It was too dark. I couldn't see a thing.

'A friend of Eliza's, I take it?'

It was the priest. He was younger than I thought. Perhaps it was his glasses that made him look older, and wiser, from a distance. Up close like this, he just looked like some first-year relief teacher. And they never knew a thing.

'If you ever need to talk, we have a counselling service,' he offered.

'In the church?'

'There's no pressure. We offer help to anyone who needs it.'

He offered a broad, easy smile, as if he had stood by a mirror in the seminary practising it for years. He had it down pat. He didn't even know who I was, but he offered me that easy, knowing smile. Perhaps he was right? I wondered. I wavered for moment. I could drop by and ask for help. No pressure.

'Such a waste,' he said.

In that split second, he destroyed all credibility. He thought Eliza's life was a waste. Her potential had been lost. A great gift had been squandered. I knew how the story went; the consequences for her actions were eternal damnation. He didn't have the guts to say it to her family, but that's what he really thought. Eliza was lost to them, in this life and the next. My blood was up. I wanted to punch him in the face.

'Get away from me. You don't know shit,' I spat.

His reaction was wonderful. His glasses fell off and he gagged on his cup of tea. It spurted out both nostrils like two little whale spouts. The brown, milky tea stained his otherwise white collar. He glared at me as he tried to wipe it off with his hanky. I could only grin. I'd damned myself now, I thought.

Dad drove us out of there. The gardens were verdant green and the sky rolled thick with clouds. Eliza would have liked this day, I thought. It had just the right mix of sun and gloom.

'I can still see her face,' I said to Dad. 'I keep expecting to see her.'

It was true. I hadn't really taken it in yet. Eliza could have stepped out in front of the car right that second and I wouldn't have given it a second thought. It would be totally explainable. They would have got it all wrong. There was a mix-up at the hospital and some other girl with blood-stained hands had been mistaken for Eliza. She had woken up in another ward, to find a whole other family waiting for her out in the hall. But their joy turned sour when they realised she wasn't theirs. Eliza, still in her hospital gown, had raced out of there and ran all the way to the funeral home to step out in front of our car. And we'd embrace once again. She'd cry and tell me she loved me and never leave me. And we'd take the ute up the coast.

Of course, I'd never see her again. Deep down, I already knew that. But hope twists the mind, and tempts you to believe the unbelievable.

Mum came home that night. As her cab pulled up in the driveway, Dad called me out to meet her by the front door. We stood on the porch, watching nervously.

She stepped out of the cab to take us in. So much had changed, I guess: the gleaming white paint, the perfectly aligned weatherboards, the son and the father who now stood side-by-side. It must have been quite a shock.

She grabbed her bag and shuffled into the house without a word. Dad and I looked at each other and wondered if we'd done something wrong. Maybe she didn't want us to fix the place up in her absence? I guess she could have taken it as a slight. She headed to the kitchen and Dad made her a cup of tea. We sat there for a time before she finally spoke.

'The house looks nice. Should have got round to that years ago,' she offered.

She liked it then. It was the gift it ought to be. A surge of relief gushed through me. She smiled at both of us. She looked different, clearer somehow, more thoughtful and connected to the world around her. It was as if she had finally woken up from a coma and realised where she was. And there was something else. She'd given up the smokes, I could tell from the tips of her fingers. They used to be tinged a dark yellow, but now they were a clean, bright pink. Her teeth seemed cleaner too. And her eyes. And her skin. Even the tips of her hair seemed to breathe in new life. It was amazing, as if every cell in her body was now younger and more alive.

Dad and I smiled. Mum drank her tea and smiled back.

She seemed happy to be home, but then I caught the look in her eye. It was the look of fear.

She glanced down the hallway towards my room and I could feel the chill in her bones. Yes, I thought. You saw it there, didn't you? You peered into the night and caught it looking back at you. Frightened and alone, you tried to succumb.

I looked to the oven, a few feet behind her. I pictured her despair. I saw her breathe in death, the shadow goading her to continue, and Dad, poor simple old Dad walking into that scene, carrying his bread and milk and pulling her back from the brink.

She went to her room and closed the door. She needed a nap, Dad told me. This wasn't like my mother at all. She used to stay awake half the night, certainly never sleep during the day. It was the medication, Dad informed me. It calmed her thoughts but meant she needed time to herself. We had to give her space.

'Why'd she come home?' I asked. 'She's not ready.'

'She wanted to be here. For you. After everything that's happened,' he said.

'She's afraid.'

'We're all afraid, Monty. At times like this, we should be together.'

I knew better. I knew the dog was lurking somewhere. If it didn't lure me to its realm, it would be perfectly happy with a substitute.

'She's not safe here,' I said.

'Monty, the doctors wouldn't let her come home if they thought she was a danger.'

'*She's* not the danger,' I told him.

Dad looked at me curiously. I could see his mind working

overtime to figure out what in the world I was talking about. He still wasn't used to having a conversation that went for more than six syllables and was struggling to get my meaning.

'You mean, you?' he asked.

'No. Something else,' I said.

I wanted to tell him so bad about the dog and the night in the tunnel and how the only thing that brought me back was thinking of him. Dad leaned back in his chair, looking thoughtful, and stroked the thick stubble on his chin. It made a harsh, crackling sound, like rubbing your fingers over dry sandpaper.

'Monty, I don't mind saying this because it's true,' he began. 'You are much smarter than me. When you were little, you'd say things no other kid would dream about. By the time you hit school, I couldn't keep up with you. Not many people could. So I let you go, to learn at your own pace. I'm proud of you, Monty. I always will be. But there's one thing you are absolutely dead-set wrong about. There is nothing else.'

He fixed me with a steely stare. I could see the bear-fisted fighter in him, all coiled up and ready to explode. I'd never seen the man angry before. Old Bob mentioned one day that my dad had once got so angry with an annoying customer that he bent a crowbar clean in half. I thought Old Bob was just having me on. Now I wasn't so sure.

'How do you know?' I asked.

'Monty, look at your mother, and where she's been. Is that what you want?'

He stood up abruptly and left, walking out the screen door to spend the afternoon in the shed. I was with my family, reunited. I had never been more alone.

Chapter Nineteen

I couldn't sleep. The dog kept its distance. I spent most nights alone with my thoughts. I kept the curtain open for her, just in case she came back. Weeks rolled by. Christmas came and went. We even gave each other presents, like a real family. New Year was a blur. She never made her appearance. Eventually I pulled the curtain closed.

The memory of her stained my every move. It coloured everything. I found myself writing her name over and over again. I tried to keep working at the shop, to keep myself busy, but I became more of a hindrance than a help. More than once I forgot to screw on someone's oil filter properly and, when they drove it out the yard, all the oil drained out of their car before they even got to the main road. Old Bob was very apologetic to his customers. He told Dad I had to go back to sweeping.

Ms Finch kept calling. She even dropped by for a coffee one day and brought over some fancy chocolate biscuits. It was an attempt to talk to me on mutual terms, I guess, to get me to open up. What was I going to say? I was responsible for Eliza's death? I couldn't forgive myself for ignoring her?

'Come back to school,' she said. 'It'll be different now. You'll be in with kids a year younger. Most of them won't know your history. You'll make new friends. And there's now a student counsellor on staff. If you have any issues, you can take it up with her.'

'I can't,' I said. 'I'm busy. Working full-time.'

'Sweeping up? Yes, your father told me.'

'That's just for now. I'll go back to working on cars again soon. It's honest work.'

'I'm sure it is. But you can do so much more. Please, don't let this ruin your life.'

'You think I've ruined my life?'

'No. I just mean you have so much to offer. I really think you could do anything. Medicine, law, science. Whatever you like. It's all there, just waiting for you to choose.'

'I'm sorry,' I said. 'I can't go back.'

Work at the shop became a chore. Since I'd been demoted back to sweeping duties, I'd become increasingly distracted and I didn't even bother to sweep much at all anymore. I just stood there like a broken statue, holding a broom. Old Bob got worried.

'He's not right. I can't have him here anymore,' he whispered to my dad.

'You know it's good for him. He needs this, Bob.'

'It won't be good for him if he gets run over. You've seen him. He doesn't even look where he's going.'

It was true. Old Bob nearly backed over me with a Mini Minor that morning. I'd been standing so still, holding that broom, that he didn't even see me in the rear-view mirror. He tooted the horn for me to get out of the way but I just stood there, looking at my broom. Dad had to come over and lead me away to a safe corner somewhere. All this happened far away from me. It was like watching pieces on a chessboard move around. Old Bob convinced Dad to give me a few weeks off. He couldn't afford to pay me while I was gone, but I didn't care. School, and now work, just seemed too hard.

Mum slept so much it was like she was hardly there. The house seemed to relax back in her presence. The place was eerily quiet. The only sounds were the birds in the street, chatting like angry neighbours on their wires. While Dad was at work, I sat on the porch to watch Eliza's house again. It was lifeless and still. I didn't hear her come out to sit beside me.

'She was beautiful, wasn't she?' asked Mum.

'Yeah. She was.'

'She was a lot like you.'

'No. She was stronger.'

'Hmm. I don't think so,' she said.

I looked over to Mum and saw her eyes roll back into her head. She was floating on a dreamy, tranquil sea. She took a lot of pills each day now, neatly arranged in little blister packs so she didn't get them confused.

'She thought you were beautiful too, Monty.'

'What?'

'I could tell, that time she came over. She thought the world of you.'

My body shuddered in silent remorse. My mother stood up and shuffled drearily back to the house, her slippers sliding over the porch. In a moment she'd be gone, back to bed for the rest of the day, and any memory of this moment would be gone.

'We all think the world of you, Monty,' she said.

Then she was gone, back to her dreams.

I took to visiting Silas again. I dropped by religiously every day. It was the only thing I had left. I watched him roll his ball down the ramp, like some mesmeric metronome.

I spent hours, days, just watching him. After a while, Erik seemed to wise up.

'I think it's time we made a move, don't you?' he asked.

'Where?' I asked.

'It doesn't matter where. We just move.'

Silas shrieked and banged his head and made the festering lump under his scalp bleed. This wasn't going to be easy.

Getting everyone into the min-van was like wrangling a bunch of mad snakes into a basket. Birdman and Keith flew about the van, looking excited. Birdman perched on his seat like some kind of parrot and it was really hard to get him to sit down to put on his seatbelt. Erik stood back and laughed. Eventually, he lent me a hand and we both managed to clip him in.

Silas was the hardest though. If you got too close to him, he'd punch you in the face. There was no malice behind it, in fact he didn't seem to notice if he hit you or not, his arms just had a mind of their own. I kind of understood what was going on; his mind was somewhere else. It was a bubble that had permanently slipped away. Without a consciousness to guide his hand, his body was left on auto-pilot. I knew what to do.

I grabbed his wrists and gently guided them for him, willing myself to govern his body. It took a few moments, but his body slowly came to the conclusion that a mind was back in control, and it gave up. He succumbed to my guidance, and I clipped him in.

Erik was astounded. He'd never seen anyone get Silas into a mini-van without sustaining at least one black eye. He told me I was a natural, and if I wanted to work with Silas, I could probably get paid for it. They were always screaming out for workers, he told me. I thought about it. It could have been a good job. I was there anyway so getting paid for it would be sensible. And I'd earn the money I needed to fix the ute.

Yet the thought of leaving Middleford without Eliza crushed me. Getting out and travelling, seeing the world, all of it, meant nothing without her. I didn't even know if I even wanted the ute anymore. I'd stopped working on it and left it in the back corner of the shop. Old Bob hadn't complained about it taking up room yet, but I knew he eventually would, and then I'd have to face the decision. I'd either give it life, or let it slowly die. I didn't know which.

We drove the entire afternoon, all around Middleford. We didn't go anywhere in particular; we just drove. The guys loved it. They stared out at the sun and the passing cars and mimicked the traffic noises. You could feel them getting more relaxed, except Silas. Something in him seemed restless, as if he was just waiting to get back to his ball.

Eventually Erik pulled in and bought soft serve ice creams. I used my new technique and guided Silas's hands to his mouth. He managed to eat it without slamming it back in my face. It was another triumph, as far as Erik was concerned, and it gave him the confidence to let the guys out for a while. It was a mistake.

The park was a wide paddock in the middle of suburbia. I pushed Silas's wheelchair and Erik was left to herd Birdman and Keith. There was a lake in the middle; a man-made puddle about two feet deep, proudly designed by city engineers and permanently filled up with duck poo. Birdman got away from Erik and ran out into the middle of the lake to become one with the ducks, I guess. He scared them all off pretty quick, and just paddled about in the green muck for about half an hour. He only came out when we offered him a packet of chips. He stank up the mini-van all the way home, but I could see the sheer delight on his face. For a few precious moments, he had flown with his flock.

Silas didn't seem to notice any of it. When he got back to the house, he promptly picked up his ball and rolled it back down the ramp. The trip may as well not have happened. It crushed me to watch. There truly was nothing for him, other than that ball and ramp. I said my goodbyes to Silas. Erik was right. With some people, no matter how much you try, the disconnection is just too great.

The summer heat seemed endless. I'd done nothing but wake up and sit on the porch for months when I realised it was my sixteenth birthday.

'Happy birthday, Monty!' beamed my mother.

'Yes. Happy birthday son,' grinned Dad.

We finally celebrated it. Well, as much as a family like mine could, I guess. Dad bought a chocolate cake from the supermarket and put some candles on it, in the shape of a sixteen. They both wanted to bring Silas over for lunch, but I told them not to bother him. It wasn't like he'd enjoy it or anything. They accepted my wishes, but it seemed like they were annoyed. That just made me all the more exasperated. They'd hidden him from sight all those years, and now we were just supposed to bring him back into our lives? It was hypocritical and they knew it. I headed to my room, unable to deal with the cake.

'You forgot your present,' said Dad.

'I don't want anything,' I told him.

'You'll want this.'

Even though I'd told myself I didn't deserve it anymore, I smiled when I saw the ute. Dad and Old Bob had finished it up. They'd even gone and put some cool looking chrome wheels on it. It looked awesome. Dad tossed me the keys.

'Go on. Start her up,' he muttered.

I couldn't do it. Starting that car seemed like going back on my word. It would mean forgetting about her. Dad sighed, sounding truly exhausted. He had put up with so much in his life. I don't know how he did it. He took back the keys gently and started it up. The ute ticked over as good as new. It sounded perfect.

'You did a good job,' he said.

'You mean, you and Old Bob did a good job,' I retorted.

'Nah. You did all the hard stuff,' he offered. 'We just finished it up for you. It seemed like you had other things on your mind.'

'Yeah, I guess.'

'Now you're old enough, you can sit your driving test. You'll ace it, no problem. I've booked you in.'

'I don't want to go,' I told him.

'It's at two o'clock. Plenty of time for you to read up. We'll take her for a spin tonight.'

I couldn't accept the car. It was too much.

I ran up the street to her house and banged on the door until Doreen answered, looking bewildered. I pushed past her and ran up the stairs to her room. Doreen called after me to stop, but I didn't listen and barged in.

The room was exactly as Eliza had left it, all pristine and neat, save for some moving boxes in the corner. I opened the top one and pulled out her hairbrush. Strands of her hair were still there, woven into little patterns. I pulled some out and held them in my hand, hoping for some memory of her to return. Nothing came to me. It was just hair. I let it fall to the floor.

Further inside the box was her phone. I quickly swiped the screen and flicked through the files. Images of Eliza stared at me, hauntingly. She was suddenly alive once again. I held her in my hands; her searching eyes, her full lips, and her faraway smile that curled away in a sombre note.

'We're giving away her clothes,' said Doreen, standing by the door. 'I can't bear to look at her things anymore. Everything's going to charity.'

'Probably for the best,' I offered.

'She wasn't the kind of girl to have a lot of things,' said Doreen. 'I always thought that was strange. Don't you?'

'Not really. Eliza knew what was important, that's all.'

Doreen smiled, as if I'd just helped her understand some small mystery. She looked at me curiously for a moment, then stepped close and hugged me. I burst into sudden, convulsive tears. I'd never been held like this before. My own mother had returned but, with her medication and everything, she was just as detached as she'd always been. She'd wished me happy birthday that morning, but that was all. No hug, no tender kiss on the forehead. Just words.

Doreen loosened her grasp, stepped back and looked at me seriously.

'Monty, I need your help.'

Doreen drove us out of Middleford. I sat beside her in the passenger seat and held the urn in my hands. It was cold and hard and made of brushed steel. Inside was Eliza. Well, what was left of her after the cremation. Her dad had kept her close, even in death. She'd been placed above the TV in the lounge room, so her father could watch her and the football at the same time. I directed Doreen where to go.

'You sure this is where she would have wanted?' she asked.

'Yeah. I'm sure,' I said.

The beach was windswept and chill. Even though it was summer, the wind coming off the ocean cooled you down instantly. It bit into you, and whipped at your sides. A punishing wind, I thought. How fitting.

The gulls on the cliffs were nowhere in sight. Perhaps they were all out at sea, or maybe breeding season was over? I wondered. We trudged up the sand to the point. Beyond lay the shipwreck, and the spot where I fell in love.

A pang of doubt rushed through me. Doreen had asked me to think of the perfect spot to spread her ashes. The only place I could think of was this beach, where we held each other, naked, under the waves. Yet was this place more important for me than it ever was for her? I guess, I'd never know.

'It's a good spot, Monty,' said Doreen. 'It's beautiful.'

'Yeah, it is,' I agreed.

We took off our shoes and waded into the waves. Together, we spread her ashes out into the ocean. Her dust billowed all around us in thick, grey furls. Eliza mixed with the waves, and dispersed into the vastness of time. She was gone now.

I watched the water until there was no more grey to be seen. Everything turned a turquoise blue again. The whitewater rushed in and fanned back out, relentless and ongoing. I pictured her ashes spreading out into the deep.

She'd merge with all the sea creatures out there, I thought. Krill and shrimp and cuttlefish would eat up her dust and, in turn, fish and dolphins and sharks would eat them up. She'd become the sea. From now on, I'd always see her face reflected in the ocean.

'Time to go, Monty,' said Doreen.

It was getting late and dusk settled in over the sea. We'd been sitting there for hours, not saying anything, just being in the moment. She took the steel urn and filled it up with sand, then screwed the lid back on. She gave me a sneaky look and I decided I liked Doreen. I wished I'd had a mother just like her.

Night fell as she drove us back to the house. As we pulled into the drive, she looked relieved that Derek wasn't home yet. She checked the time and hurried inside. She replaced the urn above the TV and positioned it just so. She was an expert at hiding her tracks, I thought. That only comes from a life lived under a watchful eye. I legged it home as quick as I could.

I bolted past Mum and Dad waiting for me at the dinner table. Dad wanted to know where I'd been, but I ignored them both and slammed the door to my room.

I had Eliza's phone. I knew it was wrong of me, but I couldn't leave it there, to be discarded. I searched through the phone. It was an invasion of her privacy but I was desperate. I just wanted to see her face again. She was gone, washed away under the waves. This was all I had of her. Then I saw it.

My gut wrenched.

I wanted to hurl.

This couldn't be right. She had two SpeedStream accounts.

One was in the name of her alias. Eliza was Gutentag.

She had been my first, and only, true friend. There, listed in the inbox, were all our midnight conversations. She was in my head the whole time and I had no idea. It all suddenly made sense; Eliza didn't know how to read my mind at all, she just had insider knowledge. I broke out into a curious, appreciative smile. But there was more. Unsent drafts. Her messages from beyond:

Alias: @Gutentag
Date: Thursday February 14, 8.25AM (UNSENT)
You don't who I am, do you Monty? I'm standing there right in front of you and you're off in some other world. Do you know how frustrating that is? BTW, happy birthday ☺

Alias: @Gutentag
Date: Friday February 15, 12.55AM (UNSENT)
I can't believe you egged Tony in the face. So brilliant. He's been asking for that for years. That takes a lot of guts, Monty.

Alias: @Gutentag
Date: Friday February 15, 3.46AM (UNSENT)
What is it with you and coconuts? You talk about girls like you're a five-year-old. Seriously. It's embarrassing. Get a life.

Alias: @Gutentag
Date: Saturday February 16, 1.33AM (UNSENT)
I showed you the tunnel today. You looked so scared,
Monty. Seriously that was pathetic. Argh! You make me
want to scream.

Alias: @Gutentag
Date: Saturday February 16, 1.38AM (UNSENT)
I'm sorry. I was mean to you. You only went to the
tunnel for me. Not for my body, just me. I know that
now. Thank you.

Alias: @Gutentag
Date: Saturday March 22, 6.45AM (UNSENT)
Don't take this the wrong way, but you don't make any
sense. EVER!!!

Alias: @Gutentag
Date: Monday April 14, 5.25PM (UNSENT)
Who the hell is Tim Smith?

Alias: @Gutentag
Date: Monday April 14, 7.50PM (UNSENT)
Your hair was so gross, Monty. I didn't want to touch it.
But I had to. I couldn't stand looking at it anymore. And
the smell was putrid! I don't know why I bother.

Alias: @Gutentag
Date: Monday April 14, 7.52PM (UNSENT)
I don't blame you. How can I? I mean, how could your
parents let you get like this?

Alias: @Gutentag
Date: Monday April 14, 11.55PM (UNSENT)
I love what you said to my dad! So brilliant. I've never seen him so angry in my life. Thanks Monty!

Alias: @Gutentag
Date: Tuesday April 24, 4.05PM (UNSENT)
I stole her phone today. They were going to destroy me.

Alias: @Gutentag
Date: Tuesday April 24, 4.05PM (UNSENT)
I took the picture of myself. I had to. They were going to take us both down. I'm sorry. Please don't hate me.

Alias: @Gutentag
Date: Sunday April 27, 9.45PM (UNSENT)
I met your mother today. You know what she told me? She said I was just out to hurt you. Me? Hurt YOU? How the hell could I do that when you don't even know I exist?

Alias: @Gutentag
Date: Monday May 5, 2.25AM (UNSENT)
Thank you for taking me to the ocean today.

It was so deep and I was so scared but you just held on to me. You were so strong, who knew? Just when you think you know everything about a person, they turn the world upside down.

Alias: @Gutentag
Date: Monday May 5, 2.28AM (UNSENT)
The ocean was so beautiful, Monty. I could live there forever. You were so strong. So sweet. I wanted to kiss you.

Alias: @Gutentag
Date: Monday May 5, 2.30AM (UNSENT)
I know you wanted to kiss me too. But I couldn't, not after everything I've done. I don't deserve it. I don't deserve you.

Alias: @Gutentag
Date: Wednesday May 28, 12.20PM (UNSENT)
Why don't you see me? I stood next to you today for half an hour before you even noticed I was there. I hate that about you.

Alias: @Gutentag
Date: Friday June 6, 3.12PM (UNSENT)
You dance funny. Hilarious!

Alias: @Gutentag
Date: Tuesday July 1, 3.25PM (UNSENT)
Cigarettes hurt. I wore long sleeves so you wouldn't see the burns. Deep down I hoped you would notice. But you didn't.

Alias: @Gutentag
Date: Thursday July 24, 7.15AM (UNSENT)
He's coming over tonight, Monty. For a big family dinner. HELP ME!

Alias: @Gutentag
Date: Thursday July 24, 7.20AM (UNSENT)
Uncle Terry. He's so big and fat and disgusting. He's grown a beard now and it just makes him look even creepier. How could they let him back in the house? How can they tell me it won't happen again?

Alias: @Gutentag
Date: Thursday July 24, 8.30PM (UNSENT)
He sat at the table with Dad and Doreen and eyed me off the whole time. I hate him. Dad noticed it, I'm sure. But he chose not to. He's family, Dad says.

Alias: @Gutentag
Date: Thursday July 24, 8.33PM (UNSENT)
They should have gone to the police when I was little. I know that now. Back then, I didn't know what was right or wrong.

Alias: @Gutentag
Date: Thursday July 24, 8.43PM (UNSENT)
All grown up now, he said. All grown up. I have to see you. I'm coming over.

Alias: @Gutentag
Date: Friday July 25, 6.45AM (UNSENT)
You helped me get through last night, Monty. You let me stay with you. You have no idea how close I was. Thank you.

Alias: @Gutentag
Date: Friday July 25, 6.56AM (UNSENT)
You were so beautiful about it. You just held me and we slept. I love you so much. I can't bear it. But I'm so sorry. I can't let anyone touch me. Not after that. Not after him.

Alias: @Gutentag
Date: Friday July 25, 9.10PM (UNSENT)
I've given you the wrong idea. I can't be with you. I know I have to let you go now. I have to be alone.

Alias: @Gutentag
Date: Saturday August 2, 8.33AM (UNSENT)
How could you do this? I know, I told you to go to that stupid party. But Pippa Wilson? I'll never forgive you. EVER!

Alias: @Gutentag
Date: Saturday August 2, 10.23AM (UNSENT)
I'm sorry. It was all a stupid set up. Pippa confessed. It was all Becky's idea. They wanted to trap you into kissing her. And you fell for it. Poor stupid Monty, taken for a ride.

Alias: @Gutentag
Date: Saturday August 2, 10.25AM (UNSENT)
I've got nowhere to go. I've got nothing left. I am endless. I am nothing.

Alias: @Gutentag
Date: Friday August 8, 1.45AM (UNSENT)
You've gone viral, you idiot. My god I don't know how you're going to survive this.

Alias: @Gutentag
Date: Tuesday September 16, 1.22AM (UNSENT)
You've been gone from school for a month now.
I miss you.

Alias: @Gutentag
Date: Wednesday October 15, 1.18AM (UNSENT)
I see you sitting on your porch watching my house.
I want to run over and hug you. I'm so sorry. I pushed
you away. I ruined your life. Please forgive me?

Alias: @Gutentag
Date: Sunday November 23, 4.43AM (UNSENT)
You see the dog too, don't you Monty?

Alias: @Gutentag
Date: Sunday November 23, 4.45AM (UNSENT)
It wants me to go back to the tunnel.

Alias: @Gutentag
Date: Wednesday November 26, 1.24AM (UNSENT)
I've dodged the train three nights in a row now.

Alias: @Gutentag
Date: Wednesday November 26, 1.32AM (UNSENT)
I feel so empty when the dog is with me, Monty. I wish
you were here right now. But the dog says you hate me.
Is that true?

Alias: @Gutentag
Date: Wednesday November 26, 1.37AM (UNSENT)
The dog says Mum is right there. I miss her so much.
It says I can be with her. Do you think that's true?

Alias: @Gutentag
Date: Wednesday December 10, 11.59PM (UNSENT)
I'm sorry Monty. I'm going now. I love you. Eliza.

I cried until I was empty. Why didn't she send them? Why
didn't she tell me?

Chapter Twenty

Derek read the messages without expression. He didn't seem surprised.

'Thank you, Monty. I'll handle this,' he said.

'You'll call the police?' I asked.

'I'll handle it.'

He closed the door and that was it. He never did call the police. I don't know what came of the phone, or the messages, but I know her Uncle Terry went free. Doreen told me he moved interstate, and got a job as a youth worker.

I was such an idiot. I should have pressed send. Then at least I'd have a copy. I'd have proof. I left her pain in his hands. I trusted him and he decided to protect the living over the dead. Family, he called it.

Doreen left him soon after that. She disappeared in the dead of night. I don't know what became of her. She didn't say goodbye, although she did leave me the urn. It appeared on our doorstep the morning she left, the metal cold and dewy from the night. The sand inside still smelled of ocean. It took me instantly back to Eliza. I'd take the lid off and breathe her in to me. I made little patterns in the sand with the tips of my fingers. Waves descended into waves. We're all just dust in the end, I thought. You could fight like hell all the way but, in the end, everything turns to dust and the world would turn as if you were never there.

'Hello Monty,' said the dog.

'Hello dog,' I replied.

'You know why I'm here?'

'Yes.'

'Good. She is waiting for you.'

'You're lying.'

'No. I can see her right beside you,' it said. 'She's calling you. Are you ready?'

'Yes.'

'Good,' said the dog.

I sat on my bed and held my life in my hands. Through my bedroom door, I could hear Mum and Dad in the kitchen, making cups of tea, discussing what to have for dinner. They wouldn't come in. They weren't suspicious of my need for privacy. They should have been.

I thought of the ramifications. I wondered how the kids at the school would react. Would there be posts for me? Would I trend? Would I become a hot topic? Would everyone say they knew Monty Ferguson, that he was a great guy? Or would it not rate a mention? Would everyone just go on with their daily lives and forget?

I thought of Mum and Dad. They'd be crushed. I didn't know if Mum would make it through. And if Dad lost her, surely he'd succumb eventually. I pictured Dad cold and alone and wandering the streets, the sole survivor of a chain of wreckage. He would look straight towards me, and in his eyes I'd see Martin's face, long dead, just a skull grinning in death. The dog would have its day. But so what? I thought. I'd be with Eliza. I wanted to believe that. I wanted to go. I wanted to trust the dog. It was another lie, I knew. It had twisted her, like it was twisting me now.

'I am here to guide you,' said the dog. 'Go now. Do it! Do it now!'

The thin steel cut easily. Hot blood gushed forward. The dog recoiled in shock; I had cut its throat instead. The dog

274

scurried across the bedroom floor, spilling blood everywhere. I watched it writhe in agony as the life bled out of it.

'Go on, dog. Die!' I said.

The dog finally went still, lying limp on the floor in a
thick pool of red. The darkness seemed to fade in its eyes.
I relaxed. I opened the urn and breathed in the salty air.
Eliza was there beside me. The dog was right about that.
But she didn't want me to go. She wanted me to keep
moving. Just keep moving.

'Nice try, Monty,' said the dog.

I looked up, astonished, to see the dog sitting back
beside me. There was no blood. There was no gaping wound
across its neck. I hadn't even touched it.

'You can't die?' I asked.

'No,' it said.

Now it was my turn. Now it was my end.

Mum and Dad came rushing in. I think they must have
heard me crying or something, I'm not sure, but they
found me. There was no blood. I hadn't managed to do anything. I just howled in pain. They held me and squeezed me
tight and told me they loved me. We cried together, I don't
know, for what seemed hours. They were so thankful.

Mum took my head in her hands and looked me eye
to eye.

'Don't ever do that again, Monty,' she ordered.
'Promise me!'

'I don't know if I can, Mum,' I blubbered.

'You can't let it take you,' she said. 'It will never go away.
You just have to learn to live with it.'

I'd never seen her strength before. She held me tight and
strong against the tide.

'You've just got to hold on,' she said. 'Do you understand?'

The dog sat behind them up the hall, waiting. Biding its time.

'Yes Mum.'

I understand.

Epilogue

A year can be an eternity. And eternity repeats itself. Eventually it just runs out of options and is forced to play the same game over and over, I guess.

I got my licence. I went back to work with Dad and Old Bob. I also finished school, by correspondence though. I couldn't bring myself to go to a new school, and going back to Middleford was never going to happen. It was just much simpler to be an external student. I only dropped in to visit the school counsellor. She was a young woman with long, red dreadlocks. Man, it took all my willpower not to spend our sessions just staring at her hair. She really helped me. She also knew exactly what I was going through; she'd lost her best friend at high school the same way. Ms Finch kept a close eye on me, and we caught up for coffee every now and then. She was so happy when I showed her the little Parisian café; we'd connected over a shared love of caffeine. She was right about me going back to school too. I scored ninety-nine percent. I could get into any course I wanted at uni. The world was open to me. I could forge my own path.

I took the year off and went up the coast in the ute. I saw mountains and rainforests and the Great Barrier Reef. I lived my dream and worked in auto shops along the way, or picked fruit, or cleaned loos at backpackers' hotels. I didn't care what the work was like, just that it gave me enough cash to get to the next town. Now I wander the country, rolling, like Silas and his ball.

I call Mum and Dad every Saturday night and we talk. It's weird. We never talked when I lived there, but now I'm gone, we spend hours chatting about anything and everything. Dolly's still going strong. She's living in my old room and still eats ham sandwiches. She'll probably outlive us all. Dad reckons they all go to visit Silas once a week to take him a new ball. It's strange how tragedy brings you together.

I've met a girl, from Germany of all places. Gaby's her name. She's tall and blonde and giggles at practically anything. She loves our country. To her the endless blue sky is like heaven. She's travelled to another planet, she reckons. I show her around, as if I know where I'm going. I don't have a clue of course, I think she knows that, but we just keep moving. We camp in the back of the ute and go swimming in waterholes and bushwalk until we're red from the sun. We're going to Darwin next. I want to see if we can get work in a crocodile farm, feeding those ancient beasts dead chooks for the tourists. We'll probably end up cleaning the loos, but who cares? Eventually, Gaby will go back home to Germany. She's going to study law, she reckons. Yeah, she's smart as a whip and loves to ponder the way of things. We stay up all night nattering about the ins and outs of the world. I might go with her to Europe. I might not. We'll see.

I'll never forget Eliza. I'll never forgive myself for not being there for her. Most of all, I know what she did was futile. It didn't change a thing. The world kept turning. The kids at school forgot about her. Her father moved on. Doreen found another life. The gulls on the rocks kept calling. The waves went on crashing.

She should have come with me. We would've been alright. We'd have gotten out of Middleford and instead of Gaby and me, it'd be me and Eliza travelling the top end. We would have been happy.

The dog still follows me. No matter where I go it always turns up, appearing in the dead of night to watch over me. But it just hangs back in the shadows now, beaten. I made my choice. Not today, dog. Not today.

Having a tough time and need someone to talk to right now?
The following services are there to listen and help you out.
They are confidential and available 24/7.

Give them a call or check them out online.

Kids Helpline 1800 551 800
www.kidshelp.com.au

headspace: 1800 650 890
www.headspace.org.au